WOMAN'S HOUR
BOOK OF
SHORT STORIES

WOMAN'S HOUR BOOK OF SHORT STORIES

Selected and introduced by Pat McLoughlin

BBC BOOKS

A BBC Radio Collection double cassette
containing readings of a selection
of these stories is also available.

Published by BBC Books
a division of BBC Enterprises Limited
80 Wood Lane, London W12 0TT
First published 1990
Copyright © in this selection BBC Books 1990

ISBN 0 563 20905 4

Set in 11/13pt Garamond by Ace Filmsetting Ltd, Frome
Printed and bound in Great Britain by Fletchers of Norwich
Jacket printed by Fletchers of Norwich

CONTENTS

———— ◆ ————

ACKNOWLEDGEMENTS

———— ◆ ————

We are grateful to the following for permission to reproduce copyright material:

Jonathan Cape Ltd for 'The Needlecase' by Elizabeth Bowen, © Elizabeth Bowen 1981; Hamish Hamilton Ltd for 'My Mistress' by Laurie Colwin, © Laurie Colwin 1982, 1983, 1984, 1986. First published in *Another Marvellous Thing*; Curtis Brown Ltd for 'Coming South' by Celia Dale, © Celia Dale 1973; Curtis Brown Ltd on behalf of Patricia Ferguson for 'The Quality of Mercy' by Patricia Ferguson, © Patricia Ferguson 1987; Hamish Hamilton Ltd for 'Lychees for Tone' by Jane Gardam, © Jane Gardam, 1980. First published in *The Sidmouth Letters*; Methuen, London, for 'Mad About the Boy' by Georgina Hammick, © Georgina Hammick 1987. First published in *People to Lunch*; A. P. Watt Ltd on behalf of the Estate of Margaret Laurence for 'The Mask of the Bear' by Margaret Laurence, © Margaret Laurence 1965; A. P. Watt Ltd on behalf of Mary Leland for 'The Swain', © Mary Leland 1987; William Heinemann Ltd for 'Nothing Missing but the Samovar' by Penelope Lively, © Penelope Lively 1978; William Heinemann Ltd for 'Other People's Bathrobes' by Shena Mackay © Shena Mackay 1987; Michael Joseph Ltd for 'The Wicked Stepmother's Lament' by Sara Maitland, © Sara Maitland 1987. First published in *A Book of Spells*; Curtis Brown Ltd for 'Vacant Possession' by Deborah Moggach, © Deborah Moggach 1987; Century Hutchinson Ltd for 'Almost Human' by Ruth Rendell, © Ruth Rendell 1980. First published in *The Fallen Curtain and Other Stories*; Peters Fraser & Dunlop Group Ltd for 'The Lost Chapel Picnic' by Margery Sharp, © Margery Sharp 1973; Jonathan Cape Ltd for 'Garter' by Lisa St Aubin de Terán, © Lisa St Aubin de Terán 1989, first published in the UK in *The Marble Mountain and Other Stories* at £10.95; William Heinemann Ltd for 'The True Primitive' by Elizabeth Taylor, © Elizabeth Taylor 1951; David Higham Associates Ltd for 'To Hell with Dying' by Alice Walker, © Alice Walker 1984. First published in *In Love and Trouble* by The Women's Press; Chatto & Windus Ltd for 'An Act of Reparation' by Sylvia Townsend Warner, © Sylvia Townsend Warner 1988.

INTRODUCTION

---◆---

Some publishers are said to believe that collections of short stories don't sell because the majority of readers don't like them; and until I began selecting serials and stories for *Woman's Hour* twenty years ago, I would have placed myself with that majority, if it exists. Certainly I never read short stories out of choice. With short stories I felt short-changed! They were over before they had begun, and I would emerge too soon from their fictional world, blinking at reality.

All that changed in 1970. At first I was horrified at the thought of having to find at least fifty short stories a year (for *Weekend Woman's Hour* existed then and featured a short story every week). In the event, being obliged to trawl through short story anthologies and collections swiftly became a pleasure and a delight. But not quite always. And that, for me, has to do with something I heard the great and the good P. D. James talk about at a recent literary festival in Hay-on-Wye.

She was speaking about her reasons for choosing crime-writing before other forms of fiction, and she said something to the effect that she was dismayed by the divide that has arisen between 'storytellers' and 'serious writers' – a divide which incidentally would have surprised the great Victorian writers who had no inhibitions about draping the brilliance of their prose on the clotheshorse of a rattling good tale. P. D. James wanted, she said, to write stories with a beginning, a middle and an end. Shock, horror! Perhaps sensing a certain literary restlessness in her audience at this dubious ambition, she then fixed us with a basilisk eye and added, 'like life'. Well, quite. Life may be untidy and unpredictable and apparently shapeless, but it does have a beginning, a middle and an end.

Like longer works, short stories, sometimes by writers who should know better, have suffered from this reluctance to 'shape' fiction, for fear of banality. As a result too many short stories are not stories at all, but a momentary happening from a longer work, or a scene setting. Well, one thinks, that was a good introduction, now where's the story? Sometimes such efforts seem more like a blueprint or a rehearsal for a story – perhaps even a rehearsal for the very act of writing?

I hope none of the stories in this collection falls into this unsatisfactory category. They are unlikely to, not least because they have been broadcast on *Woman's Hour*, and there is no crueller test than reading something aloud. It is my experience that the ear just won't accept what the eye can glide over.

But this said, where to start from the hundreds of stories that have been featured on the programme over the years? There were two ways to narrow down the selection. Although we have broadcast and do broadcast superb stories by male writers, we decided early on that a *Woman's Hour* anthology should ideally be a showcase for women writers, particularly in view of their long-standing brilliance in, and dominance of, the art of short story writing. Secondly it was decided to narrow the field further by having a theme, and that would be (*pace* Andrew Lloyd Webber) varying aspects of love. This would, of course, encompass failure and absence of love.

Within this theme, which lies at the heart of so many short stories, and indeed fiction in general, I have attempted to avoid the over-familiar, no matter how brilliant. So here, for instance, you will not find Elizabeth Bowen's 'The Demon Lover' – wonderful example of supernatural love (or hate?) though it is. Instead you will find that same author's 'The Needlecase', and I hope its quieter virtues will prove every bit as enjoyable and thought-provoking.

And to start? Where else than with early love, first love. This, in the guise of an unlikely schoolgirl crush, is the subject of Georgina Hammick's 'Mad About the Boy'. Georgina Hammick started writing short stories as recently as 1984. Her first collection, *People for Lunch*, appeared in 1987 and contained 'Mad About the Boy'. As the title implies, the object of Antonia Penrose's affection is Noel Coward. 'She had once heard Colonel Symes, an acquaintance of her father, refer to Noel as "that old pansy". This, so far as she could gather, meant that he preferred men to women in some respects. If he did, it didn't bother her.' Her passion gets her through school which she hates, and furnishes her with many an adolescent dream of opulence and success.

At fourteen, 'not just fat but spotty and greasy-haired and uncomfortably like Mrs Worthington's daughter', she realises that her only hope of interesting her hero is by 'doing something'. She embarks on a musical play called *Court Circular*, 'centred on the social round and marital difficulties, two subjects she knew next to nothing about, of a couple in their thirties'. She sends Noel the first act, having run out of steam after that. But, unaccompanied by a stamped addressed envelope, it is greeted with silence. There is no response to her annual card on Noel's birthday either, until she accidentally changes her signature . . .

Penelope Lively is a distinguished author who has won prizes for her longer works of fiction, but given the choice, I would settle for her short stories. In 'Nothing Missing but the Samovar', the title story of a collection published in 1978, the situation is the reverse of 'Mad About the Boy', in that the one who loves is older, and the beloved younger. But the object of Dieter's desire is equally unattainable, even though they are living in the same house; and the relationship is just as one-sided. Sally, the young daughter of an impoverished aristocratic family with whom Dieter spends the summer, is unaware of his passion for her, and he is as unable to make his feelings known as Antonia Penrose.

The story is lyrical (in some ways reminiscent of H. E. Bates) and very, very English; the more so, perhaps, for being seen through the eyes of a young German: 'in retrospect it was to seem always summer, those heavy static days of high summer . . . of blue sky and heaped clouds. Of straw and horseflies. Blackberries; jam for tea; church on Sunday.' The story ends with Dieter's last glimpse of the family, 'frozen in the furry yellow light of the September morning, like an old photograph'. It is beautiful writing, elegant and moving.

First love, as remembered by a young woman, is the theme of 'To Hell with Dying' by the black American feminist writer, Alice Walker. Famous for her Pulitzer Prize-winning novel *The Color Purple*, which in turn became a Steven Spielberg film, much of Alice Walker's writing is as painful and angry as you would expect from a black writer who grew up in America's Deep South. But 'To Hell with Dying' is gentler in mood. It is innocent, nostalgic and sorrowful about old Mr Sweet who was 'diabetic and an alcoholic' but 'used to call me his princess, and I believed it. He made me feel pretty at five and six, and simply outrageously devastating at the blazing age of eight and a half.'

The next section could almost be called 'courtship', but perhaps the description 'love without marriage' is more apt. For the behaviour of most of the men and women in these stories is not nearly so formal as the word 'courtship' implies. These are people getting to know and love each other, but who may or may not reach the altar.

Jack Tanner in Bernard Shaw's *Man and Superman* would have no trouble at all in recognising the heroine of Elizabeth Taylor's 'The True Primitive', for Lily ('trembling with frustrated desire') is his 'life-force' personified. Left unhampered by outside forces, she and her hapless Harry will achieve, as if ordained, 'a whole council house full of daydreams; trousseau, wedding presents, pots and pans, dainty supper dishes, baby-clothes; cradle, even a kitten asleep on a cushion'.

But then there is Harry's awesome father, Mr Ransome, for whom the phrase 'boring for England' must surely have been invented; whose 'gentle and conciliatory' wife listens to him 'evening after evening of her married life', and may just possibly have died to escape his droning voice. 'She did the best thing dying,' Lily thinks.

Mr Ransome has different ambitions for Harry. 'They are not on fire,' he mourns of his sons, 'as I have been.' When Harry met Lily he seemed, to his father, to be 'less on fire than ever'. The story ends with love momentarily routed, but my money's on Lily – 'the eternal female enemy', 'with her sly, mincing manner, her pout and her impatient sighs . . .', winding a curl round her finger and suddenly loosening it to spring back against her cheek, to distract Harry, while his father declaims. Such wickedly tongue-in-cheek malice is what delights Elizabeth Taylor aficionados. I use the word advisedly for Elizabeth Taylor, who wrote twelve novels and four volumes of short stories and died in 1975, has sadly never achieved the recognition her quietly subtle yet incisively witty writing deserves.

Margery Sharp's 'The Lost Chapel Picnic', the title story from her only collection of short stories, published in 1973, is a more decorous setting for courtship. The behaviour of her characters is more decorous too, but no less funny for that. Margery Sharp is another underrated and now almost neglected writer, yet novels like *The Foolish Gentlewoman* and *Cluny Brown* are classics of light comedy.

The Lost Chapel Picnic is an annual family picnic which *always* takes place in the rain. 'In time this became so notorious that ladies planning garden parties . . . used to enquire of my aunt in advance what date had been fixed, to avoid it.' And 'as we children grew up [these picnics] provided a wonderful testing-ground for the current objects of our affections'.

Of course the sexual mores of the 1930s and those genteel, if vigorous, middle-class pre-war outings portrayed in 'The Lost Chapel Picnic' are light years away from the 1980s characters that inhabit Shena Mackay's collection of stories, *Dreams of Dead Women's Handbags*, published in 1987. Shena Mackay, born in 1944, produced her first novel at the age of twenty, and with such a unique voice one can understand her wasting no time in embarking upon a writing career.

Her humour is the blacker humour of today where people are quite often casualties and victims. She specialises in the quirky and the eccentric (maybe she has inherited Sylvia Townsend Warner's mantle in this respect) and also the sometimes elusive divide between reality and fantasy, as suggested by the title, *Dreams of Dead Women's Handbags*. The story 'Other People's Bathrobes' is from that collection, and Adam, the central character (wearer of other people's bathrobes), is a gigolo, toyboy, conman and professional sponger.

Forced to operate in a yuppie world of designer labels and mineral water, he longs for the working-class food of his childhood: 'I'm sick of mangetout peas . . . I want proper peas, without pods, from a tin.' It's not even safe to look out of the window: 'pyracantha flung bright sprays of baked beans against the houses opposite'.

His affair with Barbara, whose lifestyle represents everything he hates, seems doomed, until he finds a photograph album. With the growing realisation that her family background is much the same as his own, comes an unexpected tenderness for her pretensions, and for her. But put away your violin. Shena Mackay's astringent humour never allows things to become mawkish.

Ireland has produced a long line of distinguished short story writers, and a comparatively recent addition is Mary Leland who was born and brought up in Cork. She began her career as a journalist there, and worked for some years in Dublin before returning to live and work in her home town. Her novel, *The Kileen*, was published in 1985 and was followed in 1987 by a volume of short stories, *The Little Galloway Girls*.

The collection included 'The Swain', which is, I suppose, about second chances in the courtship stakes. Eileen is unmarried, with several unsatisfactory affairs in England behind her: 'a sexual career that could only be described as chequered. She had not been promiscuous, but when she thought men loved her she was ready to love them back.' Returning home to small-town Ireland, she discovers that Benny Cronin has been home these past four years, after a failed marriage, also in England. When young the age gap was too big for them to be particular friends. Indeed Benny was mainly instrumental in rescuing her from the attentions of the gander on the Cronin farm. Now, older and wiser, and free to get to know one another, there are 'other ganders to pass. The Canon. Her mother.' Not least their own nervous desire to get things right this time.

The couple in Deborah Moggach's 'Vacant Possession' are in a rather similar state. Celia is an estate agent who has been having a long-standing affair with a married man. Nigel was going to leave his wife, of course. 'But not quite yet, because Vicky was doing her O-levels . . . Because his wife was depressed after her hysterectomy . . . Because, because.' In fact, her private life is a mess, as Marcus Tanner is quick to tell her. Celia is involved in selling his house because his wife has left him for her T'ai Chi instructor. ('Between you and me, a bit of a wanker. But then I'm biased.') It's just another house to sell, so why is Celia distracted by signs that a woman has stayed the night?

Deborah Moggach has taken serious themes for some of her novels, themes such as incest and surrogate motherhood, and there are serious stories too in her short story collection *Smile*, published in 1987. But there are also wonderfully funny moments in the collection, and 'Vacant Possession' is one of the best examples. She's certainly hard to surpass when it comes to the delicate art of sexual innuendo.

In the past, however, there was often a price to be paid for ephemeral sexual dalliance. 'The Needlecase' is by a doyenne of the short story, though she has also written several distinctive novels such as *The Heat of the Day* and *The Death of the Heart*. Elizabeth Bowen, who died in 1973, was a product of that stable of literary richness, Anglo Ireland. But 'The Needlecase' is set in England and features a profession which has now disappeared – the seamstress who came to country houses to 'make over' the wardrobes of female members of the household.

Miss Fox is summoned to the Forresters' house because Arthur, the eldest son, is 'bringing his new girl down'. Arthur is also the reason why the house – far too big and unheated – is kept on. Arthur 'was almost always away but liked to think of it there . . . Everyone liked Arthur.' And so Miss Fox arrives, 'that difficult class . . . Too grand for the servants, she had to be fed in her room.' But Frank and Angela and Toddy find her strangely arresting, particularly in the knowledge that, despite her 'nun-like face', Miss Fox is in fact a 'fallen' woman with a child to support. It transpires that Miss Fox has actually met Arthur before. But at what precise cost to Miss Fox only becomes clear when the photograph in the needlecase is revealed.

Jane Gardam, born in 1928 on the north-east coast of Yorkshire, was a journalist by profession before becoming a prize-winning writer of several novels and short stories. Like so many of the other writers here, her tone is individual and quirky, with a liking for the eccentric, and for the merging of reality with fantasy. She also has a particularly tender way with children in her stories, evoking all their vulnerability and freshness. Her identification with them is so complete, in fact, that it is difficult to remember that her own youth was largely pre-war. But with 'Lychees for Tone', youth is off-stage, so to speak, as in our emotional journey we reach family love, more specifically here, mother love.

Mrs James is a great worrier, particularly about her son 'Tone' and particularly when one Friday he announces, 'I's bringin' a bird home Saturday.' She admits: 'Tell you the truth my heart were like a pump. He's twenty-two and he's never brought no girls home in his life. Tadpoles yes, lads yes. Bikes yes. And now the cars . . . Always bikes and cars and lads. Girls never.'

And now Tone is bringing home not only a girl, but a foreigner, Chinese or something. 'And he's going to sleep with her . . . In this house . . . In Eastern View . . . Stepping into bed with her, just like it was on a bus!'

The difficulties of family love and life provide the theme of 'The Mask of the Bear' by the wonderful Canadian writer, Margaret Laurence, who died in 1987. It comes from *A Bird in the House*, a series of interconnected stories, published in 1970, about a family in the fictional Canadian prairie town of Manawaka. (Margaret Laurence came from a small prairie town herself and used Manawaka as the setting for several of her novels.)

'The Mask of the Bear' is narrated by a young girl called Vanessa MacLeod. She tells us about her Grandfather Connor, whom she knows as a remote and surly domestic tyrant, seemingly incapable of love, until Grandmother Connor dies. 'He wore no coat . . . although the day was fifteen below zero. He stood there by himself, his yellowish-white hair plumed by a wind which he seemed not to notice, his bony and still-handsome face not averted at all from the winter.'

The American writer Laurie Colwin's *Another Marvellous Thing* is also a series of interconnected stories, but the subject – an extra-marital affair – would not have gone down well in small-town Manawaka. It is no coincidence that these stories first appeared in the *New Yorker* magazine, for although Laurie Colwin was born in Chicago and grew up in Philadelphia, her laconic, deadpan humour is pure *New Yorker*, echoing the writings of Dorothy Parker and James Thurber.

With the story 'My Mistress', we have, of course, reached the subject of infidelity. The narrator is Francis Clemens, who is older and more elegant than Billy, his mistress, and observes the tattiness of their affair with wry amusement. Unlike 'mistresses in French movies', Billy goes off with her lover for a romantic weekend 'wearing an old skirt, her old jacket, and carrying a ratty canvas overnight bag. No lacy underwear would be drawn from it, I knew.'

Light-hearted though the treatment is here, what about the possible price of such affairs – such as the break-up of a marriage? The way in which the abandoned spouse (often the wife) reacts to the usurper (often a younger woman) is the subject of the next two stories. Celia Dale is a suspense writer whose speciality is the menace hidden within ordinary domestic lives, which she has exploited to great effect in her novels and short stories. She has written many stories for magazines and anthologies and in 1986 some of them were collected in a volume entitled *A Personal Call*.

The collection includes 'Coming South', in which apparent domestic tolerance, if not contentment, is disrupted when Frank Wisbey tells his wife that he wants to leave her for someone new. 'She kept the house nice . . . and they was as decent, respectable a couple as you could wish to meet.' The narrator is a woman who works up north as a typing pool supervisor. Celia Dale plays fair – all the clues are there – but by a judicious arrangement of pronouns the reader only gradually realises the truth.

The supplanted wife in Sylvia Townsend Warner's 'An Act of Reparation' is a very different animal. For 'Lois Hardcastle, writhing in the boredom of being married to Fenton, had snatched at Miss Valerie Fry, who had done her no harm whatever, and got away at her expense.' Fortunately for Lois, Valerie does not see herself as victimised; she feels nothing but pity for Lois, definitely middle-aged and past it. But we are in the capable – and wickedly artful – hands of a mistress of ironic humour, and it is oh-so-clear that innocent young Valerie has won a very dubious prize in fussy, old-maidish Fenton. ('Where is that appalling draught coming from? You must have left a window open somewhere.')

The middle-aged wife, delighted to pass on the burden of a staid, boring husband to a naïve young woman, comes as a refreshing change, from the accepted point of view, and this unconventionality is perhaps the common factor in all Sylvia Townsend Warner's writing. The debunking of Fenton and the idea of masculine superiority in general, is done with the subtlety and lethal elegance of a stiletto dagger. It could double as a feminist tract, except that it is far more entertaining than most.

Of course there can be other victims of second marriages. Frank Wisbey in 'Coming South' and Fenton in 'An Act of Reparation' are childless, but what if there are children? Ask Cinderella? No, says Sara Maitland in her *Book of Spells*, published in 1987. Try asking the stepmother for her side of the story for a change. Sylvia Townsend Warner would have approved.

In 'The Wicked Stepmother's Lament', Sara Maitland asks, what if Cinderella was a wimp? A born victim?

I just wanted her to *see* . . . that life is not all sweetness and light . . . that fairy godmothers are unreliable and damned thin on the ground, and that even the most silvery of princes soon goes out hunting and fighting and drinking and whoring . . . All I wanted was for her to grow up . . . and realise that life was not a bed of roses and that she had to take some responsibility for her own life . . .

Sara Maitland is one of an elite band, having won the Somerset Maugham Award with her first novel, *Daughter of Jerusalem*, published in 1978. She is a feminist writer and the feminist message is clear – be your own woman. But with or without the message, 'The Wicked Stepmother's Lament' is ingeniously entertaining.

Still, for some, there are alternatives to the messy business of emotional involvement with people. Dick, in Ruth Rendell's 'Almost Human', product of a 'drunken, savage father' and a 'mother who cared only for men and a good time', prefers dogs.

Ruth Rendell needs no introduction, if you will forgive the cliché, unless you have been constantly engaged in deep potholing or some other form of extremely isolated activity for the past twenty years. When it comes to crime-writing awards, she holds the full flush – Gold Daggers, Silver Daggers, Edgars, *et al.* And the likes of Dick in 'Almost Human' are very characteristic of her genre; in Margaret Mahy's memorable phrase, 'damaged beyond mending'.

In a Ruth Rendell story a pathological dislike of people can come in useful. In this case it almost enables Dick to realise his dream of a Highland retreat for him and his beloved dogs, where 'with luck he wouldn't hear a human voice from one month's end to another'. Ironically it is his affection for animals that momentarily undermines his ruthlessness, and postpones that dream for the foreseeable future.

There are other sublimations too, such as a caring career. This is very much the theme of Patricia Ferguson's interconnected series of stories, *Indefinite Nights*, published in 1987, following her first novel (*Family Myths and Legends*, 1985).

Patricia Ferguson is a journalist as well as a writer of fiction, and after university she trained as a nurse, which provided her with the background for *Indefinite Nights*. These stories chart the career of a nursing sister, and in 'The Quality of Mercy', the narrator works as a nurse in a male geriatric ward. There *is* a relationship with an attractive male nurse, but the main emotional pull is the old men of Mercy Ward, and nursing itself: 'They all remembered a war, old men always have a war to remember . . . there they lay . . . turning on me eyes that had seen the ships go down off Scapa Flow.' Her friend, Phyllis, also a nursing sister, asks 'Why do we stick it?' and her friend replies 'God knows.' 'But Phyllis knew too, and so did I. Love for sale.'

Finally, 'Garter' by Lisa St Aubin de Terán is from her collection *The Marble Mountain and Other Stories*, published in 1989. Lisa St Aubin de Terán is another prizewinner who, in the space of a relatively short writing career, has gathered up both the Somerset Maugham Award and the John Llewellyn Rhys Memorial Prize. The seven years she spent in the Andes on her first husband's family estate have provided colourful background material for some of her work. But the setting for 'Garter' is Clapham Common in south London, which the author knew in her childhood. It is the tender and moving story of one of 'God's innocents'. For Garter is a mentally backward road-sweeper, pathetically grateful for a young schoolgirl's friendship: 'You're the only friend I've ever had. You never laugh at me, and you gave me some cakes and I buyed you some chocolate.' For Garter, love is a luxury he can't afford, 'for sale' or otherwise. Like Miss Fox in Elizabeth Bowen's 'The Needlecase', he is a casualty of love.

Looking back at the authors of these stories, it is interesting to see that their ages range over half a century, from Sylvia Townsend Warner and Elizabeth Bowen, products of the 1890s, to Sara Maitland, born in 1950. Their writing careers have covered a period which has seen more change and progress (if that is the word) than any previous comparative timescale. And yet there is a consistency at the heart of these stories of humour, compassion and empathy. It has made them a pleasure to prepare for the original broadcasts on *Woman's Hour* and to re-read now for this anthology. I hope you will find them as enjoyable as I have done.

Pat McLoughlin
Serials Producer, *Woman's Hour*

FIRST LOVE, EARLY LOVE

MAD ABOUT THE BOY

———— ◆ ————

Georgina Hammick

He got her through school which she hated. On Saturdays, and on weekday evenings after prep, they were allowed to play the gramophone. She would take hers, a German machine in a blue-black leather case her father had found in Berlin at the end of the war, into a corner of the gym and set herself up. The inside of the gramophone had an intoxicating smell. Each time she lifted the lid she sniffed hard. Years later, searching a junk shop for something to stand plants on, she came across an old gramophone and opened it up and sniffed and was immediately taken back; she could see that German machine: the catches on the case that released the lid, the heavy head tucked safely to the side, the winder secured by two brackets inside the lid, the sliding compartment for needles, the needles themselves in their shiny tin boxes.

She was nine or ten when the passion started and her collection of his records amounted to less than a dozen. She had stolen them from her mother and her aunts. All, with the exception of 'Don't Let's be Beastly to the Germans', were pre-war and recorded before she was born. Three were twelve-inch and scenes from plays (*Private Lives*; *Cavalcade*; *Tonight at 8.30*). The rest were ten-inch and songs, sung solo by Noel with a piano accompaniment. Sometimes she listened in silence, kneeling close against the gramophone with her head inside the lid so as not to miss a syllable; more often she sang along with him in a clipped tenor as near his own as she could manage. Soon she was spending all her pocket money on records: 'Don't Make Fun of the Festival'; 'There are Bad Times Just Around the Corner'; 'Matelot'. His voice in these seemed rounder – or was it thicker? – which fitted in with his being almost bald now and not as thin as he'd been in the photographs she owned of *Private Lives*.

Noel's popularity was at a low ebb in the early 1950s, a fact she discovered from the gossip columns of the daily newspapers. He seemed to be in trouble with the press for living most of the time in Bermuda or Jamaica and thereby avoiding income tax, and he was having a rough time with the critics for writing plays which, they were all agreed, showed none of his pre-war brilliance. He was not popular at her school, Belmont, but that was because most people had never heard of him, the few that had knowing him only as a vague figure – like Fred Astaire or Jack Buchanan – from their parents' youth. The decline in his fortunes suited her very well and made her feel protective. She alone really appreciated him. She alone understood him and his problems. She alone knew, and sympathised with, the weaknesses of his literary style. These included an over-fondness for adjectives and an inability to resist, in his plays, the witty line even when it was at odds with the character who had to speak it.

By the time she was twelve she knew, she was sure, everything there was to know about him; not just about the plays – date, theatre, cast, length of run were all at her fingertips – but his private life and his character. He was kind and sentimental and generous and hardworking, someone who never put off till the afternoon what he could do in the morning. He did not suffer fools. He was of course clever, but perhaps not in an intellectual way. He was witty and funny. He had no false modesty about his talents. He was not a believer, except in himself, and this was bothering because God might strike him down. She was keen on God and often spent as much as an hour on her knees on the splintery boards of Burne-Jones (the dormitories were named after painters) before getting into bed. She had once heard Colonel Symes, an acquaintance of her father's, refer to Noel as 'that old pansy'. This, so far as she could gather, meant that he preferred men to women in some respects. If he did, it didn't bother her. It was so obvious that he liked women and that he loved them too. He was always loyal about the women he loved. She knew who they were: his mother and G. E. Calthrop (Gladys) and Lorn Loraine and Joyce Carey. And Gertrude Lawrence. She loved Gertie almost as much as she loved Noel and kept a scrap book for each of them into which she pasted newspaper cuttings, theatre programmes and notices.

In the school holidays she haunted the second-hand bookshop in the market town where her mother did most of her shopping. The shop, Burkes, had high ceilings and the bookshelves went right up to them. There were books everywhere, not just on the shelves but in untidy stacks on the floor and in parked trolleys that blocked the aisles. A rickety staircast led to more books upstairs, but she seldom climbed them because the theatre section was on the ground floor. The shop, poorly lit and with alleyways that turned corners and resembled streets, made her think of a town at dusk.

Among her finds at Burkes was a brown book with a battered spine entitled *The Amazing Mr Noel Coward* by Patrick Braybrooke. The book, in itself disappointing, had been made special by its previous owner who'd stuck photographs and press cuttings on all the available space of the end-papers. There was a caricature of Noel and Gertie taken from *The New Yorker*, a newspaper clip of Noel and Beatrice Lillie dining 'intimately' at a restaurant, and another cutting, so large it had had to be folded over, the caption of which read: 'At Goldenhurst Farm: Gertrude Lawrence, Noel Coward and Jack Wilson his Business Partner'. The photograph showed a tea party on a lawn. Gertie, sitting up very straight, poured out from a silver tea pot while a huge dog, a setter possibly, leaned across the table and licked her nose. Noel lay in a wicker chair, which was old-fashioned and had a wheel at the back. One of his knees was bent up. He held a saucer in his left hand and a cup in his right which partly obscured his face, and he eyed Gertie over the rim. The business partner who sat astride another wicker chair which did not have a wheel, was reading a magazine. Behind him a bag of golf clubs posed against a brick pillar. The domesticity of the scene was thrilling, although Goldenhurst – from the photograph all diamond panes and beams – was not to her taste.

Reading Noel was not easy to do at Belmont, where books brought back by the girls had to be passed as suitable by the headmistress, Miss Church. You put your books on an oak chest outside her drawing-room door and at some time, probably in the middle of the night for no one ever saw them go, they were taken inside. If they passed, they reappeared two days later in the same miraculous fashion, and you were then free to remove them and read them. She'd put *Fallen Angels* and *The Vortex* out once but had not seen them again until the end of term, when they were handed to her with a wan smile. After that she smuggled his plays in and kept them under a packet of sanitary towels in her underclothes drawer. She learned them, in bed and with a torch, after lights out.

Before falling asleep she invented a 'dream' about him. The dream was always the same. On a foggy afternoon she would escape down the drive (pitted tarmac and enclosed by species rhododendrons and ponticums, now glistening unpleasantly in the fog) and walk the two miles to the station and the London train. At Waterloo she'd take a taxi to 17 Gerald Road, the studio flat he lived in when he wasn't in Jamaica or wherever. He came to the door himself, peered down, saw at a glance how fascinating she was under her cloak of shyness, and invited her in for tea. Tea was crumpets in a silver dish, accompanied by light and witty conversation. She made him laugh a lot. After tea he showed her his treasures and his books and pictures (these included two landscapes he'd painted himself) until they were interrupted by actor friends dropping in for cocktails. He was proprietorial about her and introduced her to them with pride, as though he himself had invented her. Occasionally he'd pat her head, which made her blush with pleasure. When his visitors were invited to stay on for supper she stayed too and helped Cole (she knew about Cole from reading *Present Indicative*) serve it. They had cold roast mutton and baked potatoes and onion sauce and salad, followed by apple pie and cheese and biscuits. There was red wine to drink.

Coffee was served in the drawing-room. Noel ('Do stop calling me Mr Coward, there's a darling') sat down at the grand piano and played a few bars. 'Antonia!' – he beckoned her with a finger – 'Come and sing a duet with me.' They sang 'You Were There' from *Shadow Play*. She owned the record of this, and had sung Gertie's part so often, copying every idiosyncratic note, that she sounded just like her, she thought. Noel seemed to think so too. Eventually the visitors began to drift away, fetching sable wraps – the women – and capes and white silk scarves – the men – from Noel's bedroom. When she said 'I must go now,' he said 'Not in this fog dear, and in any case you've missed the last train.' So she stayed. Dressed in a pair of his pyjamas – they were slub silk and striped in pink and grey – she slept, curled up beside him in his huge double bed under a black satin quilt with scarlet roses on it.

At home she was teased about her passion, but not unkindly. Her mother – 'I was a Coward fan long before you were born' – quite liked him, and her sister Fran, who was eighteen, liked him very much. Fran's teasing often took the form of trying to trip her up on dialogue from the plays. They might be sitting at lunch when Fran would suddenly stare out of the window and point and say: 'That hedge over there is called Cupressus Macrocarpa,' to which the only possible reply (there were no hedges of the sort in their garden) was: 'Do you swear it?' Or again, she might be minding her own business in an armchair with a book, when Fran would materialise at her side and ask: 'Are you engaged for this dance?' The correct answer, which of course she always gave, being: 'I was, but I'll cut it if you promise to love me always and never let anyone or anything come between us, ever.' Her father addressed her, and often in the third person, as Lady Coward, even though Noel at the time was plain Mr. 'Some more roast beef for Lady C.?' – he would turn from the sideboard with his carving knife and his eyebrows raised. Or 'Lady Coward is in a pretty bloody mood today, it seems.' Asked for something for her autograph book, he wrote unkindly on one page: *Nobody loves a fat girl/Nobody gives me a date/The only game I play with the boys/Is sitting and guessing my weight*, and on the facing one, right in the middle: *I am a Nole and I live in a hole.* He drew a picture of the hole, and beside it a signpost on which he printed: *Montego Bay 3 miles.*

One day, feeling fat and bored and sad, she looked Noel up in the A–D volume of the London Telephone Directory, not expecting to find him there. Yet there he was, his name in ordinary print like everyone else's and there was his telephone number: SLOane 2965. For three days she did nothing except chant the number. Say she got through and managed to speak to him? A furious: 'Who are you? What do you want? Go away, please.' Click – the likely outcome – would put paid to her fantasy for ever. So she compromised. The compromise consisted of asking the operator for SLOane 2965 and then sweating with fear while the number was obtained. When it was engaged, which was often, the anti-climax was balanced by a dull relief. Whenever the operator said: 'It's ringing now, caller,' she felt sick with terror and replaced her receiver as soon as his was lifted. Sitting in her father's chair in the empty drawing-room, she would shake and speculate: Who had lifted the receiver? Was it him? Or Cole? A maid? A friend? A lover? The thrill lay in the knowledge that she had caused a bell to ring in his house and that if he were in he must surely hear it. If only in the minutest way she had affected his life. Because of something she had done he had perhaps called out: 'Answer that, Coley, would you?' or 'Who the hell's that? Tell them I'm not in.' Or, if Coley and maids and cooks and friends and lovers were absent, he himself might have padded – in his dressing-gown? – to the telephone and picked up the receiver with his own hands. The possibilities were endless.

As with a drug, the telephone episodes satisfied for a time and produced highs and lows. Soon a stronger dose was needed. So that when her best friend from school with whom she sometimes stayed in the holidays, dared her to speak to him, she decided to take on the dare. They did it from a telephone box outside the Post Office and Stores in the Suffolk village where Christina lived. There was a good deal of preliminary giggling and pinching – Christina carried on like that much of the time in any case – and scrabbling on the filthy floor of the call box for the pennies they kept dropping. Eventually the operator said: 'You're through now, caller', and after a pause and some clicks, a male voice that was not his said: 'SLOane 2965.' 'Hello,' she said. 'Could I speak to Mr Coward, please?' 'He's at the theatre at the moment, I'm afraid.' The voice sounded wary (but it could have been true, she decided afterwards. He was playing King Magnus in *The Apple Cart* that summer). 'Can I take a message?' 'My name is Amanda Prynne,' she spoke very fast, turning her back on Christina who was bent up with laughter and clutching her stomach. 'Isn't that a coincidence?' 'It certainly is,' the voice said politely, disbelievingly. 'I can't wait. I can't, I can't' Christina had started to wail. 'I'm going to do it NOW.' She wasn't sure what to say next to the voice on the telephone. Instead, it spoke to her: 'Mr Coward will be most interested to hear about you. Thank you for calling. Goodbye.' 'Wait!' she shouted, but the line had gone dead. Christina uncrossed her skinny legs and unleashed a stream of pee that struck the floor of the box as a waterfall strikes rocks, splashing their bare legs and soaking their sandals. They quarrelled all the way home to the Regency rectory where Christina lived, but by the time they reached the bathroom and were unpeeling their smelly clothes they were giggling again. 'What did he say? What did he say?' Christina aimed a loaded sponge at her and missed. 'Who's this Amanda person anyway?'

The next day she shut herself in the lavatory, and took up her pen: 'Dear Mr Coward, As you may have heard, I telephoned you yesterday . . .' She covered two whole sides. She told him how much she admired him and how she knew everything he'd ever written. She said she hoped he didn't mind her writing to him. She signed herself Amanda Prynne. The letter was written on Christina's mother's headed paper: Bumpstead Hall, nr Haverhill, Suffolk, which she hoped would impress him. Leaning out of the carriage window as her train pulled out of Audley End station, she asked Christina, as casually as she could, to forward any letters that came for Amanda Prynne.

Silence is ambiguous stuff, she discovered. Almost anything could be read into it. Sometimes he opened her letter, scanned its contents briefly, crumpled it and dropped it in a wastepaper basket. Sometimes (he did this more often) he read her letter carefully and with increasing interest, then sat down at his desk, unscrewed his Parker 51, filled it with Quink and wrote a reply. It was a kind note, quite short, and it ended with an invitation (to tea, but she knew where *that* would lead). When the weeks that went by became months and she could no longer believe in his letter, she allowed herself to think that he didn't want to spoil things by writing, but that he kept hers on his bedside table, tucked inside a favourite book – *Barchester Towers*, perhaps. She knew everything about him. She knew of his addiction to Trollope.

It was about this time that something happened to bring the real world and the fantasy world briefly if electrifyingly closer. Copies of *The Times*, the only newspaper considered suitable reading for the girls at Belmont, were kept in a Jacobean oak cradle in the hall, disproportionately large and imposing for the house which had been built at the turn of the century in baronial style for, rumour had it, a Spanish ambassador who for some reason had never arrived. The floor of the hall was on two levels, the lower level, nearest the front door, being paved with large black and white stone squares and empty except for an enormous J. Arthur Rank gong struck at mealtimes by Brooks the butler whom everybody hated; the higher level oak-boarded and part-covered by an ancient (that was easy to believe: it was almost threadbare) and, so they were always being told, priceless, Persian carpet no one was allowed to tread on. No one, that is, except for Miss Church. The cradle was on the higher level, and beside it was an oak chest you sat on if you wanted to read the paper (it was forbidden to remove *The Times* from the hall). She was seated there one morning at break, kicking her heels against the chest and giving the personal columns on the front page her usual close attention, when a small paragraph winked at her like a neon sign: 'Mr Noel Coward will be at the Times Bookshop at noon tomorrow (Tuesday) to sign copies of *The Noel Coward Song Book*.'

There was no chance of escaping in fog (it was in any case July) on the London train. She'd spent her pocket money for the term and had nothing for the fare. She did not know where the Times Bookshop was. She tore a page from her rough notebook (it was forbidden to tear pages from your rough notebook) and wrote to Fran who was doing a secretarial course in Bayswater and who lived with three friends in a basement flat off Royal Avenue:

> Darling Fran,
> Noel Coward is signing copies of the N.C. Song Book TOMOR-ROW (Tues.) at the Times Bookshop. Please get one for me in yr lunch hour. I swear I will repay. I'm sorry to be such a nuisance. Please please PLEASE!
> > T.O.L.
> > Ant.

She gave her letter to the under-matron, Miss Tankland, who shopped in the town on Monday afternoons. Miss Tankland did not like her any more than she, or any other of the girls, liked Miss Tankland, who was spiteful, two-faced, a snob and stupid (she had once said to Camilla Arbuthnot: 'I believe you're quite well connected' and had not perceived the irony in Camilla's reply: 'Yes. The ninth earl died last week'). It was quite on the cards that Tank would lose her letter on purpose.

The next day was a day of suffering. Would Fran get her letter – always supposing Tank had posted it – before she left for Bayswater? If she did get it, would she act on it? She had a feeling she hadn't told Fran what time Noel was supposed to be at the shop.

After tea, which as usual had been buns and compo strawberry jam out of a tin with woodshavings added for pips, she was searching her desk for *Geography Today Bk 3* – there was a prep on watersheds that evening – when Alice Hodges from Remove skated over the glassy boards into Vb form room. 'Antonia *Pen*rose – you're wanted in the st*u*dy.' She sang this with relish and then skated away again.

The study, which was also Miss Church's drawing-room, was furnished with highly polished Edwardian Sheraton pieces and Persian rugs. There was an ornate break-fronted bookcase full of unappetising books on one side of the fireplace, and the wall opposite to where she now stood, her back to the double doors, was taken up by a mullioned bay window, from which she could see the top of the latticed stone terrace wall and beyond it yellowing lawns sloping down to the tennis courts, on the left, and The Military Building, a leftover from the Army's occupation of the house during the war, on the right. In this dark and draughty shed (its north side was entirely open to the elements) which had a tarmacadam floor that minced your knees if you fell over, they played team games with bean bags when the weather was considered too bad for tennis or lacrosse.

Miss Church faced her from a chintz-covered armchair by the fire. She had a smallish, square head, a beaky nose and highly coloured cheeks. Her hair, cut like a man's at the back, was thick and wiry and not yet entirely grey, and it stuck out in tufts above her ears. The head sat oddly on a huge unfit body that tended to wobble in an unpleasant way when she walked and was always draped in loose navy or maroon garments, uninfluenced by fashion of any period and peculiar to Miss Church.

She had once seen a photograph of Miss Church as a young woman during the First World War. It was difficult to think of the thin and flat-chested person who held a boat-shaped tennis racquet with what looked like purpose, and who smiled at the camera from under an amusing hat, as having anything to do with the headmistress she knew. Miss Church taught English literature and scripture. She had a habit, when seated before the class, of holding her fountain pen vertically and letting her thumb and index finger slip down it to the nib. She would then about-turn the pen very slowly, tapping on the table as she did so. The action was usually accompanied by some ominously quiet instructions, apparently directed to the book in front of her: 'Jessica. I believe you learned the Gospel according to St Mark, Chapter 4, for preparation. Would you,' a pause, and she would look up at this point with a little smile that was not a smile at all, 'recite verses 10–23 for me please, darling.'

Miss Church did her pen trick now, tapping it on the notebook in her lap. She did this for some moments and then put the pen down on a little table which, when visiting parents were present, sometimes supported minute glasses of dry sherry. She opened the notebook. There was a small yellow envelope between its pages which she handed to Antonia. 'What does this mean, darling?' Miss Church asked her.

She unfolded the telegram – it had already been opened – and read: 'All is performed stop arent I a good sister Fran.'

'Yippee,' she said, and did a little jump. Miss Church looked at her unsmilingly. 'Children are not permitted to receive telegrams here,' she said, 'except on matters of the utmost gravity. I should like some explanation, please.'

She did not fancy telling Miss Church about Noel and his Song Book and what she'd asked Fran to do. It was not Miss Church's business. 'It's a private matter. Nothing to do with school,' she said brightly. 'I see,' said Miss Church, turning a nasty shade of purple. 'I'm afraid you are a rather silly and superficial person, Antonia. I think you like to imagine yourself as different from other people, superior in some way. I have to say I have not found your work to be superior. You tend to run away from anything at all difficult.' There was a pause, during which she felt uncomfortable for a moment, knowing that Miss Church referred to the music exam she'd been supposed to take last term but had refused, at the last minute, to sit because she knew she'd fail.

'It is perhaps your parents' fault that you are spineless and spoon-fed,' Miss Church went on, 'but if you can't cure this you will never achieve anything very much.'

Out of the window she could see a group of figures straggling up from the tennis courts. Caroline Timpson, or it might have been Rosemary Bailey – it was hard to tell from this distance – was bouncing a tennis ball on her racquet. Every so often the ball bounced out of the racquet's reach and rolled away over the tussocky lawn, and Caroline – or Rosemary – chased after it.

Meanwhile, Miss Church was winding up: 'You will be late for your preparation, Antonia, and must do an extra half hour. Before you return to your classroom, run up to Matron, will you, and tell her I'm sorry to have to bother her – I know how busy she is – but that I had to send you for a clean tunic because your own is so,' she looked briefly at the lentil soup and ink stains on the brown serge bosom, and then turned away, 'soiled.'

She had to wait until December 25th for the Song Book, which Fran said was her Christmas present. She made Fran go endlessly through her experience in the Times Bookshop. There had been a long queue. Noel had sat at a large table, piled with books, signing away. He'd worn a grey pinstripe suit, a pink shirt, a navy blue and white spotted bow-tie. When her turn had come, she'd said: 'Would you sign my book, please?' and he'd said: 'It will be a pleasure.' When he'd signed his name, which he did rather fast in blue biro, she said 'Thank you very much' and he'd said: 'Not at all.'

The book when it came was large and important-looking, the paper cover designed, not very well she thought, by G. E. Calthrop. The signature was eccentric and ran diagonally across the title page, fitting neatly between 'The Noel Coward Song Book' in large lettering at the top, and 'London, Michael Joseph' in much smaller print at the bottom. The flourish of the 'd' in Coward sliced through 'with an introduction and annotations by Noel Coward'. On the facing page was a portrait by Clemence Dane of Noel in a yellow jumper. His hair was unflatteringly short. His forehead and ears looked pink and cross, and his pursed mouth was a bright lipstick red.

She ran her fingers over the signature as though it had been in braille. His ballpoint pen had nearly pierced the paper on some strokes; how nearly was obvious when she turned the page over. He had written this with his pen. She copied the signature again and again in her rough notebook and was soon able to execute a perfect forgery and at speed.

It dawned on her gradually that Noel was never going to be interested in the real Antonia Penrose, who at fourteen was not just fat but spotty and greasy-haired and uncomfortably like Mrs Worthington's daughter. He could only be drawn to the Antonia Penrose she had invented for him, who was thin, attractive (not beautiful: she hadn't thought that necessary) and talented in the same sort of ways that he was. The only chance she had of winning, if not his love, then at least his respect, was by *doing* something. She removed a new exercise book from the form room cupboard and started work on a play. It was to be a musical play, she decided. She called it *Court Circular* and it centred on the social round and marital difficulties, two subjects she knew next to nothing about, of a couple in their thirties whose names were Paul and Theresa Felton.

Getting the dialogue to sound convincing wasn't as easy as she'd anticipated. But she enjoyed writing the songs, or lyrics as she always thought of them (as in 'book and lyrics by so-and-so'), and she composed the tunes and fitted the words to them while walking round and round the lacrosse pitch while supposedly 'off games'. 'Off games' was the expression employed by the school to denote the first three days of your 'period'. 'Period' was the word Matron used for what your mother called 'the curse'.

Of the songs 'Queen of Sheba':

I think you're the Queen of Sheba,
You know I do
And somehow I sort of feel a
Passion for you.
I don't care if the Atlantic's between us
So long as it's still romantic between us
I think you're a bit of my heaven come true –

had perhaps the best tune, but the smartest lyric was undoubtedly 'When the Moon is Blue':

When the moon is blue, darling,
I'll be true, darling, to you.
There are quite a few, honey,
Apart from you, honey,

I'm fond of too.
But I'll be faithful sometime,
You may be sure
When I've had my fun time,
Then I'll be your
Baby
When the moon is blue, darling,
I'll be true, darling,
To you.

The cover of her notebook said: *Court Circular*, A Musical Play in Three Acts, but she ran out of steam after the first act and wrote nothing more. Noel was not to know this, however. She copied the first act into a new notebook and wrote him a letter:

Dear Mr Coward,
I thought you might be interested to see the first act of my new musical play, *Court Circular* . . .

He would be obliged to reply now, if only to return her manuscript, and for weeks she believed this, sometimes racing to the Junior Room – the mail was given out there – at break, sometimes staying edgily in her form room in the hope that the prefect in charge of the mail would seek her out: 'Huge envelope for you, Antonia.' 'Oh thanks,' would be her bored reply as she took the packet without even glancing at it. It was years before she realised that he probably received hundreds of unsolicited manuscripts a week, and that the only ones that had even a hope of being returned, possibly accompanied by a discouraging note from a member of his staff, were those which had self-addressed and stamped envelopes attached to them.

The silence that greeted *Court Circular* marked the end of her obsession as it had been. She still loved him, and she still wrote to him sometimes, but she never posted the letters. What she did post to him, every year, was a birthday card, drawn and painted by herself. The wording never varied: 'To the Master, With best wishes for a Happy Birthday, from Antonia Penrose.' She always wrote her address on the bottom left-hand corner, just in case, but she no longer expected a reply. What was permitted was to picture him at breakfast, slitting the heaped envelopes with a silver paperknife. He hurried through them until he came to hers, exclaimed with pleasure, called everyone round to look, and then stood the card up in a place of honour on the piano.

One December when she was nineteen and teaching English and Art at a girls' preparatory school – a post she had no qualification for and had managed to get because her parents knew one of the governors – she read in the paper that he was ill in bed at the Dorchester Hotel. She read this on the 13th. There were three days to go before the birthday. She took great pains with the card, an ink and wash drawing, rather Cecil Beatonish, of an Edwardian couple walking in a park. The woman held a parasol and a little dog on a lead. Behind the couple, who walked arm in arm, was a suggestion of railings and a park bench. She pasted the picture onto a stiff blue card and wrote inside: 'To the Master. Happy Birthday. I hope you're feeling better.' She was about to sign her name as usual when she hesitated, and wrote *Anthony* Penrose instead.

Two days later she was just setting off for the school when the post arrived. Among a pile of stuff for her parents, there were two other items: a communication for her from Lloyds Bank which she did not open, and a white, square envelope addressed in blue type to Anthony Penrose, esq., The Glebe House, Monkerswell, nr Salisbury. She opened it quickly and took out a greetings card. Its entire front was taken up by a black and white photograph of Noel. He was sitting cross-legged in a white tubular chair on top of a rock in the middle of the sea. He wore a dark jacket and white trousers and espadrilles and he had a book on his knee. It was impossible to tell what book. He was seated sideways to the camera, his face half towards it with an amused expression that was not quite a smile. She opened the card. At the top, a blue seal, the sort some people stick on Christmas parcels, said: 'Merry Xmas' in fancy silver lettering above two silver holly leaves and berries. Underneath this was a signature: Noel, in red biro. There was nothing else at all.

This card, and how she came by it, became in time her 'Noel Coward story', and she told it through the years at what she judged to be the right time to the right company. It was not a story that improved with embellishment. It depended for its effect – gratifyingly hilarious, nine times out of ten – on a fast Coward delivery:

> Cue (approximate): As Noel Coward might say . . .
> A: I can't remember if I ever told you my Noel Coward Story?
> Cue: No. Do tell.
> A: I was madly in love with him from the age of eight and used to write to him from school, and ring him up – SLOane 2965 – and always for his birthday I drew him a card and he never replied. And then one year when I was about nineteen I did him a rather Cecil Beatonish card – he was in bed at the Dorchester with 'flu – and I wrote 'To the Master' at the top as usual, and was just about to sign my name 'Antonia Penrose' when I stopped and wrote 'Anthony Penrose' instead. And I got a reply by return of post.

She felt no disloyalty at telling this story, being certain that, if he could hear it, he'd laugh louder and longer than anyone else.

She had been married to James for six years and had had three of her five children when the Great Coward Revival began in the mid-1960s. She went twice to see him – his last stage appearance – in *Suite in Three Keys*. Separated from him by only the orchestra pit she was shocked to discover how like her own father, who had died the year before, he was, not just in obvious physical ways of height and shape (their ears were almost identical) but in facial expression, in speech – particularly delivery and timing – and in gesture. The way Noel sat in an armchair, for instance, one leg crossed over at the knee, his arms stretched along the chair arms, fingers lightly drumming the ends, was at once familiar, as was the way he held a cigarette, the way he inhaled smoke and released it, the way he nodded his head in emphasis. None of these similarities had been discernible from photographs. He seemed, curiously, to be more like her father – whom she had loved but had never bothered to get to know until it was too late – than her father had been himself.

Sometimes she and the children had Noel Nostalgia Evenings, when she played them all her old scratched seventy-eights. Flora, in particular, was attentive and appreciative. 'I really love Noel,' she said once, but Flora loved lots of things, and most people. James always absented himself from Noel Nostalgia Evenings, either going to bed earlier than usual, or shutting himself in the study with his dictaphone and his in-tray.

She thought about Noel whenever his name was mentioned in the press or on the wireless which was increasingly often. They were not real thoughts, more a feeling of tenderness. It was comforting to know that he was alive somewhere, getting up in the morning, cleaning his teeth, eating, making jokes. Nothing too terrible could happen in a world that contained him. But he was old and, according to reports, often ill. The day could not be far off that she dreaded when she'd turn on the wireless unsuspectingly and hear a newsreader announce: Sir Noel Coward died today at his home in Jamaica (or Switzerland; or wherever he happened to be), and then, after a brief biography, go on to give the cricket scores, as though the world were still the same place.

She was glad that he was being fêted in his old age, though a part of her felt resentful that he was everybody's darling now. There was nothing special or peculiar or different about loving Noel Coward. Even his critics had stopped being critical and seemed to think that everything he'd ever written was bloody marvellous. This was surely insulting, and a mistake she'd never made, even at ten years old.

When Christina, whom she had not seen for years, telephoned and suggested they go together to see *Cowardy Custard* at the Mermaid, she was tempted to refuse. Only Noel Coward could sing a Noel Coward song. She did not want to see a camp chorus perform dance routines with top hats and canes or hear them wreck his songs by sticking too closely to the melody in places where he would sing seconds or merely speak the lines. But she went because it would be nice to get away from James and the children for once, and she enjoyed herself because it was fun seeing Christina (fat now, hooray, whereas she had remained eight stone five – except during her pregnancies – for the past twenty years). *Cowardy Custard* itself was exactly as she'd thought it would be.

Three weeks later she got back from the afternoon school run to find a note stuck in one of the children's gumboots outside the front door:

Your telephone's out of order. We've got one spare ticket for *Cowardy Custard* on the 17th, and knowing your passion for N.C. thought of you. Please come if James can spare you. Supper in the Garrick afterwards.

After a little thought – it was very kind of the Evanses to ask her and she didn't want to seem ungrateful – she refused the invitation, explaining that James had already spared her once to see it, and suggesting the ticket should go to someone who hadn't because it was a wonderful . . . (she paused here, because the word 'show' was so disagreeable, but how else could she describe it?). She also said, which was true, that there was a parent-teacher meeting at Flora's school that evening, and that she ought to be there. Flora's maths being what they were.

On the morning of the 18th she had washed up the breakfast things, wiped some surfaces, made the beds (Jack's had to be stripped because he'd wet his sheets without telling), collected socks and knickers from the floor of every bedroom and put them in the dirty linen basket, stared out of Flora's bedroom window unseeingly for half an hour, wished she were dead, and was just about to start on the mountain of ironing she'd been avoiding for days because it was all tangled up with laddered tights and matted and odd socks, when the telephone rang. She recognised Jane Evans's voice:

'Antonia – it's Jane here. I can hardly bear to tell you this, but we were sitting in our seats at the Mermaid yesterday just before the curtain went up, when NOEL COWARD walked into our row and sat down in the seat next to yours – I mean the one you'd have been in. He got a standing ovation. The whole theatre clapped and roared for at least ten minutes. He was on his own and seemed very frail and old and his hands shook and he wept throughout the entire performance. It was rather upsetting, really, but wonderful too, of course. You never did meet him, did you? And if you'd been there you'd have sat NEXT TO HIM' (she shouted this). 'I really can't bear it!'

After Jane had rung off, she sat on her bed and stared at the floor. Tears, for sad Noel and for herself, spilled over and ran, slowly at first and then faster and faster, down her cheeks. They fell onto a join in the carpet that had come unstuck, its edges curled back to reveal the underlay. The carpet, once a subtle shade of blue, was grubby now, and needed not just hoovering but a good going over on hands and knees with a sponge and a bucket of *1001*, something she'd been putting off for months.

NOTHING MISSING
BUT THE SAMOVAR

———— ◆ ————

Penelope Lively

It was July when he went to Morswick, early autumn when he left it; in retrospect it was to seem always summer, those heavy, static days of high summer, of dingy weather and outbursts of sunshine, of blue sky and heaped clouds. Of straw and horseflies. Blackberries; jam for tea; church on Sunday. The Landers.

Dieter Helpmann was twenty-four, a tall, fair young man, serious-looking but with a smile of great sweetness; among his contemporaries he seemed older than he was, sober, reserved, the quiet member of a group, the listener. He had come from Germany to do his post-graduate degree – a thesis on nineteenth-century Anglo-Prussian relations. His father was a distinguished German journalist. Dieter intended to go into journalism himself; he was English correspondent, now, for a sociopolitical weekly, contributing periodic articles on aspects of contemporary Britain. His English was perfect: idiomatic, lightly accented. His manners were attractive; he held doors open for women, rose to his feet for them, was deferential to his elders. All this made him seem slightly old-fashioned, as did his worried liberalism, which looked not shrewd nor edgy enough for a journalist. His gentle, concerned pieces about education, industrial unrest, the housing problem, read more like a sympathetic academic analysis of the ills of some other time than energetic journalism.

It was 1957, and he had spent eighteen months in England. The year before – the year of Suez and Hungary – he had seen his friends send telegrams to the Prime Minister fiercely dissociating themselves from British intervention; he had agonised alongside them, outraged both with and for them; he had written an article on 'the alienation of the British intellectual' that was emotional and partisan. His father commented that he seemed deeply committed – 'The climate appears to suit you, in more ways than one.' And Dieter had written back, 'You are right – and it is its variety I think that appeals the most. It is a place that so much defies analysis – just as you think you have the measure of it, you stumble across yet another confusing way in which the different layers of British life overlap, another curious anachronism. I have to admit that I have caught Anglophilia, for better or for worse.'

He had. He loved the place. He loved the sobriety of the academic world in which he mostly moved. He loved all those derided qualities of reserve and restraint, he loved the landscape. He liked English girls, while remaining faithful to his German fiancée, Erica (also engaged on post-graduate work, but in Bonn). He liked and respected what he took to be a basic cultural stability; here was a place where things changed, but changed with dignity. To note, to understand, became his deep concern.

All that, though, took second place to the thesis. That was what mattered at the moment, the patient quarrying into a small slice of time, a small area of activity. He worked hard. Most of his waking hours were spent in the agreeable hush of great libraries, or alone in his room with his card index and his notebooks.

He had been about to start writing the first draft when it happened. 'I have had the most remarkable piece of luck,' he wrote to Erica. 'Peter Sutton – he is the friend who is working on John Stuart Mill, you remember – is married to a girl who comes from Dorset and knows a family whose forebear was ambassador in Berlin in the 1840s and apparently they still have all his papers. In trunks in the attic! They are an aristocratic family – Sir Philip Lander is the present holder of the title, a baronetcy. Anyway, Felicity Sutton has known them all her life (she is rather upper-class too, but intelligent, and married Peter at Cambridge, where they both were – this is something of a feature of the young English intelligentsia, these inter-class marriages, Peter of course is of a working-class background), and mentioned that I would be interested in the papers and they said at once apparently that I would be welcome to go down there and have a look. It certainly is a stroke of luck – Felicity says she got the impression there is a vast amount of stuff, all his personal correspondence and official papers too. I go next week, I imagine it will all be rather grand . . .'

There was no car to meet him, as promised. At least, he stood at the entrance to the small country station and the only waiting cars were a taxi and a small pick-up van with open back full of agricultural sacks. He checked Sir Philip Lander's letter: date and time were right. Apprehensively he turned to go to the telephone kiosk – and at that moment the occupant of the van, who had been reading a newspaper, looked up, opened the door and stepped out, smiling.

Or rather unfolded himself. He was immensely tall, well over six foot. He towered above Dieter, holding out a hand, saying my dear fellow, I'm so sorry, had you been there long – I didn't realise the train was in – I say, is that all the luggage you've got, let me shove it in the back . . .

Bemused, Dieter climbed into the van beside him. It smelled of petrol and, more restrainedly, of horse.

They wound through lanes and over hills. Sir Philip boomed, above the unhealthy sound of the van's engine, of topography, of recollections of Germany before the war, of the harvest. He wore corduroy trousers laced with wisps of hay, gumboots, a tweed jacket. He was utterly affable, totally without affectation, impregnable in his confidence. Dieter, looking out of the window, saw a countryside that seemed dormant, the trees' dark drooping shapes, the cattle huddled in tranquil groups, their tails lazily twitching. The phrase of some historian about 'the long deep sleep of the English people' swam into his head; he listened to Sir Philip and talked and had the impression of travelling miles, of being swallowed up by this billowing, drowsy landscape.

Once, Sir Philip stopped at a village shop and came out with a cardboard carton of groceries; the van, after this, refused to start and Dieter got out to push. As he got back in, Sir Philip said, 'Thanks so much. Very old, I'm afraid. Needs servicing, too – awful price nowadays, a service. Oh, well . . .' They passed a pub called the Lander Arms, beetle-browed cottages, an unkempt village green, a Victorian school, turned in at iron gates that shed curls of rusting paint, and jolted up a long, weedy, rutted drive.

It could never have been a beautiful house, Morswick: early seventeenth century, satisfactory enough in its proportions, with a moderately ambitious flight of steps (now cracked and crumbling) to the front door, but without the gilding of any famous architectural hand. The immediate impression was of a combination of resilience and decay: the pock-marked stone, the window frames unpainted for many years, the pedestal-less urns with planting of woody geraniums, the weeds fringing the steps, the rusted guttering.

They went in. Dieter had a muddled impression of welcoming hands and faces, a big cool hallway, a wide oak staircase, perplexing passages and doors culminating in a room with window looking out onto a field in which a girl jumped a large horse to and fro over an obstacle made from old oil-drums. He changed his shirt, watching her.

Only later, over tea, did he sort them all out. And that took time and effort, so thunderstruck was he by the room in which it was eaten, that bizarre – preposterous – backdrop to brown bread and butter, Marmite, fish paste and gooseberry jam.

It was huge, stone-flagged, its exterior wall taken up with one great high window, as elaborate with stone tracery as that of a church transept. There were family portraits all round the room – a jumble of artistic good and bad – and above them jutted banners so airy with age as to be completely colourless. The table at which they sat must have been twelve feet long; the wood had the rock-hard feel of immense age; there was nothing in sight that was new except the electric kettle with which Lady Lander made the tea. ('The kitchen is such miles away, we do as much as we can in here . . .')

He stared incredulously at the banners, the pictures, at pieces of furniture such as he had only ever seen before in museums. These, though, were scarred with use, faded by sun, their upholstery in ribbons: Empire chairs and sofas, eighteenth-century cabinets, pedestal tables, writing desks, bureaux. Bemused, he smiled and thanked and spread jam on brown bread and was handed a cup of tea by his hostess.

She was French, but seemed, he thought, poles removed from any Frenchwoman he had ever known – there was nothing left but the faintest accent, the occasional misuse of a word. And then there was the mother-in-law, old Lady Lander, a small pastel figure in her special chair (so fragile-looking, how could she have perpetrated that enormous man?) and Madame Heurgon, Lady Lander's mother, and the two boys, Philip and James, and Sophie, the old French nurse, and Sally, who was sixteen (she it was who had been jumping that horse, beyond the window).

He ate his tea, and smiled and listened. Later, he wrote to his father (and forgot to post the letter): 'This is the most extraordinary family, I hardly know what to make of them as yet. The French mother-in-law has been here twenty years but speaks the most dreadful English, and yet she never stirs from the place, it seems – I asked her if she went back to France often and she said, "Oh, but of course not, it is so impossibly expensive to go abroad nowadays." The boys go away to boarding school, but the girl, Sally, went to some local school and is really barely educated at all, daughters are expendable, I suppose. And they are all there, all the time, for every meal, the old nurse too, and in the evenings they all sit in the drawing-room, listening to the wireless – comedy shows that bewilder them all, except the children, who try to explain the jokes and references, all at once, so no one can hear a word anyway. The old ladies, and the nurse, are in there all day, knitting and sewing and looking out of the window and saying how hot it is, or how cold, and how early the fruit is, or how late, day after day, just the same, there is nothing missing but the samovar . . . Sir Philip is out most of the time, in the fields, he is nothing if not a working farmer, tomorrow I shall help him with some young bullocks they have up on the hill.

'I have not yet looked at the papers.'

That first day there had been no mention of the papers at all; and he had not, he realised, as he got into bed, given them so much as a thought himself. After tea he had been shown round the place by Sally and the boys: the weedy gardens where couch grass and bindweed quenched the outline of tennis court, kitchen garden, and what had once been a formal rose garden with box hedges and a goldfish pond. From time to time they met Lady Lander, hoeing a vegetable bed or snipping the dead heads from flowers; she worked with a slow deliberation that seemed appropriate to the hopeless task of controlling that large area. To go any faster would have been pointless – the forces of nature were winning hands down in any case – to give up altogether would be craven. There was no gardener, Sally said – 'The only men are Daniels and Jim, and Jim's only half really because he's on day release at the tech and of course Daddy needs them on the farm all the time.'

They toured the stables (a graceful eighteenth-century court-yard, more architecturally distinguished than the house) and admired the Guernsey cows grazing in a paddock nearby. Sir Philip came down the drive on a tractor, and dismounted to join them and explain the finer points of raising calves to Dieter: this was a small breeding herd. 'Of course,' he said, 'it doesn't really make sense, economic sense, one never gets enough for them, but it's something I've always enjoyed doing.'

Sally broke in, 'And they *look* so nice.'

He beamed at the cows, and his daughter. 'Of course. That's half the point.'

A car was approaching slowly, taking the ruts and bumps with caution, a new model. Sir Philip said, 'Ah. here's George Nethercott, we're going to have a chat about those top fields.' He moved away from them as the car stopped, saying, 'Good evening, George, very good of you to come up – how's your hay going, I'm afraid we're making a very poor showing this year, I'm about 300 bales short so far. I say, that's a very smart car . . .'

His voice carried in the stillness of the early evening; it seemed the only forceful element in all that peace of pigeons cooing, cows cropping the grass, hypnotically shifting trees.

Sally said, 'Mr Nethercott's land joins our farm on two sides. Daddy may be going to sell him the three hill fields because we've got to have a new tractor next year, it's a pity, you oughtn't to sell land . . .' Her voice trailed away vaguely, and then she went on with sudden enthusiasm, 'I say, do you like riding? Would you like to try Polly?'

'You will never believe it, I have been horse-riding,' he wrote to Erica. 'Not for long, I hasten to say – I fell off with much humiliation, and was made a great fuss of. They are such a charming family, and have a way of drawing you into everything they do, without ever really bothering about whether it is the kind of thing you are fitted for, or would like . . . So that I find myself leading the most extraordinary – for me – life, mending fences, herding cattle, picking fruit, hay-making.

'Next week I must get down to the papers.'

Sir Philip had taken him up to the attics. 'I really don't know what we shall find,' he said. 'Things get shoved away for years, you know, and one has very little idea . . . I've not been up here for ages.'

There were pieces of furniture, grey with dust, and suitcases, and heaps of mouldering curtains and blankets; a sewing-machine that looked like the prototype of all sewing-machines; gilt-framed pictures stacked against a wall; a jumble of withered saddlery that Sir Philip picked up and examined. 'I wonder if Sally mightn't be able to make use of some of this.'

Dieter, looking at an eighteenth-century chest of drawers pushed away beneath a dormer window, and thinking also of the furniture with which the rest of the house was filled, said, 'You have some nice antique pieces.' Sir Philip, still trying to unravel a harness, said, 'Oh no, Dieter, not really, it's all just things that have always been here, you know.' He put the harness down and moved away into another, inner attic room with a single small window overlooking the stable-yard. 'I have a feeling the stuff we're looking for is in these boxes here.'

Later, Dieter sat at a small folding green baize card table he had found in a corner, and began to open the bundles of letters and papers. It was much as Felicity Sutton had predicted: there were family letters all mixed up with official correspondence both from and to the Sir Philip Lander of the 1840s. It was a research worker's gold-mine. He glanced through a few documents at random, and then began to try to sort things out into some kind of order, thinking that eventually, before he left, he must suggest tactfully that all this should be deposited in the Public Record Office or some other appropriate place. In the meantime it was just his own good luck . . .

Curiously, he could not feel as excited or interested as he should. He read, and made a few notes, and yawned, and beyond the fly-blown window small puffy clouds coasted in a sky of duck-egg blue, the garden trees sighed and heaved, and if he lifted himself slightly in his chair he could see down into the stable-yard where Sally was in attendance on that enormous horse of hers, circling its huge complacent rump with brush and comb. Presently Sir Philip drove the tractor into the yard, and, with one of the boys, began to unload bales of hay. Dieter put his pen down, tidied his notes into a pile, and went down to help.

He had never known time pass so slowly – and so fast. The days were thirty-six hours long, and yet fled by so quickly that suddenly he had been there for two and a half weeks. Much embarrassed, he went one morning to find Lady Lander in the kitchen and insist that he should pay for his keep.

She was making jam. The room was filled with the sweet fruity smell; flies buzzed drunkenly against the windows. Astonished, she said, 'Oh, but of course not, we couldn't hear of such a thing, you are a guest.'

'But I am staying so long, originally Sir Philip suggested a few days, and with one thing and another it has got longer and longer. Please, really I should prefer . . .'

She would have none of it.

He hardly knew himself how it was that his departure was always postponed. Of course, he had done no work at all, as yet, on the papers, but he could get down to that any time. And always there was something that loomed – 'You must be sure to be here for the County Show next week,' Sir Philip would say. 'You'll find it amusing if you've not seen that kind of thing before – do you have the equivalent in Germany, I wonder?' Or Sally would remember suddenly that the first cubbing meet was in ten days' time. 'You'll still be here, won't you, Dieter? Oh, you must be – honestly, if you've never seen a meet . . .'

He protested to Lady Lander – 'Please, I would be happier . . .', but could see that there was no point in going on. 'In any case,' she said, turning back to the pink-frothing pan on the stove, 'you have been most helpful to my husband, he is always short-handed at this time of year, I am afraid only that we drive you into things you would never normally dream of doing. You must say, you know, if it bores you – we tend to forget, down here, that not everyone lives this kind of life.'

And she, he wondered, had she not once been someone quite different? On Sundays, both she and her mother appeared for church in quite unfashionable but recognisably expensive clothes – silk dresses and citified hats of pre-war style. In these incongruous outfits, they walked down the lane to the village church. The family filled the whole of the front pew; Sir Philip's confident tenor led the sparse congregation; afterwards they would all stand, every week, for the same amount of time, chatting to the Vicar. Then back to Morswick, stopping again from time to time to talk with village people.

He had thought, when he first came, that it was feudal, and had been amused. Now, his perceptions heightened, he saw otherwise. 'It is not that they are not respected,' he wrote to his father. 'Far from it – people are deferential to them – a title still means something, and they have always been the big family in these parts. But it is as though they are runners in a race who are being outstripped without even realising it. I think they hardly notice that their farming neighbours have new gadgets they have not – washing machines, televisions – that theirs is the shabbiest car for miles around, that the Morswick tractor is so out of date, Nethercott (the neighbour) declined the loan of it when his broke down. And why? you will be saying, after all they have land, a house, possessions. But the land is not good, a lot of it is rough hill-grazing, I suppose that is at the root of the problem – and a mansion and a family past are not very realisable assets. I certainly can't imagine them selling the furniture. But when you come down to it – it is as though there is also some kind of perverse lack of will, as though they both didn't know, and didn't want to know.'

The children were where it most showed. Beside their contemporaries – the sons and daughters of the local farming families (many of them at private schools, their country accents fast fading), they seemed quaint, too young for their ages, innocent. Sally, talking to other adolescent girls at an agricultural show, was the only one without lipstick, a hair-do, the quick glancing self-consciousness of young womanhood. She seemed a child beside them.

At the cubbing meet – held outside the village pub – he found it almost unbearable. Standing beside Lady Lander, he watched her. Lady Lander said, 'She's not well mounted, I'm afraid, poor darling – we've only got old Polly these days.'

It was a huge horse, with a hefty muscularity that suggested carthorse ancestry. Seated on it, Sally towered above the dapper ponies of the other children. Beaming, unconscious of the vaguely comic figure she cut, she yanked the horse's head away from a tray of glasses that was being carried around, and waved at Dieter. She wore her school mac over grubby breeches and a pair of battered hunting-boots. The other girls were crisp in pale jodhpurs, tweed jackets and little velvet caps.

Dieter was wrenched by pity, and love.

He adored her. With horror he had recognised his own feelings, which smacked, it seemed to him, of paedophilia. She was sixteen; her rounded features, her plump awkward body, were raw with childishness. He was obsessed by her. He forced himself to contemplate her ignorance, her near-illiteracy. He thought of Erica, of her sharp clever face, the long hours of serious discussion, the shared concerns, and it did no good at all.

And Sally had not the slightest inkling, nor ever would, of how he felt. She jostled him in puppyish horse-play; she worked beside him in the harvest field, her breasts straining at her aertex shirt, her brown legs as shiny with health and vigour as the rump of that incongruous horse she rode; he could hardly take his eyes off her, and was appalled at himself.

In the evenings, he played board games with the two boys, held skeins of knitting wool for old Lady Lander as she wound the balls. Sometimes, he took a book from the great high cases that lined the walls of the drawing-room. They held an odd assortment: bound volumes of *Punch*, row upon row, Edwardian books about hunting and fishing, the classic Victorian novelists, books of humorous verse, Henty and Buchan and Rider Haggard. He read with perplexity novels like *The Constant Nymph*, *Precious Bane* and *Beau Geste* that seemed to fit not at all with the concept of English twentieth-century literature that he had formed after two years' carefully selective leisure reading. Scanning the titles on the shelves, he had a confusing impression of being presented with a whole shadow culture of which he had been unaware. Yet again he felt his own judgements and perceptions to be hopelessly inadequate. Sir Philip, standing beside him at the bookcase one evening, said, 'Glad to see you're making use of the library, Dieter – I'm afraid none of us get much time for reading.' There was hardly a single recent edition, not an untattered dust-cover to be seen.

On a day of sullen rain clouds, when the whole landscape seemed sunk in apathy, the old tractor broke down with more than usual finality. For hour after hour, Sir Philip and Daniels crawled around it, oiling and adjusting; Dieter, on edge with vicarious anxiety (it was needed for several urgent jobs), watched in frustration, cursing his lack of mechanical knowhow. The worry on Sir Philip's face distressed him greatly; he longed to help. Eventually, the tractor sputtered into fitful life, and everybody stood back smiling. Sir Philip said, 'Well, Daniels, we shan't have any of these crises next year, when we've got the new one, I hope.' And Daniels said, 'That's right, sir, we'll be in clover then,' and added, looking down the drive, 'here's Mr Nethercott now.'

Nethercott had come, though, not to talk about fields but to look at the bull Sir Philip proposed selling. It was a young bull, whose performance was proving unreliable. Daniels was in favour of going over to artificial insemination. Sir Philip had reluctantly concurred, as they stood side by side at the gate, a few days before, watching the bull at work among the cows in a steeply sloping field opposite. Sir Philip said, 'You're right, Daniels, I'm not too happy about him either.'

'Silly bugger don't realise he got to do it downhill.'

Sir Philip turned away. 'Oh well, there's nothing to be done – he'll have to go. Now, George Nethercott's wanting a bull, I know – I'll give him a ring tonight.'

And now Nethercott too stood at the field-gate, studying the bull. Other matters were talked of for a while, then he said, 'How much were you thinking of asking for him?'

Sir Philip named a price.

Nethercott nodded. There was a brief silence and then he said with a trace of embarrassment, 'He might well work out more satisfactory than he looks just now – but the fact is, what I'm looking for's going to cost a fair bit more than that. Thanks for letting me have a look at him, though.'

A week or so later, they heard through the postman that Nethercott had paid five hundred pounds for a bull at the Royal Show. Sir Philip said, 'Well, good heavens! Lucky fellow.' He was standing with Dieter in the front drive, the two or three brown envelopes that the postman had brought in his hand. 'I really don't know how people manage it, these days. He's a good chap, Nethercott – they're a nice family. His grandfather used to work here, you know, for mine – stable-lad he was, I think. Well, I suppose we might get on with that fencing today, eh?'

Up in the attic, the sun striking through the window had browned Dieter's single page of notes; there was a faint paler stripe where the pencil lay.

At the beginning of September, the boys went back to boarding school. The corn was down, the blackberries ripening, the green of the trees spiced here and there with the first touch of autumn colour. Since he had come here, Dieter realised, the landscape had changed, working through its cycle so unobtrusively that only with an effort did one remember the brimming cornfields of July, the hedgerows still bright with wild flowers, the long light evenings. Now, the fields were bleached and shaven, the hedges lined with the skeletal heads of dried cow-parsley and docks, the grass white with dew in the mornings. It came as a faint shock to realise that the place was not static at all, that that impression of deep slumber was quite false, that change was continuous, that nothing stood still. That he could not stay here for ever.

There was a dance, in the local market town, in connection with some equestrian activity, to which he went with Sally and her parents. It was the first time, he realised, that he had ever been anywhere with them when the whole family had not come, grandmothers and all. Sally wore an old dress of her mother's that had been cut down for her; it did not fit and was unbecoming, but she shone with excitement and anticipation. In the hotel where the dance took place, the other young girls were waiting about in the foyer in sharp-eyed groups and he was stricken again at Sally's frumpish looks in contrast to their fashionable dresses, their knowingness. But she was quite happy – laughing, greeting acquaintances.

He danced with her once at the beginning, and then left her with a group of her contemporaries. But later, the evening under way, whenever he saw her she was dancing with friends of her parents, or sitting alone on one of a row of gilt chairs at the edge of the room, holding a glass of lemonade, but still radiant, tapping her foot in time to the music. After a while he went over and sat beside her.

'Are you having a good time, Sally?'

'Marvellous!'

'Let's dance, shall we?'

She was clumsy; he had to steer her round the room. She said, 'Sorry, I'm hopeless. We did have dancing lessons at school but it's quite different when it's a real man, and anyway I always had to take man because of being tall, so I'm no good at being the woman. I say, Mummy says perhaps I can go to the Hunt Ball this year – will you still be here?'

He said, 'I'm afraid not. I have to go back before the term begins in October.'

'Oh, what a pity.' They danced in silence for a minute or two and then she said suddenly, 'What are you going to do after you've finished your – your what's-it, the thing you're writing?'

'I shall go back to Germany and get a job. I expect I shall get married,' he added after a fractional pause. He had never spoken of Erica at Morswick.

'Will you?' She looked amazed. 'Gosh – how exciting. Do write and tell us, won't you, so that we can send a present.'

She beamed up at him; she smelled of toothpaste and, very faintly, of a cheap scent that she must have acquired in secrecy and tentatively used. He had seen, once, into her room; there had been a balding toy dog on the pillow, photographs of horses pinned to the walls, glass animals on the windowsill. She said, 'Do you know, they want me to go to a sort of finishing school place in Grenoble next year.'

'I should think you would like that.'

She said, 'Oh no, I couldn't possibly go. I couldn't bear to leave Morswick. No, I can't possibly.'

Dieter said, 'Sally, I think you should, I really do.'

She shook her head.

Later, back at Morswick, he sat with Sir Philip in the drawing-room; Sally and her mother had gone to bed. Sir Philip had taken a bottle of whisky from the cupboard and poured them both a glass; it was almost the first time Dieter had ever seen alcohol produced at Morswick, except for the glass of sherry offered to their rare visitors. Sir Philip said, 'Quite a successful evening, I thought. Of course, you get rather a different kind of person at this sort of do now – it's not really like before the war. I daresay my father would be a bit taken aback if he was still alive.'

He began to talk about his wartime experiences in Italy and France; he had been with the Sicily landings, and then in Normandy shortly after D-day, advancing through France and into Germany. Remembering suddenly the delicacy of the subject, he looked across at Dieter and said, 'I hope you don't . . . of course, one realised at the time how many people like yourself, like your father . . . What a wretched business it all was, so much worse in many ways for you than for us.'

Dieter said, 'I think you would be interested to see Germany now. I wish you would come to visit us – my father would be so delighted to make arrangements, if all of you could come, or perhaps at least the boys and Sally.'

'How awfully kind. We really must try to – you know, I can't think when we last had a holiday of any sort. Yes, we really must.' He swilled the whisky in his glass, peering down into it. 'Yes. Of course, one is so awfully tied up here, being pretty short-handed nowadays. I daresay things will pick up in time, though. I must admit, it is getting a bit hard to manage just at the moment – still, we keep our heads above water. Anyway, I really mustn't burden you with our problems. By the way, I hope you didn't mean what you said earlier about leaving us next week – I'd imagined we'd have you with us for some time to come. There's the Harvest Festival on Sunday week – I'm sure Jeanne was intending to rope you in for one thing and another.'

'I have to get back – the term begins soon, you see. My supervisor – well, they must wonder what on earth has become of me. And in any case, you've been far too kind already, too hospitable. I don't know how to thank you enough.'

'I'm afraid what with one thing and another you've not had all that much time to put in on those papers. They've been of some interest, I hope?'

Dieter said, 'Oh yes, extremely interesting.'

The day before he was to leave he went to the attic to clear up the green baize table. His note-pad, with its single page of notes, was curled at the edges now, and dusty. Insects had died on the opened bundles of letters. Beyond the window, the landscape had slipped a notch further into autumn: there was a mist smoking up from the fields, and long curtains of old man's beard hanging down the wall beside the stable-yard. He tied up the letters again and put them away in the trunk, folded the card table, gathered up his own things. He opened the window for a moment, with some vague notion of airing the place, and heard, faintly, Sally whistling as she did something out of sight in one of the loose boxes.

His departure for the station was delayed for a few minutes by the arrival of Nethercott. Sir Philip stood with him at the field-gate nodding and listening. When at last he finished, and Nethercott, apologising for turning up at what was obviously an inappropriate moment, had driven away, the whole family was gathered on the steps to say goodbye to Dieter. He had shaken hands with them all, several times; everyone was smiling and interrupting. Sir Philip came across the drive to them and said, 'Sorry about that – had to have a word or two since he'd taken the trouble to come up.'

Lady Lander said, 'What was it about?'

'Oh, just the fields – you know, the hill fields. He'd like to make an offer for them but I'd got things a bit wrong, I'm afraid – they're worth rather less than I'd imagined, on the current market. Rather a lot less, I'm afraid. George was awfully apologetic – you'd have thought it was his fault. He's a good chap.'

'Oh dear, does that mean no new tractor?'

'I suppose it does. I don't know how I'm going to break that to poor Daniels. Well, anyway,' he went on cheerfully, 'we'll be able to send the old one for a thorough overhaul, we'll have to make do with that. Now, Dieter, we'd better be on our way, hadn't we, where's your case . . .'

He saw them like that, in his mind's eye, for long after – the women – standing on the front steps waving and smiling. 'It's au revoir, anyway,' Lady Lander had said, 'because we shall see you again, next time you're in our part of the world, shan't we?' And her mother-in-law, that frail old lady in her pale floppy clothes and regimental brooches, had piped up, 'Oh yes, we're always here, you know, you'll always find us here,' and Sally was calling out not to forget to let them know about the wedding. She had given him a hug and a kiss; the feel of her arms, her warm soft face, the smell of her, stayed with him all the way to the station, and beyond. And the sight of them, and of the house behind, frozen in the furry yellow light of the September morning, like an old photograph – the figures grouped around the steps, the house with its backdrop of fields and hills and trees.

At the station, Sir Philip shook him by the hand. 'We've enjoyed having you, Dieter. You must get down to us again sometime. You'll find everything goes on much as ever at Morswick. And the best of luck with your doctorate.'

In the train, Dieter began a letter to Erica, and then sat staring out of the window at that placid landscape (the landscape of Constable, he told himself, of Richard Wilson, of the English novelists) and saw only the irresistible manifestations of change: the mottled trees, the tangle of spent growth in the hedgerows.

TO HELL WITH DYING

◆

Alice Walker

'To hell with dying,' my father would say. 'These children want Mr Sweet!'

Mr Sweet was a diabetic and an alcoholic and a guitar player and lived down the road from us on a neglected cotton farm. My older brothers and sisters got the most benefit from Mr Sweet, for when they were growing up he had quite a few years ahead of him and so was capable of being called back from the brink of death any number of times – whenever the voice of my father reached him as he lay expiring. 'To hell with dying, man,' my father would say, pushing the wife away from the bedside (in tears although she knew the death was not necessarily the last one unless Mr Sweet really wanted it to be). 'These children want Mr Sweet!' And they did want him, for at a signal from Father they would come crowding around the bed and throw themselves on the covers, and whoever was the smallest at the time would kiss him all over his wrinkled brown face and begin to tickle him so that he would laugh all down in his stomach, and his moustache, which was long and sort of straggly, would shake like Spanish moss and was also that colour.

Mr Sweet had been ambitious as a boy, wanted to be a doctor or lawyer or sailor, only to find that black men fare better if they are not. Since he could become none of these things he turned to fishing as his only earnest career and playing the guitar as his only claim to doing anything extraordinarily well. His son, the only one that he and his wife, Miss Mary, had, was shiftless as the day is long and spent money as if he were trying to see the bottom of the mint, which Mr Sweet would tell him was the clean brown palm of his hand. Miss Mary loved her 'baby', however, and worked hard to get him the 'li'l necessaries' of life, which turned out mostly to be women.

Mr Sweet was a tall, thinnish man with thick kinky hair going dead white. He was dark brown, his eyes were very squinty and sort of bluish, and he chewed Brown Mule tobacco. He was constantly on the verge of being blind drunk, for he brewed his own liquor and was not in the least a stingy sort of man, and was always very melancholy and sad, though frequently when he was 'feelin' good' he'd dance around the yard with us, usually keeling over just as my mother came to see what the commotion was.

Toward all of us children he was very kind, and had the grace to be shy with us, which is unusual in grown-ups. He had great respect for my mother for she never held his drunkenness against him and would let us play with him even when he was about to fall in the fireplace from drink. Although Mr Sweet would sometimes lose complete or nearly complete control of his head and neck so that he would loll in his chair, his mind remained strangely acute and his speech not too affected. His ability to be drunk and sober at the same time made him an ideal playmate, for he was as weak as we were and we could usually best him in wrestling, all the while keeping a fairly coherent conversation going.

We never felt anything of Mr Sweet's age when we played with him. We loved his wrinkles and would draw some on our brows to be like him, and his white hair was my special treasure and he knew it and would never come to visit us just after he had had his hair cut off at the barbershop. Once he came to our house for something, probably to see my father about fertiliser for his crops because, although he never paid the slightest attention to his crops, he liked to know what things would be best to use on them if he ever did. Anyhow, he had not come with his hair since he had just had it shaved off at the barbershop. He wore a huge straw hat to keep off the sun and also to keep his head away from me. But as soon as I saw him I ran up and demanded that he take me up and kiss me with his funny beard which smelled so strongly of tobacco. Looking forward to burying my small fingers into his woolly hair I threw away his hat only to find he had done something to his hair, that it was no longer there! I let out a squall which made my mother think that Mr Sweet had finally dropped me in the well or something and from that day I've been wary of men in hats. However, not long after, Mr Sweet showed up with his hair grown out and just as white and kinky and impenetrable as it ever was.

Mr Sweet used to call me his princess, and I believed it. He made me feel pretty at five and six, and simply outrageously devastating at the blazing age of eight and a half. When he came to our house with his guitar the whole family would stop whatever they were doing to sit around him and listen to him play. He liked to play 'Sweet Georgia Brown', that was what he called me sometimes, and also he liked to play 'Caldonia' and all sorts of sweet, sad, wonderful songs which he sometimes made up. It was from one of these songs that I learned that he had had to marry Miss Mary when he had in fact loved somebody else (now living in Chica-go, or De-stroy, Michigan). He was not sure that Joe Lee, her 'baby', was also his baby. Sometimes he would cry and that was an indication that he was about to die again. And so we would all get prepared, for we were sure to be called upon.

I was seven the first time I remember actually participating in one of Mr Sweet's 'revivals' – my parents told me I had participated before, I had been the one chosen to kiss him and tickle him long before I knew the rite of Mr Sweet's rehabilitation. He had come to our house, it was a few years after his wife's death, and was very sad, and also, typically, very drunk. He sat on the floor next to me and my older brother, the rest of the children were grown up and lived elsewhere, and began to play his guitar and cry. I held his woolly head in my arms and wished I could have been old enough to have been the woman he loved so much and that I had not been lost years and years ago.

When he was leaving, my mother said to us that we'd better

sleep light that night for we'd probably have to go over to Mr Sweet's before daylight. And we did. For soon after we had gone to bed one of the neighbours knocked on our door and called my father and said that Mr Sweet was sinking fast and if he wanted to get in a word before the crossover he'd better shake a leg and get over to Mr Sweet's house. All the neighbours knew to come to our house if something was wrong with Mr Sweet, but they did not know how we always managed to make him well, or at least stop him from dying, when he was often so near death. As soon as we heard the cry we got up, my brother and I and my mother and father, and put on our clothes. We hurried out of the house and down the road for we were always afraid that we might someday be too late and Mr Sweet would get tired of dallying.

When we got to his house, a very poor shack really, we found the front room full of neighbours and relatives and someone met us at the door and said that it was all very sad that old Mr Sweet Little (for Little was his family name, although we mostly ignored it) was about to kick the bucket. My parents were advised not to take my brother and me into the 'death room', seeing we were so young and all, but we were so much more accustomed to the death room than he that we ignored him and dashed in without giving his warning a second thought. I was almost in tears, for these deaths upset me fearfully, and the thought of how much depended on me and my brother (who was such a ham most of the time) made me very nervous.

The doctor was bending over the bed and turned back to tell us for at least the tenth time in the history of my family that, alas, old Mr Sweet Little was dying and that the children had best not see the face of implacable death (I didn't know what 'implacable' was, but whatever it was, Mr Sweet was not!). My father pushed him rather abruptly out of the way saying, as he always did and very loudly for he was saying it to Mr Sweet, 'To hell with dying, man, these children want Mr Sweet' – which was my cue to throw myself upon the bed and kiss Mr Sweet all around the whiskers and under the eyes and around the collar of his nightshirt where he smelled so strongly of all sorts of things, mostly liniment.

I was very good at bringing him around, for as soon as I saw that he was struggling to open his eyes I knew he was going to be all right, and so could finish my revival sure of success. As soon as his eyes were open he would begin to smile and that way I knew that I had surely won. Once, though, I got a tremendous scare, for he could not open his eyes and later I learned that he had had a stroke and that one side of his face was stiff and hard to get into motion. When he began to smile I could tickle him in earnest because I was sure that nothing would get in the way of his laughter, although once he began to cough so hard that he almost threw me off his stomach, but that was when I was very small, little more than a baby, and my bushy hair had got in his nose.

When we were sure he would listen to us we would ask him why he was in bed and when he was coming to see us again and could we play with his guitar, which more than likely would be leaning against the bed. His eyes would get all misty and he would sometimes cry out loud, but we never let it embarrass us, for he knew that we loved him and that we sometimes cried too for no reason. My parents would leave the room to just the three of us; Mr Sweet, by that time, would be propped up in bed with a number of pillows behind his head and with me sitting and lying on his shoulder and along his chest. Even when he had trouble breathing he would not ask me to get down. Looking into my eyes he would shake his white head and run a scratchy old finger all around my hairline, which was rather low down, nearly to my eyebrows, and made some people say I looked like a baby monkey.

My brother was very generous in all this, he let me do all the revivalling – he had done it for years before I was born and so was glad to be able to pass it on to someone new. What he would do while I talked to Mr Sweet was pretend to play the guitar, in fact pretend that he was a young version of Mr Sweet, and it always made Mr Sweet glad to think that someone wanted to be like him – of course, we did not know this then, we played the thing by ear, and whatever he seemed to like, we did. We were desperately afraid that he was just going to take off one day and leave us.

It did not occur to us that we were doing anything special; we had not learned that death was final when it did come. We thought nothing of triumphing over it so many times, and in fact became a trifle contemptuous of people who let themselves be carried away. It did not occur to us that if our own father had been dying we could not have stopped it, that Mr Sweet was the only person over whom we had power.

When Mr Sweet was in his eighties I was studying in the university many miles from home. I saw him whenever I went home, but he was never on the verge of dying that I could tell and I began to feel that my anxiety for his health and psychological well-being was unnecessary. By this time he not only had a moustache but a long flowing snow-white beard, which I loved and combed and braided for hours. He was very peaceful, fragile, gentle, and the only jarring note about him was his old steel guitar, which he still played in the old sad, sweet, down-home blues way.

On Mr Sweet's ninetieth birthday I was finishing my doctorate in Massachusetts and had been making arrangements to go home for several weeks' rest. That morning I got a telegram telling me that Mr Sweet was dying again and could I please drop everything and come home. Of course I could. My dissertation could wait and my teachers would understand when I explained to them when I got back. I ran to the phone, called the airport, and within four hours I was speeding along the dusty road to Mr Sweet's.

The house was more dilapidated than when I was last there, barely a shack, but it was overgrown with yellow roses which my family had planted many years ago. The air was heavy and sweet and very peaceful. I felt strange walking through the gate and up the old rickety steps. But the strangeness left me as I caught sight of the long white beard I loved so well flowing down the thin body over the familiar quilt coverlet. Mr Sweet!

His eyes were closed tight and his hands, crossed over his stomach, were thin and delicate, no longer scratchy. I remembered how always before I had run and jumped up on him just anywhere; now I knew he would not be able to support my weight. I looked around at my parents, and was surprised to see that my father and mother also looked old and frail. My father, his own hair very grey, leaned over the quietly sleeping old man, who, incidentally, smelled still of wine and tobacco, and said, as he'd done so many times, 'To hell with dying, man! My daughter is home to see Mr Sweet!' My brother had not been able to come as he was in the war in Asia. I bent down and gently stroked the closed eyes and gradually they began to open. The closed wine-stained lips twitched a little, then parted in a warm, slightly embarrassed smile. Mr Sweet could see me and he recognised me and his eyes looked very spry and twinkly for a moment. I put my head down on the pillow next to his and we just looked at each other for a long time. Then he began to trace my peculiar hairline with a thin, smooth finger. I closed my eyes when his finger halted above my ear (he used to rejoice at the dirt in my ears when I was little), his hand stayed cupped around my cheek. When I opened my eyes, sure that I had reached him in time, his were closed.

Even at twenty-four how could I believe that I had failed? that Mr Sweet was really gone? He had never gone before. But when I looked up at my parents I saw that they were holding back tears. They had loved him dearly. He was like a piece of rare and delicate china which was always being saved from breaking and which finally fell. I looked long at the old face, the wrinkled forehead, the red lips, the hands that still reached out to me. Soon I felt my father pushing something cool into my hands. It was Mr Sweet's guitar. He had asked them months before to give it to me; he had known that even if I came next time he would not be able to respond in the old way. He did not want me to feel that my trip had been for nothing.

The old guitar! I plucked the strings, hummed 'Sweet Georgia Brown'. The magic of Mr Sweet lingered still in the cool steel box. Through the window I could catch the fragrant delicate scent of tender yellow roses. The man on the high old-fashioned bed with the quilt coverlet and the flowing white beard had been my first love.

LOVE WITHOUT MARRIAGE

THE TRUE PRIMITIVE

◆

Elizabeth Taylor

Lily had not considered culture – as a word or anything else – until she fell in love. As soon as that happened it, culture, descended on her. It was as if all the books Mr Ransome had ever read were thrown at her one after the other – Voltaire, Tolstoy, Balzac – the sharp names came at her, brutal spondees, brutally pronounced. She thought, though, that she hated Dostoievsky most of all. 'Yes, Dad,' Mr Ransome's two sons continually said, agreeing to rate Zola higher than Dickens if he wished them to, promising to remember what he had told them about Michelangelo. Painters' names were also part of the attack, but Lily thought they sounded gentler. She had felt curiosity about someone called Leonardo when first she heard him mentioned and had wondered if he were Harry's cousin. When she asked Harry he laughed and referred her to his father, which meant three-quarters of an hour wasted, sitting in the kitchen listening, and then it was too late for them to go for their walk. Trembling with frustrated desire, she had learnt her lesson; she asked no more questions and sat sullenly quiet whenever the enemy names began again.

Only winter courting seemed to be allowed: then, with the Thames Valley giving off impenetrable vapours or taking in, day after day, torrents of rain until the river rose and spread over the fields, Harry was free to take her out; except, of course, for his two evenings at the art school. They held hands coming back in the bus from the cinema, kissed beneath dripping trees in the muddy lane, choked and whispered in the fog.

'Silly notion, venturing out tonight,' Mr Ransome would tell them. 'You've no right, letting her catch her death, Harry.'

'I think it's easing up now,' Lily would say. 'Just the clearing-up shower. And a spot or two of rain doesn't do anyone any harm.'

Mr Ransome, with a daunting-looking book open in front of him, would be hurriedly unfolding his spectacles.

'We ought to be going,' Lily whispered.

'Man is a political animal,' boomed Mr Ransome, wanting to throw as many words at them as he could before they escaped, but Lily had gone, was through the scullery and already standing in the wet garden and Harry sent an apologetic smile back at his father and followed her.

'Good Lord,' said Lily. 'Once he gets going.'

'He's a wonderful old man,' Harry said.

'You're both afraid of him, I think – you and Godfrey.'

'We *respect* him,' Harry said sententiously. 'He's been a good father and since Mother died he has no one to read to in the evenings. He misses that.'

'She did the best thing, dying,' Lily thought.

Mr Ransome was a lock-keeper. He and his sons lived in a red-brick cottage at the side of the lock. On hot summer afternoons, the garden was what people going through in their boats called a riot of colour. The primary colours assaulted the eye – salvias, geraniums, lobelias, calceolarias were made all the more dazzling by everything being whitewashed that Mr Ransome could lay his brush on – flower tubs, step-edges, the boulders round flowerbeds, the swinging chains round the little lawns. In winter-time, it seemed that it could not really have been so bright.

Now, when all the locks down the river were closed, the cottage was lost in a cauldron of steam and the sad sound of the weir came drearily through the fog. Mr Ransome wondered how Harry and Lily could prefer the sodden lanes to a nice fire and a book to read beside it. He read so much about great passions, of men and women crossing continents because of love, and enduring hardship and peril, not just the discomforts of a dark, wet night – but he could not see Harry and Lily go out without feeling utter exasperation at their fecklessness.

'It will be lovely when the summer comes,' Lily sometimes said; but Harry knew that it would not be, if by 'lovely' she meant they would have long evenings together in the golden meadows or walking along the towing-path. 'He does like us to get out with our sketching, Godfrey and me,' he said.

'I don't mind. We can go miles away. You can sketch with one hand and I'll sit beside you and hold the other.'

'We couldn't very well do that, you see, because Dad likes to come out with us.'

'I can't think why you bother with it when you've got such a nice job.'

Harry knew why he bothered. His father, self-taught painter, had once had a picture hung in a local exhibition – an oil-painting, moreover. 'I jib at nothing,' he had explained. The bright, varnished scene hung in the parlour now. 'It was not for sale,' he said, when no one bought it. Jibbing at nothing, he had used a great deal of paint and had, in some way, caught the hard, venomous colours of his own garden. 'The Towing Path of A Sunday' was inscribed carefully on the frame. The white chains stood out thickly, like icing piped on the canvas; the chestnut trees had pink cones of blossom stuck about them and dropped down sharp ovals of shadow on the emerald grass. 'If I had of had tuition,' Mr Ransome so often said. He would see to it, he added, that his sons should not look back and have to say the same. In their earliest days they had been given paintboxes and sketching-blocks; he had taken them to London to the National Gallery and shown them the *Virgin of the Rocks* and, standing in front of it, lectured them on Leonardo. They had not known which was most painful – their embarrassment or their shame at their own disloyalty in suffering it. Young as they were at the time, they realised that he was much stared at – the thin, fierce man with his square beard and so old-fashioned clothes – but they could not help feeling that he deserved it, booming away as he did in the echoing gallery. They even began to think that he expected to be noticed and took pleasure from it.

Harry and Godfrey, articled in respectable offices in the nearby town, were not quite yet a disappointment to him; for many great men mature late, their father reminded them, reach their height after middle age: Voltaire, for one. They went on with their art classes at evening school and were painstaking enough in their desire to please; but, sometimes, looking at them and then at their feeble paintings, Mr Ransome could not help thinking that passion was missing from them.

'They are not on fire,' he mourned, 'as I have been.'

Then Harry met Lily and seemed, to his father, to be less on fire than ever. 'But it will come,' he encouraged his sons. It must come. What had been in him so powerful a desire, so bitterly a failed attempt, could not be wasted, must be passed on, and in greater strength, too, if things were to turn out as he considered just.

Lily, impinging on his plan with her sly, mincing manner, her pout and her impatient sighs, was the eternal female enemy. He had built a bastion, a treasurehouse for his sons, with all the great names they had heard from the cradle, the learning he had struggled for to make their inheritance. It had come too easily, he realised now, and Harry would rather spend an evening talking inanities, lowering his mind to Lily's level. His attitude towards her was vexing, suggesting that he was willing, eager to learn something from her and even that she might be able to teach it: suppliant, receptive he was with her; yet it was surely for him to instruct, who knew so much, and dominate, being a man, and to concede, whatsoever he felt inclined to concede; not beg for favours.

Mr Ransome thought of his own happy married life – the woman, so gentle and conciliatory, listening to him as he read. Into those readings he had put the expression of his pleasure at being able to share with her the best he had discovered. She had sat and sewed and, when she raised her eyes to look for her scissors, she would also glance across at him and he, conscious of her doing so, would pause to meet this glance, knowing that it would be full of humble gratitude. She had never been able to comprehend half of what he had offered her, she had muddled the great names and once dozed off after a few pages of Stendhal; but something, he thought, must have seeped into her, something of the lofty music of prose, as she listened, evening after evening of her married life. Now he missed her and so much of the sound of his own voice that had gone with her.

How different was Lily. The moment he began to read aloud, or even to quote something, down came her eyelids to half-mast. An invisible curtain dropped over her and behind it she was without any response, as if heavily drugged. He would have liked to have stuck pins in her to see if she would cry out: instead, he assaulted her – indecently, she thought, and that was why she would not listen – with Cicero and Goethe, Ibsen and Nietzsche and a French poet, one of his specials, called Bawdyleer. Having removed herself, as it were, she would then glance at the clock, wind a curl round her finger and suddenly loosen it to spring back against her cheek. Distracted by this, Harry would murmur, 'Yes, Dad, I remember you telling us.' So Mr Ransome had lost them both. Come here, Lily seemed to be enticing his son. Come behind my invisible curtain and we can think of other things and play with my hair and be alone together.

Sometimes, but very rarely, Mr Ransome would manage to catch her unawares and force one of the names on her before she had time to bring down the curtain. Then her manner was rude and retaliatory instead of vague. 'And who, pray, is Dosty what's-is-name when he's at home?' She knew that Mr Ransome was her enemy and felt not only malice in his attitude towards her, but something she might have defined as obscenity if she had known the meaning of the word.

He – for he was at heart puritanical – had once or twice delighted to indulge in a bout of broadmindedness. She should learn that he and some of the great thinkers of the world could face the truth unflinchingly and even some of the words the truth must be described in. To the pure, he said, all things are pure: he watched Lily's look of prim annoyance, implying that to her they obviously were not. He was defeated, however, by the silence that fell – Lily's and his son's. His remark, made to seem blatant by being isolated and ignored, repeated itself in his own head and he felt his cheeks and brow darkening. He did not want to appear to have any impurity in his own mind and quickly bent down and rearranged the coals on the fire.

The spring was beginning; the puddles along the rutted lanes were blue, reflecting the bright sky, and lilac trees in cottage gardens bore buds as small as grape-pips. Although the darkness fell later, the interval of daylight after tea was of no use to Lily, for Mr Ransome had his two sons out, whitewashing and weeding and trimming. 'We shall have no time to do it once the season has begun,' he said.

'But what about us?' Lily asked Harry.

'I can't help but give him a hand of an evening. It wouldn't be right to leave it all to Godfrey.'

'It sounds as if the summer's going to be just as bad as the winter.'

All along, Harry had known it would be worse.

In the summer, the lock was always full, boats jostled together, smart women in motor launches stared through their dark glasses at men in rowing-boats wearing braces and knotted handker-chiefs on their heads: in the narrowness of the lock they were all resentful of their proximity to one another, and were glad, when the water had finished rising or falling, to see the gates open-ing slowly. The locks were an ordeal to be negotiated, not made easier by the passers-by on the tow-path who stopped to watch them lying exposed below and hoped that they would ram their craft into the gates, or take the paint off one of the white launches.

Steamers came through at intervals and then the lock was a well of noise with someone thumping at the piano in the saloon and cheery messages thrown from deck to towing-path; glasses of beer were held up to tantalise and the funny man of the party, wearing a yachting cap, sang 'A life on the ocean wave is better than going to sea.'

The pretty stretch of river with its willows hanging down to the water and the brilliance of the lock garden brought artists, with folding stools and easels, who took up much of Mr Ransome's time. Such an odd character they thought him, forgetting – as, of all people, the English should not – that characters are encouraged at the cost of their families' destruction. He showed them his own painting of the same scene and they were enraptured, they called him a true primitive and talked of the Douanier Rousseau.

On summer evenings, after days of advising these amateur artists, talking about himself, bringing in a great deal about Leonardo, Mr Ransome behaved as if he had been drinking too much. He boasted, belaboured his sons with words and then, from too much excitement, surrendered to self-pity. It suddenly seemed to him that he had wasted his life: he had seen this on the face of one stranger after another. 'You!' they had been thinking, 'a man who has all the great masters at his fingertips and can summon from memory one thundering phrase after another, who would expect to find you in such a backwater, living so humbly?'

'You two, my sons, shall make up for me,' he told them. 'Then I have not lived in vain.' 'I am the teacher of athletes,' he intoned. 'He that by me spreads a wider breast than my own proves the width of my own. He most knows my style who learns under it to destroy the teacher.'

'Yes, Father,' said his sons.

'Walt Whitman,' he added, giving credit where credit was due.

Lily, who had given up working in a shop to become a laundress, now had Saturday afternoons free. The full significance of this she told Harry when they were lingering over, postponing from minute to minute, their farewell embrace in the dark lane near her home. To draw apart was so painful to them that, as soon as they attempted it, they suffered too much and flew together again for comfort.

'It must be gone eleven,' she said. 'Dad's tongue will curdle the milk. But guess what, though. Did you realise?'

'Realise what?' he mumbled, and lifted her hair from her shoulders and kissed underneath it, along the back of her neck, with busy little nibbling kisses. In a curious and contradictory way, she felt that he was so intent on her that she no longer existed.

'Why, Saturday afternoons, of course,' she said. 'You'll be free: now I'll be free as well.' She could not help noticing that the kissing stopped at once.

'Well, you do know weekends in the season I have to give Dad a hand,' Harry said.

'It isn't the season yet. We'll have a fortnight before that. I can meet you any time after dinner. Sooner the better,' she whispered and raised herself on tiptoe and put her warm mouth against his. He was unhappy and she became angry.

'Say about teatime?' he suggested.

'Why not earlier?'

She knew, although of course she could not see, that he was blushing.

'Ever since we were little, Dad's liked us to be together on Saturday afternoons.'

'What for, pray?'

'Just to have a quiet time together. It's a family custom.'

Now she could feel him blushing.

'If you ask me, he's round the bend,' she said loudly. 'And even if you don't ask me, he is.'

She pushed Harry away and began to walk down the lane towards her home. He followed her. 'And so are you,' she added. She did not turn her head as she spoke, but the words came back to him clearly. 'No wonder that girl Vera Webster gave up going out with Godfrey. She could see the way the wind was blowing. "Dad likes this and Dad likes that." I'm sick and tired of Dad and one of these days I'll tell him so. "You and your Bawdyleer," I'll say, "you boring old . . ."' her voice rose and trembled, '"codger"' she cried. 'And you, too,' she had reached her gate, threw it open and hurried up the path.

'Saturday teatime then?' he called after her anxiously.

'Saturday nothing,' she shouted back, and she lifted the latch and went in boldly to face her father's sarcasm.

'You're in early this morning,' he said. 'The milkman hasn't been yet.'

The next day her beautiful anger had dissolved. She had enjoyed it while she indulged in it, but now her words haunted and alarmed her. Perhaps they had meant the end of Harry's love for her and, so, of all her hopes. Her future life with him dissolved – a whole council house full of daydreams; trousseau, wedding presents, pots and pans, dainty supper-dishes, baby-clothes; cradle, even a kitten asleep on a cushion. She imagined him going to work and then on to his evening class, his head tilted proudly back, the stain of anger on his cheeks. The day after would be Saturday and if it turned out that he had taken her at her furious word, she could not endure to go on living.

'Not going out with Harry?' her mother asked her, when Lily began to wash her hair at the kitchen sink on Saturday afternoon.

'I think love's sweet song has run into a few discords,' her father said. '*Very* hoity-toity words coming up the path the night before last.'

Lily poured a jug of water over her head and so her tears were hidden.

By four o'clock her hair was quite dry. Harry had not come. She was restless and felt herself watched by her mother and father. Soon she decided that there was, after all, nothing to stop her walking along the towing-path for a breath of fresh air. It was a public way and there was no one who could stop her. It would be a sorry thing if, just because of Harry Ransome, she could never walk along the river bank again.

It was a bright and blowy evening. She met no one. At every bend in the lane, she expected to see Harry come hastening, full of apologies, towards her. Then she came to the river and still no one was in sight. The water was high, after the winter's rain, and flowed fast, covered with bubbles, bearing away scum and twigs and last year's leaves. The sound and look of it completed her depression.

With her head turned towards the river and not in the direction of the cottage, she walked along the lock-side. She went on beyond it a little way and then turned and sauntered back. The kitchen window was dark, but from the parlour a light fell faintly through the wooden shutters which had been drawn across the outside of the window. This seemed quite strange to Lily, for it would not be dark for some hours to come and in all the months she had known Harry she had never seen anyone go into the parlour except to fetch a book. She remembered Harry's shame and reluctance when she had tried to make plans for this afternoon and an unreasonable suspicion overtook her that he was in that shuttered room making love to someone, that he had known beforehand that he would be doing so, and knowing, had gone on kissing Lily; though he had had, she admitted, the decency to blush. She stepped quietly onto the little plot of grass and hesitated, glancing round her. There was no one in sight and not a sound except for the river. She went softly across to the window and listened there; but there was a shameful silence from within. Her heart beating with great violence unnerved her and only the extreme tension of her jealousy enabled her to lay her hand on the shutter and move it gently towards her.

The light in the room was not so very bright; but standing upright in a strange stiff pose with hand on hip and one knee slightly bent, she could see Mr Ransome facing her not two yards away, his beard jutting forward and his expression fixed. A rosy glow from an oil-stove fell over his completely naked body.

Their eyes met, his widened with surprise, Lily's with horror. Then she slammed back the shutter and leant against it for a moment, sick and trembling. Through the narrow slit between the shutters she had not seen the two sons, sitting unwillingly but dutifully behind their easels. Terror, in any case, had quite put the thought of Harry out of her mind. She was afraid that Mr Ransome would come leaping out of the house after her and chase her down the towing-path, naked and mad as he was, shouting Balzac and Voltaire after her. She summoned all her strength and turned and ran across the lawn, as fast as she could go, away from the cottage and her legs were as heavy as lead, as if she were running in a nightmare.

THE LOST
CHAPEL PICNIC

—— ◆ ——

Margery Sharp

Faced with so enormous and complex a subject as the Lost Chapel Picnic (six miles each way, on bicycles), one hardly knows where to start. To any member of the Bly family it is like starting to write about the French Revolution, or the United States of America – there is so much to bring in. Nor can one safely generalise; even the statement that it took place every summer, for instance, at once calls to mind the summers when it didn't, such as 1927 (chicken-pox) and 1940 (Battle of Britain). Only its essential characteristic was constant: the Lost Chapel Picnic always took place in rain.

Even for England, it was remarkable. Lost Chapels – an abbreviation also employed in such constructions as 'to go on a Lost Chapel', or 'to go Lost Chapelling' – happened invariably, and only, in August, when we children were home from school and friends stayed holidaying round about; but however brilliant the weather before and after, it always rained for Lost Chapel. In time this became so notorious that ladies planning garden parties, or Vicars organising fêtes, used to enquire of my aunt in advance what date had been fixed, to avoid it. Theoretically, of course, it should have been possible to wait for a really fine afternoon, fling together sufficient provisions, and set off *à l'improviste*. But that wouldn't have suited us Blys at all. A Lost Chapel was not only a serious event, to be looked forward to for at least ten days, but also, so to speak, a serious *sporting* event, which we would have scorned to rig. Moreover, one of its most important and beloved features, the pony-cart, had to be hired ahead of time. No one rode in the cart, but we needed it to carry enough kindling and firewood to build a good big fire. The fire was to dry ourselves at, because it always rained; and if there was a sort of circular lunacy about the whole scheme, no Bly ever seemed to notice. Getting first wet through and then rough dried, was what one *did*, on a Lost Chapel.

Who first found the Lost Chapel, my cousin Bryan or my cousin Sarah?

Bryan's juvenile claim was that he actually lived there, for several months, when at the age of six he left home to become a bandit. No one took this seriously, since he was well known to have been back in time for tea. If he saw the Lost Chapel at all, he didn't mention it at the time. Sarah, rather cleverly, was completely vague; she said she'd just found Lost Chapel one day when she was out by herself, and thought she'd told everyone, though she mightn't have. This point remains mysterious. In any case, by about 1924 we were going there regularly.

No one knew either who first gave the place its name. It almost certainly wasn't a chapel at all, but the barn of a pulled-down farm. Nor was it lost, in the sense of being hidden or unknown: it could be seen, high up on a spur of moorland, from any point in our village. It was still remote. Of the six miles we had to cover to reach it, only three lay along a proper road; at the third milestone one had to turn through a gap and pedal desperately up a narrow slippery track. (From this point the pony was led.) Here heather grew on either hand, thinning as one ascended, then thinning out again to what was called the tundra-line – beyond which there was only grass again, much shorter and less lush than the grass below. (When the sun shone it must have been very hot up there. But we went to Lost Chapel only for the picnic, only once a year. It was one of those rules children make for themselves in their perennial quest for stability.) Then the last fifty yards or so flattened out, and there the farm and its buildings must once have stood. Now only the barn was left, big and high, stone-floored, and very dark inside . . .

Solemnly dark; the first few moments, before we lit the fire and set up the oil-stove, were always rather hushed. We children would fling down our bicycles and race in, panting and noisy, sweating under our wet mackintoshes – and for a moment be hushed. It was the moment, in a way, we came for; we always tried to arrive before the adults. (Actually this was easy, the last half-mile on grass winded them so.) For a moment we would all stand silent, by ourselves, savouring the solemn dark; perhaps it was in the first of such moments that we gave the place its name. It was just *like* a chapel. As a matter of fact, my cousin Alan Bly got married in it. He didn't tell me this till many years afterwards, but at the 1926 picnic, while the rest of us were cooking sausages, he took a little girl called Sybil Addis aside, proposed, was accepted, and immediately twisted a paper-clip round her finger, announcing 'With this paper-clip I thee wed.' He was then twelve, and Sybil ten; he had been immensely struck by both her curly red hair and her uphill cycling, and felt she shouldn't be missed. His instinct was absolutely sound: they were remarried in '38, on which occasion I stood bridesmaid.

But to leap to such an episode, in the history of Lost Chapels, is like leaping to the execution of Marie Antoinette in the history of the French Revolution, or to the Boston Tea-Party in the history of the United States . . .

The nucleus of all Lost Chapels – the Pilgrim Fathers, so to speak – consisted of my Aunt Mary and Uncle James, my cousins Alan, Bryan and Sarah, and myself. The friends we children invited varied from year to year, especially as we grew older, but numbered usually five or six. There were also several adults, known as Steadies, who had somehow got involved.

The leading Steady was Miss Pargiter, an elderly spinster who spent most of the year in Italy, but whose hardy frame had successfully resisted all Capuan blandishments: one of our best cyclists on the flat, and very game uphill.

Mr Adrian, also elderly, there was some slight mystery about. The village believed he'd been in jail. Whether or not this was true – he certainly led a very solitary life, painting watercolours in a cottage like a picture-postcard – my aunt had long decided there was no harm in him. Mr Adrian loved Lost Chapels, because they were the only things he was ever invited to, and did the view from the hill each year. (Another reason why we had to have the pony-cart: to tote Mr Adrian's easel. He was a watercolourist of the old school, with an immense amount of baggage.)

The third Steady was comparatively young – kind Mr Gore-Willoughby, for eleven months of the year a London stock-broker, whose ridiculous name we children used to chant in unison as he toiled up the last lap. Someone, I forget who, said he Lost Chapelled simply to get his weight down, but this was a lie, because he always brought, and partook of, a large box of marrons glacés. They were the only marrons we ever set tooth to, but we liked him for himself as well, in a rather offhand, patronising way, and his bicycle had a three-speed gear.

All participants wore their oldest clothes, under mackintoshes.

It was considered legitimate in an adult to dismount for the last lap, but absolutely no one was let ride in the pony-cart. And no one, however wet or tired, could expect sympathy if they grizzled.

Here we come to something really important about Lost Chapels. (The Tennis-Court Oath, the Declaration of Independence.) As we children grew up, they provided a wonderful testing-ground for the current objects of our affections. Alan, as has been related, grasped this point extremely early; but his brother Bryan between '31 and '36 tried out at least five possibles. They all, with the exception of Milly Blanchard, started fairly level: nice, pretty girls every one, all of course with bicycles, and all with an abundance of goodwill. My cousin Bryan was an extremely taking youth. Milly Blanchard was nice only technically – as it were in the eyes of a jury of matrons. Her father was our chemist, and so quite hopelessly in trade. Only one damsel, as I remember, failed to complete the course, but two were literally washed out at the post. They looked, said Bryan disgustedly, *wet*. Of course they *were* wet, poor creatures, but we all knew what he meant. The fourth entry failed on sensibility. We Blys never thought of ourselves as in the least artistic, in fact we rather derided Art – poor Mr Adrian's hobby. It never occurred to us that one reason we so loved Lost Chapel was for its romantic beauty. But when Cecilia White called it *pokey*, every Bly hackle rose. So Milly Blanchard was left with a clear field. She was full of running anyway. She hadn't even a permanent wave, but she braided her long wet hair like a Red Indian's, and wrapped herself in a rug, and did a war-dance all round the oil-stove. She was undeniably rowdy. She also, in due course, made my cousin Bryan an excellent wife.

The most exciting thing that ever happened on a Lost Chapel was when the oil-stove caught fire. No one ever discovered the cause; simply all at once, in an instant, blue and yellow flames were running swiftly across the flagstones *after Miss Pargiter*. It was this that made the excitement: we were all tough, experienced Lost Chapellers, perfectly capable of estimating the comparative slightness of the danger – the floor, as has been said, was stone, all we had to do was stand clear until the oil burnt itself out. But they ran, the little blue flames, *after* Miss Pargiter – one really couldn't believe without a conscious sense of fun. Because Miss Pargiter, instead of making sensibly for the door, skipped back and back directly in their path. 'Sideways, you Juggins!' shouted my cousin Alan. 'Jump sideways, and let 'em go by!' This was the first time any one of us children had ever shouted at an adult, and Alan wasn't even made to apologise. The episode opened new vistas all round – as my aunt subsequently lamented; but some fifteen years later I myself most profitably shouted, 'Down, you Juggins!' at a full general caught beside me in the street during a London blitz.

The most scandalous thing that ever happened was the snatching of a quite personable millionaire by the Vicarage Kids' new governess. An episode (1930) not strictly Bly, but Bly by repercussion.

He was staying, Mr Richards, at the local inn: to cast a casual, millionairish eye over the inn itself, and a couple of farms, which he'd been left (in the way millionaires do get left such trifles), by a comparatively poor relation. My aunt invited him to Lost Chapel out of pure kind-heartedness, because she thought he looked lonely. Sarah and I were both still in the schoolroom – as I dare say Mr Richards knew, at fifty he was still unmarried, which shows how knowing he'd been for years. It was also out of sheer kind-heartedness that my aunt invited Miss Dove. I remember how all we children protested, saying she'd never get up the hill. We disliked Miss Dove, which in a way was odd, since we also disliked the Vicarage Kids; as a rule any governess who gave them hell had our enthusiastic support. But in fact everyone rather disliked Miss Dove. Though of English parentage she had been born and reared in Paris; which of course gave her a wonderful French accent, but also, in some mysterious way, enabled her to dress quite unsuitably well. She turned up for Lost Chapel in beautifully cut tweeds, also a small felt hat with a pheasant's wing. My aunt and Miss Pargiter wore sou'westers, tied firmly under the chin. Even Cecilia White had worn a skiing cap. 'Haven't you a mackintosh, Miss Dove?' enquired my aunt solicitously. 'It's almost certain to rain. And won't your pretty hat be quite spoiled?' Miss Dove said smilingly that she would risk it.

The rest of the party as usual looked like a bunch of tramps. I remember that Mr Adrian had had the brilliant idea of putting his head in a sponge-bag. He was undeniably a little odd. But wait! – his hour is yet to come.

Miss Dove, as she gracefully mounted her bicycle, cut an extremely elegant figure; and all we children cheered up at the thought of seeing her drenched.

Mr Richards my aunt provided with the bicycle of our garden-boy. I think he found the whole affair pretty surprising: he didn't know about Lost Chapels, and I dare say had anticipated some far milder excursion. When he realised the awful truth, he in fact at once suggested using his Rolls. But after we explained how soon the proper road ended, he resigned himself – all too literally – to his fate. For exactly at the proper road's end, though it was hardly raining at all, Miss Dove dismounted from her bicycle and *stopped*.

We could hardly believe it. No one ever *stopped*, on a Lost Chapel. 'A little *riposo*?' called Miss Pargiter, pedalling gamely by. 'Don't think it's going to clear!' warned Uncle James cheerily. 'Best foot forwards, Miss Dove, best foot forward!' 'I'm going home,' replied Miss Dove, calmly propping her machine against the hedge. 'Come, come, come, come, come!' piped Mr Adrian – flat over his handlebars. Cool as a cucumber, and with a brazenness to take the breath, Miss Dove neatly cut out Mr Richards from the tail of our convoy and asked him to cycle back and get his car, and take her home.

Nothing succeeds like audacity – especially if one is practically a Frenchwoman. Mr Richards, offered this splendid excuse for abandoning the whole project, at once reversed direction. We heard later that they spent the rest of the day driving about in his Rolls, inspecting his various properties, also taking tea at an hotel. Miss Dove had about four hours' clear run, and at the end of it killed. For if Mr Richards didn't actually propose that afternoon, or if what he did propose wasn't actually marriage, Miss Dove undoubtedly quitted the village at the same time as he did – rightly confident, as it proved, of bringing him to the legal point in due course.

The Bly aspect of this was that during Mr Richards' call of apology, to say how sorry he'd been to miss Lost Chapel, the conversation somehow turned to the shipping industry, in which Mr Richards had large interests, and in which my cousin Alan now does so well.

Perhaps there was a repercussion on my cousin Sarah also. If I have as yet barely mentioned Sarah, it is because she was in general so self-effacing. Her clever claim to the discovery of Lost Chapel is remembered for its unusualness – as a rule she didn't claim so much as a pet rabbit, just let each litter be divided among the rest of us, and fed them when we forgot. She was the perfect elder sister, elder cousin; her kind plain face perfectly reflected, except in beauty, a disposition very nearly angelic. But she really was plain, and when in 1934 a new young doctor came to flutter every female heart, we Blys frankly regretted that Sarah hadn't a hope. Because we all liked Dr Henderson at once, and would have welcomed him into the family – whereas if Sarah went on not getting engaged, and she was then twenty-one, we feared she might well end up with the curate.

Dr Henderson Lost Chapelled and liked it. (One of the reasons why we approved of him.) He came *again* ('34, '35 and '36). And at the '36 Lost Chapel my cousin Sarah, possibly remembering how well audacity had succeeded with Miss Dove, quietly and self-effacingly proposed to him.

If self-effacingness and audacity hardly chime together, let us say that Sarah performed the audacious deed as self-effacingly as possible.

The rest of us were all gathered round the fire. It was one of the wettest Lost Chapels I remember. But even dripping, Dr Henderson still looked wonderfully handsome. Sarah looked her plainest; but at least, so to speak, *indestructible*. With her mouse-brown hair pushed damply back from her forehead, without a trace of make-up on a face just scrubbed dry – there Sarah stood, take her or leave her, and suddenly asked Dr Henderson to come outside. It was pouring cats and dogs. Rain drove into the turf, if the turf hadn't been so sodden the rain would have bounced off. But out Dr Henderson went. And out in the rain, keeping her gaze firmly fixed on the storm-swept valley below, Sarah said, 'I love you with all my heart. I think I would make a very good doctor's wife. If you'll never want to marry me, will you please say so now, so I can go into a convent and be a nun.'

No doubt it was a very different approach from Miss Dove's. It happened to be just what Dr Henderson would have ordered for himself. (He often told us afterwards how bedevilled he'd been by too many attractive patients.) Of course neither Alan nor Bryan nor I thought of eavesdropping, we were most honourably *not* eavesdropping; what Sarah said she told me herself in case it might ever be useful to me. But we were somewhere near the door, and we did happen to see Dr Henderson suddenly take Sarah's hand, and hear him call her 'My splendid honest girl . . .'

They came in again almost at once. They had to, because it started to hail as well, and Mr Adrian ran out with his umbrella. And Sarah cooked Dr Henderson's sausages very carefully, and he tried to make her eat them, and that has been the pattern of their lives ever since.

Mr Adrian's hour of glory. This struck some time in the thirties, when he astonishingly induced a small London gallery to exhibit a batch of his watercolours. They were all of the same view, in rain. (Naturally; all executed on Lost Chapels.) More astonishingly still, he won a small but definite *succès d'estime* : the novelty of such monotony, as it were, struck several critics to admiration, and four of his wettest gems actually found purchasers. As a result Mr Adrian's social life quite bloomed, and besides going on Lost Chapels he went out to tea right and left. He didn't, however, as we half expected, lay his heart and press-cuttings at the feet of Miss Pargiter; they remained individual Steadies to the end.

Kind Mr Gore-Willoughby I married myself; to my immense surprise, he turned out to be no more than twelve years my senior. And we too plighted our troth, like Alan and Sybil, and Bryan and Milly and Sarah and Dr Henderson, on a Lost Chapel – I apparently looking like a mermaid, and he without doubt resembling a seal. For of course it was pouring cats and dogs as usual, because Lost Chapels always took place in rain . . .

They still do. We still take the pony-cart (though with a new pony), to carry sufficient firewood and kindling to build a good big fire. Mr Adrian and Miss Pargiter no longer pedal gamely beside us, nor my kind uncle and aunt; we have acquired several fresh Steadies, however, and of course there are the children. Alan's three boys come, and Sarah's boy and girl, Bryan's two daughters, my own twins and their elder sister.

Obviously the subject is too vast. There is too much to bring in. It's like writing the history of the French Revolution, or of the United States – writing about our Lost Chapel picnics, six miles (by bicycle) each way.

OTHER PEOPLE'S BATHROBES

◆

Shena Mackay

Her underwear slipped through his fingers in silky shoals of salmon and grayling; stockings slithered like a catch of rainbow eels. He moved about the bedroom like an assassin, although he was alone in the flat, as if he was watched by eyes other than his own which glanced off the mirror's surface like fish scales reflecting the rainy morning light. Several times when he and Barbara had been together, he had felt that they were not alone; over his shoulder an invisible circle of her friends was whispering, condemning him, warning her. He imagined their nights laid out on lunchtime restaurant tables shrouded in white linen, and dissected with heavy silver knives and forks. He did not know what he was looking for as he went through her things – some evidence as dangerous as a gun lying in the silken nest, that he could possess and use to destroy her when it suited him.

Last night they had come out of the cinema knock-kneed with grief, holding on to each other against the pain of someone else's tragedy. The restaurant smelled of fish and lemon, and clouds of steam banked the lower halves of the windows and evaporated in rivulets down the black glass. He was hungry throughout, and after, the meal. She had eaten almost nothing and her refusal of wine had inhibited his own intake, as the spring water bubbling glumly in its mossy green glass dampened his desire, although her stockinged foot, slipped from its shoe and stroking his leg under the table, suggested that it had refreshed hers.

'I'm sick of mangetout peas,' he had grumbled. 'I want proper peas, without pods, from a tin.'

She had smiled at him indulgently, as at a child, although his petulant mouth was in danger of becoming merely peevish. Meanwhile he salivated discontentedly in memory of the food of his brief happy childhood. A low-slung moon hung in the North London sky as she drove them home; the golden crescent of a pendulum slicing the blackness; it would taste of melon if sucked, a wedge of honeydew. He sat beside her, in silence, aware that he was, as always, in the passenger seat.

There was nothing in the bedroom to incriminate her: dresses gave evidence of nothing that he did not know, shoes were mute and jewellery jangled to no purpose, scent left false trails and no glove pointed the finger. Books that might have betrayed her were not called to witness.

'There are some robes you can use,' she had told him on the first night he had spent with her. That had been three weeks ago and he was still there, still wearing borrowed bathrobes and dressing gowns. This morning he was dressed in a blue kimono with a red and gold dragon writhing up its back and tongues of flame licking his shoulders. He went to the window and lifted the corner of the blind. The trees in the street were hung with leaves the colour of cooked swede, and mashed swede lay in heaps in the gutters; pyracantha flung bright sprays of baked beans against the houses opposite. In his twenty years he had worn too many dressing gowns belonging to other people. He sighed and pulled the sash tighter around his diminishing waist and padded into the kitchen.

He opened the fridge and the freezer compartment and then slammed them shut, sending shivers through the bottles of mineral water shuddering in the door. There wasn't even any real coffee, just that stuff that you had to muck about with filter papers, and a small jar of decaffeinated powder, and a tiny tin of sweeteners instead of sugar. He shook four or five white pellets into a cup and added coffee and a dash of skimmed milk as he waited for the kettle to boil.

'No bleeding bread of course . . .'

He microwaved the lone croissant into a blackened shell and smeared it with low-fat spread. He could have murdered a fried egg sandwich washed down with a mug of hot sweet tea. She, of course, had breakfasted on her usual fare of a tisane and half a dozen vitamin and mineral tablets. He lit a cigarette and took it and the newspaper into the main room of the flat – he never knew what to call it: front room, although it was, or lounge, were wrong – and pushed aside the white vase of black porcelain roses and white plastic tulips and put his feet up. Smoking was frowned on almost to the point of a total ban, but since the early morning when she had sensed his absence in the bed and come into the kitchen and screamed at the sight of his legs sprawled on the kitchen floor, his head wedged firmly in the obsolete cat-flap, a forbidden cigarette clamped in his lips spiralling smoke helplessly into the dawn chorus, she had relaxed slightly the interdiction. She had thought he was dead. It had taken an hour, a lot of soap, and finally a screwdriver to release him.

When he had bathed he would run the Hoover over the carpets; there was little for it to vacuum up except a light frosting of the low-fat crisp crumbs which he had consumed while she got ready for bed. It was the Hoover which had brought them together: he had arrived in response to her inquiry to a cleaning agency and had stayed on to help her prepare for a dinner party, as she moved about the kitchen with a brittle energy that teetered over into panic, her pale hair crackling with electricity in the stormy light pouring through the window. When the first guest arrived it was he who opened the door, a glass of wine in his hand, and entertained them until she emerged from the bathroom where she had fled. She could hardly have arrested in mid-arc the bowl of salted pumpkin seeds he was proffering to her friends and explain that he was the cleaner, and so he had stayed. It was not until they all sat down to eat that she realised that an extra place had been set already at the table.

After the Hoovering he would take her italic list and a plastic carrier bag, as well preserved and neatly folded as if it had been ironed, and wander down to the shops. He took the radio and another cup of coffee and his cigarettes into the bathroom and as he idled in the scented oil watching mingled smoke and steam being sucked through the extractor fan on the window he could not avoid remembering the previous night.

She had wanted both of them to go to bed early because she had had a hard day before they met in the evening, and she was nervous about a sales conference the following morning. The publishing company for which she worked had been taken over recently, and anxiety about losing her job and treachery within the firm had smudged blue shadows under her eyes; and bitten nails, spoiling her gloss, betrayed her fears. By the time Adam had joined her in the bedroom she had fallen asleep; her hair frazzled out like excelsior on the pillow, the tag of a sachet of camomile tea drooping over the rim of the mug on the bedside table. He slid into bed, smelling the sweet-sour odour of the infusion on her breath as he leaned over her face and took her, all flowers and mineral water, in his arms and slowly and cynically began to make love to her. Their hip bones clashed; the morning would see his faint bruises mirrored in milky opals on her skin. He thought that her ambition was to be the thinnest woman in London this side of anorexia, and he remembered reading of a young girl who had almost achieved sainthood by dint of never eating; people had flocked to witness this miracle and marvel at the beautiful and holy maiden pink and white as roses and angel cake, sustained on spiritual food, until one night a nun had been caught sneaking into her room with a basket of goodies. He wondered sometimes if Barbara, too, was a secret snacker but there was never any evidence. He licked the whorls of her ear, as cold as one of her porcelain roses, with the tip of his tongue, while in imagination he piled a plate with processed peas swimming in their bluish liquor, pickled beetroot staining the fluffy edges of a white instant-mashed potato cloud, a crispy cluster of acid yellow piccalilli; he added a daub of ketchup to his garish still-life, and then he had to stifle a laugh in her shoulder as she responded because only he knew that the rhythm they moved to was that of a song that had been running through his head since they had got home. Food, glorious food . . . dah da da da dah dah. He had forgotten some of the words he had sung as a ruby-lipped treble taking the lead in *Oliver!*; backstage, after the last performance before the last tremulous tear had been flicked from the lashes of the departing audience, Adam had been expelled for extortion. Food, fabulous. Food, beautiful. Food, glor-i-ous food!!! Pease pudding and saveloy, what next is the question? While we're in the mood – Glenn Miller took up the baton with a flash of brass and buttons, or Joe Loss, sleek as an otter in a dapper dinner jacket or tuxedo. 'Tuxedo Junction'. And then Adam and Barbara expired together in an ecstasy of cold jelly and custard and he let her drop back on to a steaming heap of hot sausage and mustard. She traced with her finger his lips which were parted in a grin.

'Darling.'

'Best ever?' he asked.

She nodded, smiling and showering the pillow with pease pudding from her hair as he licked the dollop of mustard from her nose.

He had slept badly in an indigestion of shame. Bits of bad dreams lay on his mind, as unappetising as congealing food left overnight on a plate. He watched beneath half-closed lids as she gathered up the clothes she would assume as silken armour against her threatening day, moving quietly so as not to wake him, but each door, each opened and closed drawer hissed her panic. He felt her hover over him for a moment after she had placed a mug of coffee on the coaster on the floor beside him, then with a jangle of keys, a revving of the car, she was gone and he was left floundering in the billows of the duvet trying to sleep away part of the long morning. He wished to spend as little time as possible in the company of someone he disliked as much as himself.

People who had encountered Adam as an angelic-looking child had assumed that he was a good little boy. He shared their estimation of himself until at the age of six years he had been surprised by impulses that were far from good. A girl in his class at the infants' school brought in, one morning, to show the teacher, a dolls' chest of drawers that she had made by gluing four matchboxes together and covering the top, back and sides with glossy red paper, the sort of paper that they made lanterns from at Christmastime. The handles of the drawers were yellow glass beads. Adam coveted and coveted this object all morning. She had allowed him to hold it at dinner play, as long as he didn't open the drawers, and had made him give it back. It was beyond the price of the Matchbox tractor which he had offered in exchange. He could not have said why he wanted the chest of drawers so much: he had no use for it beyond the pleasure of opening and closing the drawers. He could keep matches in it, he had decided, if he had had any . . . perhaps it was because it was so tiny and perfect and because he could not have contrived so neat an artefact with his own clumsy fingers, which behaved in craft lessons like a bunch of flies on flypaper – his Christmas lantern had been a disaster, with the slits cut the wrong way, and had ended up, shamefully, in the waste-paper basket. He brooded through the afternoon story and squinted at it through the steeple of his fingers as they sang, 'Hands together, softly so, little eyes shut tight', plotting. He had hidden behind a hedge after school and jumped out on her from behind, pulling her knitted hat over her eyes, and snatched the chest of drawers and run off. The school was a very short distance from home, with no roads to cross. He was out of sight, although not out of earshot of her wails, by the time she had freed herself from her hat.

'What's this?' His mother was waiting for him at the entrance to the flats.

'I made it at school.'

'Isn't that lovely. Just like something they make on *Blue Peter*,' she had said as they went up in the lift.

'It's for you,' he had heard himself say. There was even a pink ring from a cracker in one of the drawers, which fitted her little finger, just above the second joint.

So, eating tinned spaghetti on toast in the afterglow of his mother's kiss that afternoon, he had realised that he could assault and rob and lie; arts which he had polished over the years, after his mother's death when he was ten years old, during his six years in care and throughout his sojourns in squats all over London.

'That's that,' he said to himself as he rewound the Hoover's flex. 'Now for the next item on my thrilling agenda.' As he stowed it away in what she called the 'glory hole', although a neater glory hole than this one with no cobwebs and everything stacked on shelves could not be imagined, his eye fell on a cardboard carton. He pulled it out, not knowing what he expected to find. His heart beat faster as he opened the flaps – a baby's shoe perhaps, a bottle of gin or the heads of her former lovers, as in Bluebeard's Castle, their beards dripping blood. What it contained was books: children's books, schoolgirl annuals, an illustrated *Bible Stories* whose red and blue and gold illuminated sticker stated that it had been presented for regular attendance at St Andrew's Sunday School in a year before Adam had been born, a stamp album with a map of the world on its cover, that released a shower of shiny and brittle stamp hinges like the wings of long-dead insects when Adam set it aside with the thought that it might be worth selling; the books that heap trestle tables at every jumble sale, even to the copy of *The Magic Faraway Tree* by Enid Blyton, with the statutory request in faded and wobbly pencil that if this book should chance to roam, box its ears and send it home, to: Barbara Watson, 59 Oxford Road, Canterbury, Kent, England, Great Britain, the Northern Hemisphere, the World, etc., etc., *ad tedium*. Barbara had been crossed out and Brenda substituted; then Barbara had deleted Brenda, but in vain. The names fought each other in sisterly rivalry all down the page and it was not clear at the end who had triumphed; Adam heard slaps and tears, and the pulling of hair. *Britain's Wonderland of Nature* : a large green volume with a butterfly embossed on its cover and glossy colour plates which must have been her best book, Adam thought. It had been given to her by Uncle Wilf in 1960.

At the bottom of the box was a photograph album. He lifted it out and took it into the black and white room. Perhaps this was what he had been looking for. He lit a cigarette to heighten the experience.

The album had a faded blue cover and crumpled spider's web paper separated the leaves; the small photographs affixed to the storm-grey pages had crimped edges, like crinkle-cut chips, and there, flies in amber and butterflies in glass, was Barbara's past. It seemed that she had spent all her childhood on a beach against an unfailingly grey sky. The photographs were captioned in a loopy adult hand. Here were the infant Barbara and Brenda, the tangled strings of their sun-bonnets blowing towards a sullen sea; a comical snap of Barbara in giant grown-up sunglasses, mouth open in dismay, holding an empty cornet whose unstable scoop of ice cream had evidently just fallen to the beach. Here was Uncle Wilf, with Aunty Dolly at Tankerton – he must have been a widower then, when he had purchased *Britain's Wonderland of Nature*, Christmas 1960. Adam pictured him entering the glass doors of W. H. Smith, sleet, like a dandruff of sorrow on the stooping shoulders of his black coat, to buy books for his nieces, the icy wind, or memories of the time he had rolled his trousers and Dolly tucked her skirt up round her knees and stood with the sea gushing between their toes smiling into the camera before she had vanished off the edge of photographs, bringing a tear to his eyes. At Whitstable, Dad, whose name was Ron, Adam discerned, had for some reason come without his trunks and, presumably unable to resist the call of the sea, was wearing what looked suspiciously like his wife's bathing suit rolled to his waist. All the sad south coast resorts were represented in shades of black and white and grey; Adam sat in the room whose colour scheme echoed the childhood tints, his cigarette burning unnoticed in a cube of black onyx striated with white, turning the pages. He had the family sorted out now, grandparents, uncles, aunts and cousins, Mum or Mavis in white shoes, Dad; Brenda and Barbara so close in age as to be almost twins, and no longer bothered to read the captions.

By the age of four or so Brenda had become noticeably plump; beside her Barbara was as frail as an elf. Brenda swelled with the years like a raisin soaked in water; she grew into a quite unfortunate-looking kid. There was one shot of her that arrested him: she stood scowling, with her bare feet planted apart on the shifting pebbles, thighs braced, her solid little body eggcup-shaped, straining the rosettes of her ruched cotton bathing suit, her candy-floss hair parted at the side, and caught in an ungainly bow blowing in the wind that blurred the sails of the toy windmill in her hand, every line of her face and body expressing such defiance and discontent that Adam found himself smiling. Behind her the horses of a merry-go-round galloped in a frieze refrigerated by time. Someone had added a comment in pencil to her mother's writing. Adam took the album to the window the better to see.

'Barbara is a fat pig,' it said, and a pencilled arrow pointed undeniably to the photograph and was corroborated by the words, 'singed Brenda'. It was impossible. 'Barbara is a fat pig, singed Brenda.' So Barbara had been the fat plain one all along. Adam sat down heavily and lit another cigarette. He felt cheated, as if Barbara had deceived him deliberately. Under that designer exterior there was a common little fat girl. It was all a sham. She was no better than he was. He snapped the album shut. Instead of feeling triumphant at finding the weapon he had sought, he felt sad, almost like crying. Then he began to feel angry with Brenda. He flicked through the pages again and noticed that Brenda in each photograph had pushed slightly in front of Barbara, and she was often dressed in organdie and flounces of artificial silk while Barbara was in cotton. Why was Brenda always wearing party dresses to the beach, and an angora bolero, while Barbara was in print with a school cardigan?

'It seems to me, Brenda, that it was you who were the pig. And you couldn't spell,' he said to the Christmas-tree fairy with her bucket and spade. He wondered how many times Barbara had been singed by Brenda. What were Mum and Dad, Mavis and Ron, doing to have such a discrepancy between their daughters? He hoped Uncle Wilf had loved Barbara the best.

He closed the album and put it away in the carton with the other books and closed the cupboard door. He found Barbara's shopping list and shopping bag and set out for the shops. He could not rid himself of the picture of Barbara in the bathing suit with Brenda's cruel caption, and the quotation – he had played Viola in *Twelfth Night* – 'Thus the whirligig of time brings in his revenges', spun round in his mind like the windmill in her hand and the merry-go-round in the distance, and above the jangle of fairground music he heard the teasing voices of Mum and Dad and all the aunts and cousins, and Brenda's taunting laughter. He had been wrong in thinking that Barbara was no better than he was: she was much better. Everything she had she had earned for herself, while he was driven through life in the passenger seats of other people's cars and lounged in other people's bathrobes. More, she had created herself. He stopped dead in his tracks on the pavement, colliding with a woman with matted hair, draped in a shawl of black refuse sacks.

'I'm in love,' he told her.

'Piss off.'

'Yes. Yes I will,' he said and gave her a five-pound note from Barbara's purse, which was clawed into her shawl as she spat at his feet. Something amazing had happened. He had fallen in love, for the first time, with a cross little girl holding a windmill at the end of her goosefleshed arm. If she had been singed by Brenda he would erase the burns, like scorch marks from a table. If she wanted revenge he would oblige, on the whole pack of them. If she wanted a white wedding with all the family there, including Brenda whose childhood had been entwined with hers like the strings of two sun-bonnets on a windy day, that was all right with him too. He went into the shop; for him the best part of the movie had always been when the guy arrived at the girl's apartment with a paper sack of groceries with a fifth of bourbon sticking its neck out: to him that was New York: romance. Unbeknownst to herself, Barbara bought herself a bottle of champagne. As he walked home with his love feast in a plastic carrier bag he saw that the pavement was strewn with lychee shells, broken to show their sunset pink interiors, like shells on a beach in the rain. Outlined against the hectic light everything assumed a poignancy; a bag of refuse and a broken branch of blue eucalyptus made a haiku on the wet kerb. He felt healed, as if someone had poured a precious jar of alabaster over him.

He was in the kichen when he heard her key in the lock. She stepped inside, all unawares, in her black raincoat rolling with ersatz pearls, coming home to a steaming bowl of Heinz vegetable soup, just like mother used to make.

THE SWAIN

◆

Mary Leland

'Your swain,' her mother had called him. At first it had been gently ironic, there was no sting in it, the older woman had no expectation. And now it was all right. Eileen knew it fitted him, Benny was her swain.

It had nearly not happened. They had left the town within a few years of one another, Benny first as the elder graduate, taking a degree and a boat in the same week and lost for years thereafter to the talk of the town. It was said as easily as these things are said always that his departure had broken his father's heart, but it was more likely that the old man had choked on his avid acres. And then it was said that Benny's irregular marriage – no marriage at all as it turned out – had brought on the stroke. Married in an office abroad in London, with a strap of a one who had already brought down the name of a priest on the island!

As that had been the death of him, Benny's father had no more to fear from further reported irregularities, such as divorce, but the town had anxieties which surfaced when Benny himself arrived home single but not a widower. 'Wiser in their generation,' was all the Canon had to say when questioned about the young man's Catholic eligibility. No one knew whether to be relieved or scandalised.

Eileen knew nothing of all this.

'Did I see Benny Cronin in the town today?' she asked her mother as they prepared an evening meal together.

'How would I know?' Her mother's approach to life these days was laconic. Her last joy had been Eileen's return after fourteen years in England. Her next delight, in the nature of things, should be the girl's marriage and children, but Mrs Tuohy accepted that these could not be regarded as imminent.

'Well, is he home in Manortreacy, that's all I'm asking? If I knew he was back I'd know whether it was him I saw or not.'

'He's been back working the farm for four years now.' Mrs Tuohy's tone was dry. She had been a poor letter-writer, and anticipated the next question.

'– yes, I never told you, I suppose I thought you'd pick it up for yourself over there. You would have too, if you hadn't been too grand for Kilburn! Anyway the girl ran away after a few weeks; she came from Clanboffin, so I suppose it was all you could expect – not that I believe all I hear about her.'

Eileen could only laugh at the number of targets her mother had pelleted.

'Come on, Mum, we've been over and over that Kilburn thing. Sure what was the point of going to England if I was only to be going to meet the same people I'd see here? And maybe Benny's wife was not all bad – why must it have been her fault?'

Mrs Tuohy did not reply as she put the shining delft on the table, but the nod of her head and the pursed mouth were enough to remind Eileen that if she had bothered with the Irish community in London she could have met a grand big builder and be living in Hampstead now like her sister instead of back here in Manortreacy as plain as when she left it and, so far as she could see, not half so Catholic.

'What I will say, Miss, is that nobody here has a bad word to say to Benny Cronin. He has a man and a boy working out there for him now and he's never seen with a drop too much or with a cigarette in his mouth. And his bull took a first prize in Leixlip last year!'

For a second her educated mind tempted Eileen to question the significance of Benny's bull as part of this list of recommendations, but she sighed to herself as she prepared for a meeting later that evening, thinking 'poor Benny' before grabbing her folder of notes for the teachers she was to talk to. In the darkening street, with the sleet wind pushing winter into her bones as she walked, he came into her mind again and she smiled at the rueful thought of himself, and herself, after their different journeys, both back where they had started.

She wondered if his return had been a matter of choice, like hers. Did his marriage mean he had found romance, as she had – although, as she fervently and frequently thanked God, she had not felt the need to marry in order to keep hold of what she had found, and now she was free. Older, but free.

Now was all that true? Would she have married if she had been asked? Was there nobody whom she had wanted to marry? Impatient with herself and her habit of constant assessment, Eileen told herself that whether it was true or not now she'd had enough of it all anyway. Enough, as she scanned the marriages of the friends she'd left behind her, to last her lifetime. 'I'm finished with all that,' she told herself, and did not ask herself if it were true, and God did not strike her dead with a thunderbolt.

To give her her due she earnestly wanted to be free of emotional complexities. The odd thing was – and it was odd, she had admitted that much to herself long ago – that her studiously progressive professional life had been carried on against a sexual career that could only be described as chequered. She had not been promiscuous, but when she thought men loved her she was ready to love them back. Now it amounted to no more than a tedious passage of her life which concluded with her voluntary self-immurement in a small school in the Scottish highlands.

It was hardship I needed, she thought when she thought about it. And the shame of seeing people live easily in a land which seemed so bleak, providing for themselves without help from elsewhere; I needed to learn that one could live anywhere.

For years she had waited to see some grand design, some place for herself in a pattern. Instead she had come to understand that it is one's own pattern-making which makes the whole, and that the design of her life could be determined only by herself. That took courage, and besides, she was a slow learner. Trembling on a surging highland promontory she had remembered her grandmother's adage: experience is a hard school, but fools learn in no other.

She had learned enough to be able to respond to a newspaper advertisement for a position in the new library in Manortreacy sent without comment by her mother. She applied successfully and went home to an unsurprised town which had somehow carried on without her; few people understood why she had left Manortreacy, even fewer wondered why she came back to it.

As a librarian with teaching qualifications the service for schools was Eileen's special responsibility, and she did not spend much time in the public lending rooms. However, it was there that she met Benny Cronin, on a day of howling grimness when the building stank of damp warmth. He had brought back a Frederick Forsyth and an Anthony Trollope, he was taking out a Canon Sheehan and an Anthony Trollope, and her task was to tell him that his request for an inter-library loan of *Orley Farm* had not yet been filled.

'Eileen?' He was uncertain, but there was a tentative smile. 'Eileen! I'd heard you were back, but it's really good to see for myself – how are you?'

'Glad to be here. I think. I enjoy the work anyway. I gather things are going nicely for you too? You seem to have lots of time for reading, these days.'

Was it strange that there was no shyness between them? He confessed that he loved old-fashioned books now that he had to run a modern farm. As a child Eileen had accompanied her mother on visits to his mother, and anticipated some changes since then.

'Yes, there are changes, of course. But I let the stream alone, and I keep a few animals on a small scale, ducks and a few geese and hens.'

'And a gander?' That belligerent beak had terrified the small Eileen; Benny would be sent out to bring her safely past the bird.

They had never been particular friends, he was bigger and older and more solitary than she was as a child, and when school events or family visits had brought them together he had been kind to her, but no more. That left some liking between them, and now they were so much older, some curiosity.

With a patiently knowing line of customers lining up behind him, Benny suggested talking over their adventures. It was settled as a visit to Eileen's home, for tea with her mother.

'I suppose you arranged all that before the whole town,' was Mrs Tuohy's comment, but she had no real fear of Eileen being talked about, the girl was past the age for it.

When Benny came the winter had turned, and from his car he brought bunches of early daffodils for Mrs Tuohy which so disarmed her that she didn't see the small but elaborate box of chocolates he handed to Eileen in the hall. The evening went well: he ate enough to endear him to Eileen's mother, and to Eileen for her mother's sake. Although his talk was slow and deliberate he was not dull, and he and Eileen spelt out stories of their early, innocent London days. Mrs Tuohy talked about the people of the town, and together they remembered her husband, Eileen's father, and the children of the family now all spread throughout the country – indeed, the world.

'Except for Eileen,' Mrs Tuohy said once, and Benny turned to look at the brown-haired, brown-eyed young woman, graceful now where she had been neat, amused where she had been merry, and smiled his pleasure at her presence.

New because it was unexpected, this added ingredient in Eileen's life of telephone calls, a film, a walk, gave a new dimension to the comforts of normality. It was nice after all, she thought, to be among real friends.

It was when her mother had seen the primroses, wrapped in damp moss and delivered in a box by the postman, that Mrs Tuohy had first called Benny the swain.

'My God, girl,' she said drily, 'what are you doing to that boy at all? He's like a swain, sending flowers to the house!'

Her face lightening as she read the little card over her breakfast coffee, Eileen said only that he knew she preferred flowers to sweets, that was all. It wasn't all. The card reminded her that she had once delighted in the primroses gleaming along the green banks of the stream below Benny's pastures. No more than that, though it was a notice that there was more to life than friendship.

She bought Wellington boots, took her car on hazardous mountain tracks, sweated as she helped with a difficult calving, not thinking much of what she was doing except that it was a kind of sharing. Perfume came in the post, a book found in Westport, a letter explaining an absence.

'A letter from your swain!' Eileen's mother called one morning, and on the hall table Eileen found the familiar writing stroked across the patch of envelope. It was the early, mellow beginning of a balmy day in April, and Eileen felt that lifting of the spirit which seemed to come these days when she thought of Benny. She held the envelope lightly, and the big black letters were a mirror through which she could see him, the dark brown hair crusted with grey, the long shape of him in his careless flannels or correct tweeds, the hazel eyes sober in his weathered face. His mouth, thinner now, was still as beautifully cut as she had noticed in adolescence, the nose as straight, the brows as sleek. She felt as she mused that he was looking at her, and she could not meet his eyes.

He had never touched her. She had had no expectation of it, and it had never happened. Now she wondered. A fan of radiant flowers on the wall reflected the warming light in the window above the door, and in its glow she realised that she had never written to Benny, never given him anything. Here she felt, she suspected, that he was hoping for something.

Sitting down to her egg she opened the letter. He was taking a Jersey cow to Dublin, one of her pets. If she could get leave, would she like to accompany him?

Quickly, the answer was no. She decided she could not get the time off, but without asking, or taking time. To refuse nicely she searched the town for a card which might take the sting out of the message: the print was of a child in a field of corn, both child and grain blessed and golden with ripening sun. Again she stood with a message in her hands, unable again to think of looking at him.

Posting it, she said, 'I'm caught.' She would not go, but as she walked back along the street to the library, she knew she wanted to be with him. There was still something in herself which made her want to see what would happen. 'To be in his power,' and she quivered as if to a remembered sting. Setting briskly to work she tried to keep her mind off the image of him, blocking it with the mounds of books before her, the accounting slips and invoices, the destination of each parcel. There was a request for *The Way We Live Now*, one of Benny's favourite Trollope novels. She turned over the pages, finding again the sad suit of Roger Carbury: 'After all, though love is a wonderful incident in a man's life, it is not only that he is here for.'

Duties. 'When did you realise you were stuck?' he had asked her as they walked, hands in anorak pockets, down a hill path.

'When I bought the car with my mother, so that we could "get around together". Then, I knew.' Lightly said.

For Benny it had been when he took on John Joe Sweeney.

'Not only did I have someone relying on me for wages, I gave him the bawn house. And when you give a man wages and a roof over his head, you're stuck. So I settled myself to it then.'

He had halted to light his pipe, and the tiny curl of flame lit up the slender black hairs of his eyebrows, the deep crease between his gathered eyes. The wet track was bedded with leaves, with twigs and mosses and bordering weeds. The cool of the spring evening had its own scent, but over that lay the velvet aroma of tobacco. This was what she scented as she counted and checked through the volumes. It was his smell that came, not the spicy earth or the chill. He had tossed aside the spent match and ground it into earth that was his own.

He was settled. Was she? How badly she wanted to think she was. After all, this was not new to her, this heightened sense of a being beyond her own. She knew what was happening. After all those mistakes it seemed that while she could hold to her resolution for herself she could not forbid it for others. She had made that error with Benny, the error of assumption.

'Everyone knows about my mistakes,' he had said, weeks ago only. They sat in a lounge bar and drank amiable pints of beer on their way home from the annual Head of the River race.

'You must admit, being the death of my father was a hard act to follow – but I followed it, and everyone knows all about it. What mistakes did you make? Is there a great secret?'

He was pretending a mystery of her own to show that he accepted her knowledge of him, but there was hurt in what he said although he said it almost gaily, making light of it. Sugar crystals sparkled on the dark, coffee-ringed table-top between them, a white brightness which linked itself in her mind with the hint of damage in his voice. She felt forced to honesty, beyond it, to the search for some truth in herself.

'I was lucky, Benny,' she said. 'Just lucky. I made the silent kind of mistakes, the kind you recognise afterwards, but that seemed worth the risk at the time. All that happened was that I lost my taste for it, hadn't the courage any more, I suppose.'

'Was that why you went to Scotland?' His question was gentle, but it surprised her. He had been studying her. Only the instinct of understanding read through their casual conversations but she wasn't sure she wanted to be understood. Yet Benny deserved the truth if she could tell it.

She hesitated over it. 'More than that. I mean, yes, I was afraid I wouldn't want ever again to meet challenge. And I badly needed to feel that I could live with myself. By myself.'

'And can you?'

'Yes. Yes, Benny, I can.' She looked at him squarely then. He might as well know she was independent, looking for nothing. He might as well know everything.

'There is one mistake that wasn't so lucky. Just plain stupid, really. And I kept on making it.'

He was still, sitting easily back from the table, his hands in his pockets.

She went on quickly:

'I slept with men who didn't love me. I thought they did. I always thought they did.'

She thought the silence trembled between them. Then he said, 'But you didn't marry.'

Again she was surprised.

'Marry? No, of course not. I found out in time.'

'Well,' Benny said, the words serious but somehow light, 'that's the difference between us. You found out in time. I didn't.'

Kneeling between the books in the library, Eileen knew that he had absolved her. He was the only one in Manortreacy who knew about her life in England, and he had equated it with his own, saying they were different in the same way.

She had posted the rejecting card on her way to work. Going home later she wished she could recall it. Many times in the days after that Eileen wished harder, wrenched with a kind of hopeless regret. Then when it was time for Benny to be back from Dublin and days after that time again, a kind of fright took hold of her. When the telephone rang in her office she jumped and steadied herself before answering. It was never him. Her mother noticed.

'I hear your swain won all round him in Dublin.' She was reading the *Chronicle* by the light of the window, but pretended her information came through more natural, subtle channels.

'Is he coming in to town at the weekend?'

There was a black slug of jam at the edge of Eileen's plate; the blackcurrants had cropped heavily and the kitchen was still full of the bright warm smell of their cooking. The house was comfortable, a well-used, well-kept building, characteristic of the town in its main-street elegance. At this time of evening the summer light was deepening to gold, and the geraniums in their old china pots were stippled as if with sequins. Getting up heavily and rinsing the dishes before washing them in the sink, Eileen wondered if this would be enough for her for the rest of her life. She had chosen it; would it be enough?

'I don't know what Benny plans to do this weekend,' she said to her mother, casually as if to give the impression that he and she together had talked about it. Mrs Tuohy wasn't fooled for a moment, saying only that she had a lot of gardening and preserving to do so wouldn't want to be taken anywhere in the car if Eileen was wondering. Her daughter was free, in other words, to make plans.

Freedom was a very relative thing, Eileen reflected as she went for a searching, restless walk in that most poignant time of a summer evening, when soft purple rain soaks perfume from the lime trees and the white globes of philadelphus hang heavy and sweet. From the boat club came submerged music from the Friday night dance, and the alleys and angles of the town smoked with blue dusk. She returned soused in self-pity, but there was the beginning of shame underneath it, an awareness of selfishness.

Without Benny, and missing him dreadfully because she was uncertain, she had begun to count. The letters, the cards, the bunched or potted flowers, the walks and the drives, all had come from him. That could be said to be in the nature of things, perhaps, but somehow to remember it now made her uncomfortable. Bigger than that, however, was the patience of his attentions. There was a generosity in him and she had accepted it. Beyond all that there was Benny himself, the person that he was, not so much his value although she valued him, but his essence.

That had been offered too. And what had she thought she preferred? Her own calm stoicism. That, instead of the sense of him in her blood, the way her pulse thumped at this incisive thought of him as a man as she had known men, lusty and endearing but different because he was Benny.

'In the morning,' she promised herself, 'I'll take the car and go up to him. I can do that much. I'll go to him and see what happens.'

It was almost exciting, going to bed with that thought. The optimism of her resolution kept her awake with dreams of what would happen, but the cheerful dawn found her at last chill, no longer sure, dreaming all done. Six o'clock was too early, even for a farmer. As the hours grew she felt her purpose draining. By eight she still could have gone, by nine the thought of her mother's questions held her back, by ten it was the fear of making a fool of herself.

What right, after all, did she have to be asking for explanations? The man was his own boss, they were both adults, he had only stayed away from her for a few days. Ten and a half days. At his age he wouldn't like to have to answer for himself in that way.

At her age, too. 'Thirty-six,' she said to herself, 'that's not the age to be taking risks. It would be better to leave it, we'll meet around the town and it'll be all right.'

Except that she'd never find out what had happened. Never atone. There was that side to being an adult, too. The duties of maturity. Attempting to put right was one of them, wasn't it? Reparation took courage – and she had thought she had that. It was strange too, disquieting, to feel the need for courage with Benny. Now there were all sorts of needs stampeding at her, needs she had recognised and banished and which now came clambering back into her consciousness and above them all, clamouring most insistently, was the need for Benny himself. It was a risk, it would be a risk, he might not want her, but she was ready to give anything he wanted.

What could she bring him? The white geraniums grown from seed on the sitting-room window. Pots of the currant jam glazing the pantry shelves, a blue-leaved bunch of the striped and dappled pinks all spiced and giddy-smelling, that paperback of Cobbett's *English Gardener* she'd discovered. And wine, the bottle bought in case he came to dinner and never opened. A good year, she hoped.

Brushed and bare-legged in a skirt of improbably flowered cotton and chaste white shirt, feeling brave and wretched at the same time, she drove too soon over the six miles to the farm. Getting out to lift the latch of the first gate she felt her hands damp against the wrought iron.

'I know what I'm doing,' she told herself sharply against her clenched eyes, and she went on over the cattle grid and up the drive until the house stood square and uncompromising before her.

Benny had seen her coming, and pounded up from the small barn, his ecstatic collie dancing under his feet, nearly tripping him. He slowed before he reached her so that she would not see him red and sweating with haste. She stood by the car, her arms like a belt between the flowers of her skirt and the heaving blossoms she held. Above them her face shone, she couldn't help it, she was so glad to see him.

'Oh, I am so *glad* to see you, Benny!' she cried, and he laughed out loud at the joy in her voice, and reached out to grasp her. He could have congratulated himself that at last she had come to him but instead he held on to her so that book and flowers and parcels rolled and tumbled onto the gravel as the upright bodies met. Spirit and flesh blazed between them like the morning's second sun; their rapture was filtered through the green of the bounding fields, through the brick-red barns and the true and limpid river winding below the hill of the farmhouse to the grey distance of the town.

'By God, girl,' was all Benny could say. 'By God!' His voice was unsteady against her hair. 'I thought I'd gone the wrong way about it . . .'

'I thought I'd never make it past the gander!' She was able to laugh at last, although still frightened, frightened now that she had nearly not made it.

Benny had to remind her that there would be other ganders to pass. The Canon. Her mother.

'Ah, Benny, we'll make it now. As for my mother, she knows that every blessing is a mixed one, and she doesn't much care what the mix is any more!'

They did Mrs Tuohy an injustice. She would have no trouble at all in accepting Benny as a son-in-law. She knew Eileen, and knew how dangerously her daughter had been living. And besides, she had always had a soft spot for the swain.

VACANT POSSESSION

Deborah Moggach

S ome people call us cynics. Us, being estate agents. With a chortle they quote our advertisements: 'STUDIO FLAT,' they read. 'You mean a bedsit. EASILY MAINTAINED GARDEN. You mean four square yards of concrete.'

I'm not a cynic. In fact, I'm the opposite. I'm a romantic. I see the possibilities in the meanest property. I don't just see it; I believe it. For instance, I don't tell myself that a garden is surrounded by buildings, I tell myself it's secluded. If a flat overlooks Tesco's loading bay I tell myself it's convenient for the shops.

And to my surprise it works. If you're blind to the disadvantages, you pull other people along with you in the warm slipstream of your vision. Next time you're in the Fulham area, drive around and have a look at all those boards up saying FOR SALE: PREWITT, CUDLIP & LITTLE. Cudlip's me.

Oh yes, this optimism has got me a long way professionally. In my private life, however, it's been a different matter. Only the most foolish of romantics, the blindest of fools, would believe that a married man, working for the Department of the Environment, with three teenage children, would ever leave his wife.

Nigel was going to, of course. But not quite yet, because Vicky was doing her O-levels and he'd never be able to forgive himself if she failed. Because his wife was depressed after her hysterectomy and he couldn't bear to upset her just yet. Because, because.

They had gone on for four years, these becauses, and meanwhile I'd see him once a week or once a fortnight, when I was known as a conference in Southampton or a meeting in Hull. I'd been every major town in the British Isles. Once, for a couple of days, I was actually a summit meeting in Brussels.

Work is easy, isn't it, compared to everything else? I would sit in my beige office with its warbling phones and its window display of dream houses which I passed from one stranger to another. I would drive around in my shiny Metro, making valuations on the properties of Fash Fulham. I worked out percentages on my calculator; how cool those numbers were, how simple the soft bleeps of my sums.

If you want to know what sort of properties we handle, then Marcus Tanner's house was typical. I'd already acted for several clients in Foster Road, a street once occupied by the humble. A few still remained, with their net curtains and polished front steps, the chrysanths carefully staked in the gardens. But they were a vanishing species, outnumbered by the middle classes who knocked through their ground floors, called to each other in fruity, confident voices and filled up the street with their double-parked Renaults.

It was a morning in May that I went to Marcus Tanner's house to make a valuation. I guessed the reason for selling when I saw that the tubs on each side of the front door were choked with weeds. After six years in the house trade, I can recognise a divorce.

'Think you can shift it?' he asked. 'Quick?'

I nodded. 'No problem. These houses always sell. They're so sweet.'

'You mean small.'

'I mean sweet. Bijou. Perfect for –' I stopped.

He sighed. 'It was.'

Blushing, I gazed around the lounge. It was a typical late-seventies job – open plan; William Morris wallpaper; corduroy sofa; pub mirrors; Maggie Thatcher candle.

I paced the carpet. 'Hold this, will you, please?' I gave him one end of the tape measure. 'Immaculate through-lounge,' I murmured.

'Immaculate?' He raised his eyebrows. 'Looks a bit battle-scarred to me.'

I ignored him. 'Period features retained.'

'You mean these grotty old cupboards?'

I looked at him. 'You want to sell this house or not?'

He grinned. 'For a moment I thought you were a romantic.'

'Oh no. I'm a businesswoman.'

We went into the kitchen. 'Compact,' I muttered.

'You mean it's a cupboard. Hey, don't lean on those shelves, I put them up.'

'Everything within reach,' I said, measuring it.

'Shall I tell you about the dry rot?'

'No.'

We went outside.

'Even you can't pretend this is a garden,' he said.

'No, but it's a suntrap patio.'

He paused, picking a weed out of the wall. 'I'll miss this place. It's full of single-parent actresses. On Sundays you hear them learning their lines. And then there's the Sloane girls who've been bought their houses by Daddy. On summer evenings you can hear the pop of Waitrose hock bottles and the rustle of After Eights.'

'Now who's sounding romantic?'

'No. Just over-sexed.'

We went inside.

'It's an up-and-coming area,' I said.

He sighed, and inspected himself in the passage mirror. 'Look at these period features.'

He looked all right to me: a big chap, I would say in his early forties. Big but not fat – beefy. A lived-in, humorous face. I seem to have a weakness for older men. He wore a tired-looking jacket and corduroy trousers.

We went upstairs. Halfway up, I paused and looked out on to the extension roof. There was a flowerpot there, with shrivelled foliage.

He asked, 'What are you writing?'

'Roof terrace.'

We went into the bedroom. Being an estate agent, I've become an expert on divorces: weeds in the tubs, cracks in the walls. To me, the outsider on the inside, entering their lives at a moment of stress, they divide into two sorts. The ones who say nothing (men) and the ones who say too much (women). But Mr Tanner, unlike most men, wanted to tell me about it.

'Spacious fitted cupboards throughout,' I murmured, writing it down.

He opened one. It was full of dresses. 'She's coming for them tomorrow. It'll look even more spacious then.'

'What about the carpet?'

'Oh, get rid of the lot.' He paused, gazing at the bed. A cat lay curled there, its fur lit by sunlight. 'Looks peaceful, doesn't she?'

I gazed at the cat nestling on the daisy-patterned duvet, and nodded.

'She left me for her T'ai Chi instructor.'

'What?'

'Chinese martial arts.' He shut the cupboard with a snap. 'Spiritual self-defence. She was taking classes.'

'So he's Chinese?'

'No. From Tufnell Park. Between you and me, a bit of a wanker. But then I'm biased.'

There was a moment's silence. We stood in the bedroom, listening to the far strains of Radio One coming from the opposite house, which was being done up. No doubt another couple was moving in there, full of hope. I thought of the wheel of fortune, turning. Couples rising, and the casualties fallen by the wayside. Him, for instance; and me. I was not becoming a cynic.

'Enough maudlin talk,' he said. 'How much can we ask?'

'Sixty-eight,' I said briskly. 'Are you open to offers?'

He grinned again. 'Depends who's offering.'

He worked at the BBC, so he was out all day. Over the next week I showed prospective buyers around the house. After all these years I still feel intrusive, letting myself in through somebody else's front door. Particularly when that person lives alone; their solitary possessions seem vulnerable when exposed to strangers.

I showed round young couples who lingered, arm in arm. 'Lime-green!' said one girl. 'What a ghastly colour for a bathroom.' In the kitchen, an officious young man prodded the shelves. 'What a wally job. Wonder who put these up.'

I felt prickly. I told myself it was simple jealousy. These people were couples, and they were actually buying a house. They would walk down a street together, arm in arm, in broad daylight.

I looked at the bowl of half-eaten Weetabix and wondered if Marcus Tanner always ate his breakfast standing up in the kitchen. I wondered how he passed his evenings. In the lounge one day, while the floorboards above creaked with yet another couple, I found an open *Time Out* next to the phone; various cinemas had been underlined. He'd been doodling in the margins, and he'd drawn specs on Helen Mirren.

The cat, disturbed from her bed, came downstairs and rubbed herself against my legs. I fetched a tin and fed her. Even though I didn't know her name, I felt at home then.

It was Thursday. That evening I was expecting a visit from Nigel. We were going to a suburban cinema, where we couldn't be spotted, to watch *Gandhi*. I realised how I had been changing recently. Once I would have resented *Gandhi* because it was three hours long and that meant three hours missed when I could have had Nigel to myself, in bed. Now I just wanted to see the film. I thought: I'm curing myself. The cure is working.

But in the end it was immaterial because he phoned up with his call-box whisper, and said he couldn't come because his son had been sent down from Oxford for possessing cannabis and they had to have a family confrontation.

So I went to *Gandhi* alone, at my local. At least I didn't have to travel all the way to Orpington. The next morning he sent me a bunch of roses in apology. I shoved them into the swing-bin, jamming down their heads in a crackle of cellophane.

When I went to Marcus Tanner's house that morning there were two empty wine glasses on the table. In the kitchen I found two coffee cups; it wasn't his usual Nescafé, he'd made proper coffee in his cafetière. Two breakfast plates, with toast crumbs. Irritably I thought: what a mess. How's he going to sell his house if he leaves it like this?

I was called upstairs then. The people wanted to know if the blinds went with the house. I answered them, gazing at the bed. Beside it were two glasses and a half-empty bottle of Calvados. And his Maggie Thatcher candle, burnt down to a pair of sloping blue shoulders. She must have been important, for him to have burnt his candle.

'Pardon?'

'I said,' the man repeated, 'is the seller open to offers?'

I replied: 'Apparently.'

A week later an offer was made, and accepted. I spoke to Marcus Tanner on the phone.

'Come out and celebrate,' he said. 'Say you will.'

'You only got sixty-two thousand.'

'I knew you were an optimist. A romantic.'

'I'm a businesswoman.'

'Forget business,' he said. 'I'll give you a meal.'

He took me to a Fulham Road bistro. The evening got off on the wrong foot when one of the waiters looked at me, then winked at him.

'I see you're known here.'

'Oh yes,' he said blandly. He was wearing a red shirt and a bright blue tie. In the candlelight he looked caddish; a divorced man on the loose.

'Have you found somewhere else?' I asked.

'I'm looking. A flat in Barnes, I thought. Lots of BBC people in Barnes.'

'Lots of actresses.'

'Lots.'

I looked down and ordered veal, the most expensive thing on the menu.

The wine arrived. He said: 'Glad I didn't get Prewitt or Little.'

'Watch it. They're my partners.'

'But they're not as pretty.'

'They're blokes.'

'I don't go for blokes.'

'I've gathered that.'

He laughed. My neck heated up. I sipped my wine and thought of the breakfast coffee cups, and despised myself. Why shouldn't the chap enjoy himself?

I thought: catch me becoming another melted portion of Maggie Thatcher. Blushing harder, I thought: What on earth am I thinking?

We ate our antipasto. For a while it went all right. He wanted to know how I'd got into the business and I told him about my flat, and my brother's awful wife who hoovered under his lifted feet, and what I'd thought of *Gandhi*. I hadn't talked so much for ages; he made the words come into my head. I found I was entertaining even myself.

Then he said: 'Who is he?'

'Who's who?'

'There must be some lucky bloke, somewhere.'

I paused. 'Well . . .' I speared an anchovy.

'Go on. I've been longing to ask.'

'It's all . . . well, rather difficult.'

'Ah. That sort of difficult.'

I glanced up sharply. 'No!'

'Jesus,' he said. 'What a waste.'

'It's not!'

'How long has it been going on? Do you mind me asking?'

'Yes. No.' I ate a green bean. 'Four years.'

'Four? That's appalling.'

'It's not appalling. It's . . . difficult.'

'So you sit by the phone, and when it rings there's that pip-pip-pip?'

I said coldly: 'You're obviously speaking from experience.'

He ignored me. 'And all weekend you wash your hair, and hear the hours ticking away, and watch the families in the park —'

'Marcus, shut up!'

'And he keeps promising he'll leave her, and sometimes he even breaks down and cries –'

'Look –'

'– a grown man, and that makes you feel even worse.'

'Marcus –'

'And so you throw yourself into your work, and sublimate –'

Furious, I shouted: 'What a stupid, sexist remark! You wouldn't say that if I were a man.'

'I wouldn't feel like this if you were a man.'

I pushed an olive around my plate. 'It's none of your business.'

We fell silent. After a while we started talking politely. It was Wimbledon fortnight and we discussed McEnroe, but the zest had gone.

Outside, he offered to drive me home but I said I would rather walk. I thanked him for the dinner.

He took my hand. 'Sorry.'

'It doesn't matter.'

'It does.' Lorries rattled past. He was gazing at me, frowning. 'Four years is a long time. I just feel . . . you ought to be more honest with yourself. Not such a romantic.' He paused. 'You should face up to reality.'

'I do!'

He smiled. 'You and your suntrap patios.'

On the way back I stopped outside the office. We were doing so well that we'd had it refurbished. In the window, each photo was mounted in a plastic cube, lit from within . . . glowing from the heart. CHARMING PERIOD HOUSE . . . DELIGHTFUL GARDEN MAISONETTE. Beyond them I could see the shadowy room and my dark desk.

I thought of Marcus's words. Why was he such an expert, when he'd made such a mess of his own life?

I worked harder than ever the next couple of weeks. Houses move fast in July; people are restless.

I was restless too. I felt hot and cramped in the office. I spent a lot of time in my car, driving clients around and visiting new properties. Once I drove to Holland Park, just to see if I could pass down Nigel's street without my stomach churning. I stopped outside the house. The blinds were down; he had taken the family on holiday.

I knew that, of course. For the first time in four years, however, I didn't know where they had gone. Or even how long they would be away. I hadn't asked him.

For the first time I gave the house a long, honest look. I saw it for what it was: an imposing, terraced mansion with a pillared porch. There it stood, large and creamy. A family fortress.

I drove away. I had three appointments that afternoon, meeting prospective buyers at various empty properties.

Two of them passed without incident. At five o'clock only the last remained. It was not until then that I fished the third key from my bag, and found the piece of paper, where my secretary had noted down the person's name.

He was waiting outside in the street.

'It's you,' I said stupidly.

He grinned. 'It's me all right. I'm glad it's you.'

'What?'

'Not Prewitt or Little.'

'No. It's not them.'

We stood there by the front gate. Trying to collect my thoughts, I fiddled with the gate-latch. There was a moment's silence, then he pointed up at the house.

'Which floor's the flat?'

'The second. Didn't you know?'

'I just saw the board up, with your name on it. So I phoned.' He picked at the blisters on the fence. 'On impulse.'

I felt hot. I said: 'Thought you were looking in Barnes.'

'I looked. Everyone's married.'

'Even the actresses?'

'Even them.'

We stood there. He popped the blisters in the paint. He wore his tired-looking jacket.

'Didn't you go to work today?'

He shook his head. 'Went round looking at your boards.'

I moved towards the door. 'You won't like this flat.'

'Why?'

'Just being honest.'

We went upstairs. The flat was a new conversion. It had been flashed up with magnolia paint and woodchip wallpaper.

'Cowboy job,' I said.

'You are being unromantic today.'

We stood in the empty room.

'Vacant possession,' he murmured.

'Oh yes, it's that all right.'

He looked at me. Then he said: 'How are you, Celia?'

I gazed at the floorboards. 'All right.'

'How's things?'

I looked up at him. 'Oh, they're over.'

'Are they?'

I nodded. There was a silence.

Later we had a meal. Not at the bistro place; somewhere else. He said: 'I don't want that flat.'

I shook my head. 'No.'

'It's cheap and nasty.'

I nodded. 'Yes.'

'Are we both telling the truth now?'

'Yes.'

Afterwards we sat together in my Metro. The car shook as lorries rumbled down the Cromwell Road.

I said: 'You feel so warm.'

'Oh yes,' he replied. 'I'm fully central-heated.'

CHARMING GARDEN-LEVEL FLAT. That's what he bought, and it means a basement, of course. It had a COUNTRY-STYLE garden which meant full of nettles but I've been seeing to those.

It is charming, too. I'm not just saying it. I've come to know every corner, over the past few weeks. It charms me.

THE NEEDLECASE

———— ◆ ————

Elizabeth Bowen

The car was sent to the train – along the straight road between dykes in the late spring dusk – to bring back Miss Fox, who was coming to sew for a week. Frank, the second son of the house, had come suddenly back from town; he was pleased to find the car there, which was more than he hoped, but appalled to see Miss Fox, in black, like a jointed image, stepping in at the back. Frank had, and wished to have, no idea who she was. So he sat in front with the chauffeur, looking glumly left at the willows and dykes flitting by, while Miss Fox, from the back, looked as fixedly out at willows and dykes at the other side of the road. No one spoke. They turned in at the lodge gates and the avenue trees closed in.

When the car drew up at the hall door, Frank got out and shouted. It embarrassed him having come home, and he did not want to explain. His sister Angela, sitting up at her window, heard, shot downstairs, and flung her arms round his neck, nearly knocking him over, like far too big a dog, as though he had been away two years instead of two days. This pleasure she over-expressed was perfectly genuine; Angela was effusive because she was often depressed; she could not be bothered being subtle with Frank, whom she knew far too well, and whose chagrins she often shared. So she kept up this rowdy pretence that everything was for the best.

'Had-a-good-time?' she said.

'No.'

'I'm sure you did really,' said Angela.

'No doubt you know best,' said Frank. 'Who in God's name's that in there?'

'Oh, that's Miss *Fox*,' explained Angela, peering into the car, where Miss Fox sat like an image, waiting to be let out. Angela rang the bell wildly for someone to come and cope. The chauffeur carried Frank's bag and the sewing-woman's strapped-up brown paper suitcase up the wide steps. The front of the house loomed over them, massive and dark and cold: it was the kind of house that easily looks shut up, and, when shut up, looks derelict. Angela took Frank's arm and they went indoors, into the billiard-room, the only place they could be certain of meeting nobody else. The room had a dank, baizey smell, and a smell of cold anthracite from the unlit stove: four battered green shades hung low over the sheeted table. It was not cheery in here. Frank sat on the fender-stool with his shoulders up and stared through his sister Angela heavily, uninvitingly. Had he wished to be quite alone he would not, however, have shouted.

'What did you do?' said Angela.

'Nothing special,' Frank said. He had been up to London to meet a man who might get him a job if he liked the looks of him, and the man clearly had not. The man had seen Frank to do Arthur a good turn: unfortunately the brothers did not resemble each other. Everyone liked Arthur. And Frank had stayed up in London, and had hoped to stay longer, because of a girl, but that had been a flop too: he had run through his money; that was why he was home. Angela had the good sense to ask no more. Leaning against the table and screwing her left-hand white coral earring tighter (she always looked rather well) she said nonchalantly: 'The Applebys have been over. Hermione's after Arthur. They want us for tennis on Monday. The vet came about Reno; he says it's nothing – oh, and Mother has heard from Arthur; he's coming down Friday week and bringing his new girl. So then Mother wired to hurry on Miss Fox. She's going to make us all over – first the drawing-room covers, then Mother's black lace, and then do up Toddy and me – cut some dresses and run up some tennis frocks. She's our one hope for the summer. No doubt she sews like hell, but we really couldn't look worse. Could we, Frank? I mean, could we?'

'Yes,' said Frank. 'I mean, no.'

'We heard of her through Aunt Doris,' said Angela, chatting away. 'She's one of the wonderfully brave – she's got a child to support that she shouldn't have. She trained somewhere or other, so I suppose she *can* make. She's been on these rounds for years, going down in the world a bit. She seems dirt cheap, so there must be something fishy. She used to work, years ago, for the Fotheringhams, but Aunt Doris only got on to her after she fell.'

'You surprise me,' said Frank, yawning drearily, wanting a drink more than anything in the world.

Miss Fox's arrival, though perfectly unassuming, had left quite a wake of noise: she had been taken up and put somewhere, but doors went on opening and shutting, Frank's mother stood out in the hall giving directions, and his elder sister Toddy began shouting for Angela. As Frank crossed the hall his mother broke off to give him her vivid mechanical smile and say, 'Oh, you're *back*.' The house – far too big but kept on for Arthur, who was almost always away but liked to think of it there – had many high windows and a white stone well staircase that went, under a skylight, up and up and up. This would have been an excellent house for someone else to have lived in, and heated; Frank and Angela could then have visited comfortably there. As it was, it was like a disheartened edition of Mansfield Park. The country around it was far too empty and flat.

Miss Fox was not to work tonight; they left her to settle in. But Toddy was in such a hurry to get in first with her things that she slipped upstairs, unobtrusively, as soon as dinner was over. She found Miss Fox still smoking over her supper tray. She was of that difficult class that has to have trays all the time. Too grand for the servants, she had to be fed in her room – one of those top bedrooms in any Georgian house with high ceilings and windows down by the floor. It looked rather bleak in the light of two hanging bulbs. A massive cheval glass, brought from downstairs today, reflected Miss Fox's figure sitting upright at the table. Deal presses stood round the walls, dress-boxes tottered in stacks and two dressmaker's dummies – one stout and one slimmer – protruded their glazed black busts. A sewing-machine with a treadle awaited the dressmaker's onslaught. In the grate, a thin fire rather uncertainly flapped. What should be done had been done to acclimatise Miss Fox. But her purpose here could be never far from her mind, for she rigidly sat at the table where she would work. A folded-back magazine was propped on the coffee pot: when Toddy came in she lifted her eyes from this slowly, but did not attempt to rise.

Her meek, strong, narrow, expressionless face, with heavy eyelids, high cheekbones and secretive mouth, framed in dusty fair hair brushed flat and knotted behind, looked carven under the bleak overhead light. Its immobile shadows were startling. Toddy thought: 'She's important.' But this was absurd.

Toddy kicked the door to behind her and stood stock still, a cascade of tired dance dresses flung over one arm, two bales of gingham for tennis frocks balanced under the other. Success this forthcoming summer was deadly important, for Toddy was now twenty-four. She felt Miss Fox held her fate in the palm of her hand. So she stood stock still and did not know how to begin. She had quieter manners, a subtler air than Angela, but was in fact a rather one-idea girl.

'I hope you have all you want,' she said helplessly.

'Yes, thank you, Miss Forrester.'

'I mustn't disturb you tonight. But I thought you might like some idea –'

'Show me,' said Miss Fox politely, and pushed her chair back from the table.

'My red tulle is ripped right round. It caught on a spur –'

She stopped, for Miss Fox was looking at her so oddly, as though she were a ghost, as though it were terror and pleasure to see her face. Toddy's looks were not startling, but were, like her brother Arthur's, pleasant enough. No one, no man, had been startled this way before.

'It caught on a spur,' she said, on a rising note.

Miss Fox's eyes went quite blank. 'Tch-tch-tch,' she said, and bent quickly over the stuff. She had unpacked and settled in – Toddy saw, looking round – screens hid her bed and washstand, the facts of her life, away, but one or two objects had appeared on the mantelpiece, and a fine, imposing work-basket stood at her elbow. Toddy, who loved work-baskets, had a touch of the jack-daw, so, while Miss Fox was examining the martyred red dress, she flicked back the hinged lid of the basket and with innocent, bird-like impertinence routed through its contents. All sorts of treasures were here: 'souvenir' tape-measures, tight velvet emery bags, button-bags, a pincushion inside a shell, scissors of all sorts in scabbards – and oh, such a needlecase! 'As large as a family Bible,' said Toddy, opening it, pleased. And, like a family Bible, it had a photo stuck inside. 'Oh, what a nice little boy!' – '*Thank you*,' exclaimed Miss Fox, and with irresistible quickness, a snatch, had the needlecase back. The movement so surprising, it seemed not to have happened.

'That looked such a dear little boy,' Toddy went on, impenitent.

'My little nephew,' Miss Fox said impenetrably.

It was odd to think she had a child, for with such a nun-like face she had looked all wrong, somehow, smoking a cigarette. The dusty look of her hair must be the effect of light, for Toddy, standing above her, looked down and saw how well brushed her hair was. Her fingers looked as though they would always be cold, and Toddy dreaded their touch on her naked spine when the time would come to try on her evening dresses. And felt frightened alone with her, at the top of this dark, echoing house. They saved light everywhere, you had to grope up the stairs, for this well of a house drank money. So its daughters, likely to wither, had few 'advantages'. Everyone knew, Arthur knew, that Arthur must marry money. Toddy was sick of the sacrifice. She was in love this year, baulked all the time, and her serene, squarish face concealed a constant, pricking anxiety.

'I've *got* to look nice,' she said suddenly.

'I'll do all I can,' said Miss Fox, flashing up once again that odd, reminiscent look.

'How *like* you, Toddy,' Angela cried at breakfast.

'What was like Toddy?' Frank asked, scrawling a maze among the crumbs by his plate. He seldom listened to what his sisters were saying, but sat on at table with them because he had nowhere special to go next.

'Creeping up there, then poking about in her things. You really might give the poor old creature a break.'

'She's not so old,' said Toddy, serene. 'And the child looked about seven.'

'What was it like?'

'I only saw curls and a collar – I tell you, she snatched it away.'

'What child?' said Frank. He pushed his cup across vaguely and Angela gave him more coffee, but it was cold.

'The child she had,' said Toddy.

'Oh God,' said Frank, 'is she fallen?' But he did not care in the least.

'I told you she was, last night,' said Angela, hurt.

That morning, Miss Fox was put in the drawing-room to work. Bales of chintz were unrolled and she cut out the new covers, shaping them over the backs of the chairs with pins. In cold, windy April sunlight, she crawled round and round the floor, with pins in her mouth. The glazed chintz looked horribly cold. Frank, kept so short of money, not only thought the rosy-and-scrolly pattern itself obscene, but found these new covers a frenzied extravagance. But now Arthur's most promising girl was coming to stay, and must at all costs be impressed. If she did marry Arthur, she'd scrap these covers first thing. Any bride would. Frank leaned in the doorway, letting a draught in that rustled under the chintz, to watch Miss Fox at work on her thankless task. She magnetised his idleness. Their silence was fascinating, for if he spoke she would have to spit out those pins. The drawing-room was full of tables covered with photographs: Arthur at every age. He watched Miss Fox dodge the tables and drag her lengths of chintz clear.

Then she sat back on her heels. 'How fast you get on,' Frank said.

'I give my whole mind to it.'

'Don't your hands get cold, touching that stuff?'

'They may do; I'm not particular.'

She put pins back in her mouth and Frank wondered how she had ever been seduced. He picked up her big scissors idly and snipped at the air with them. 'This house is like ice,' he said. 'Do you know this part of the world?'

She was round at the back of the sofa and nothing came for some time; she must be eyeing the pattern and chewing the pins. Then her voice came over the top. 'I've heard speak of it. It seems very quiet round here.'

'*Quiet* –' began Frank.

But, hearing his voice, his mother looked in and said with her ready smile: 'Come, Frank, I want you a moment. We mustn't disturb Miss Fox.'

That same afternoon, the sun went in. Sharp dark clouds with steely white edges began bowling over the sky and their passing made the whole landscape anxious and taut. Frank went out riding with Angela; the wind, coming up and up, whistled among the willows; the dykes cut the country up with uneasy gleams. The grass was still fawn-coloured; only their own restlessness told them that it was spring. It *was* quiet round here. They jogged tamely along, and Angela said she saw no reason why things should ever happen, and yet they did. She wished they saw more of life. Even Miss Fox in the house was *something*, she said, something to talk about, something going on. 'And of course I do need those clothes. But when we *are* all dressed up, I don't know where we're to go. Oh hell, Frank. I mean, really.' She rode hatless, the wind stung her cheeks pink: Frank bitterly thought that she looked like some Academy picture about the Morning of Life.

'Do you think Arthur'll marry that girl?'

'I daresay he'll try,' said Frank.

'Oh, come. You know, Frank, our Arthur's a big success . . . It's terrible how we wonder about Miss Fox. Do you think we are getting prurient minds? But the idea's fantastic.'

'Fantastic,' Frank agreed, feeling his own despondency ironed into him. Angela shot off and galloped across the field.

That night, in a wind direct from the Ural mountains, the house began to creak and strain like a ship. The family sat down-stairs with as few lights on as possible. It was Angela who slipped up to talk to Miss Fox. The handsome work-basket was present but hasped shut, and Angela, honourably, turned her eyes from it. She really did want to talk. She sat on the rug by the grate; the wind puffed down the chimney occasional gusts of smoke that made her eyes smart. Miss Fox sat at the table, puffing away at a cigarette with precision. Perhaps she was glad of company. Noth-ing showed she was not. Her head, sculptured by shadows, was one of the finest heads Angela had ever seen.

'You must see a lot of funny things, going from house to house.'

'Well yes, I do. I do see some funny things.'

'Of course, so do hospital nurses. But people must be much funnier trying on clothes. And some families are mares' nests. I wish you'd tell me . . .'

'Oh well, that would hardly do.'

'You know nurses aren't discreet . . . My brother Frank thinks you're a witch.'

'Gentlemen will have their fun,' said Miss Fox, with an odd inflection, as though she were quoting. Meeting Angela's eye, she smiled her held-in, rigid smile. Angela thought with impatience of gentlemen's fun that they must have – and, in this connection, of Arthur, who had his share. She heard the wind gnaw at the corners of this great tomb of a house that he wouldn't let them give up.

'It's all right for Arthur,' she said.

'Those photographs in the drawing-room – they are all your Mr Arthur?'

'Of course,' said Angela crossly.

'Miss Toddy favours him, doesn't she?'

Angela hugged her knees and Miss Fox got no answer to this. So the sewing-woman reached out her cold hand across the table, shook out of the packet and lit with precision another thin cigarette. Then: 'I've seen Mr Arthur,' she said.

'Oh yes, I've seen Mr Arthur. He was staying one time in a lady's house where I worked. There were several young gentlemen there, and I wasn't, of course, in the way of hearing their names. They were a big party, ever so gay and high-spirited, dodging all over the house, they used to be, every night, and in and out of my workroom, playing some game. I used to be sitting alone, like I sit here, and they used to stop for a word as they went through, or sometimes get me to hide them. Pleasant, they all were. But I never did catch any names. Mr Arthur took a particular fancy to one of my dummies, and asked me to lend it to him to dress up for some game. I should have known better; I ought to have known my place.

'But it was eight years ago. The last night, I let him take the dummy away. They did laugh, I heard. But there was an accident and Mr Arthur let it drop on the stairs. The pedestal broke and some of the skirt-wires bent. He came back, later, to tell me how sorry he was. He *was* sorry, too. He said he'd make it all right. But he went off next day, and I suppose something happened to put it out of his head. My lady was not at all pleased, as she had had the dummy made to her own figure, and her figure was difficult. I didn't work there again.'

'How like him!' exclaimed his sister, savagely reclasping her hands round her knees.

Miss Fox, immensely collected, let out a cloud of smoke. 'He meant no harm,' she said stonily.

Frank came upstairs in the dark, feeling his way by the handrail and calling, 'Angela?' It gave him the creeps when anyone disappeared. And downstairs Toddy was fumbling on the piano. 'Here,' called Angela. Frank knocked once, and came in. 'You look very snug,' he said, rather resentfully. This room's being inhabited gave the house a new focus. Soon they would all be up here. He came and stood by the fire and watched his sister rocking and hugging her knees. He saw by her face that he had cut in on a talk. His own superfluity bit him.

'Miss Fox once knew Arthur, Frank.'

'A ladder's run right down your stocking,' said Frank with angry irrelevance.

'Damn,' said Angela vaguely.

'Best catch it up,' said Miss Fox.

She looked from Frank to Angela. There was a pause. Then, in the most businesslike way, she put down her cigarette, opened her work-basket, glanced at Angela's stocking and, matching it with her eye, drew a strand from a mixed plait of darning silks. Then she took out the big black needlecase. 'Mr Frank . . .' she said. He went over and, taking the case, brought it across to Angela. She knelt upon the hearthrug; he rested a hand on her shoulder and felt the shoulder go stiff. 'What a lot of needles,' she said mechanically. She and Frank both stared at the photograph of the child. They saw, as Toddy had seen, its curls and its collar. Like Arthur's collar and curls in old photographs downstairs. And between the collar and curls, Arthur's face stared back again at the uncle and aunt.

'I should take a number five needle,' said Miss Fox calmly.

'I have,' said Angela, closing the needlecase.

'Ladders down stockings break one's heart,' said Miss Fox.

FAMILY LOVE

LYCHEES FOR TONE

◆

Jane Gardam

'Eh, Mum,' he says, standing up and scratching hisself (I'm sorry but that's Tone), 'I's bringin' a bird home Saturday.'

'Saturday's tomorrow,' I says.

'That's it,' he says, bending down and pulling out the telly plug. We'd been watching the James Bond. Tell you the truth my heart were like a pump. He's twenty-two and he's never brought no girls home in his life. Tadpoles yes, lads yes. Bikes yes. And now the cars. He's dug this great hole in the front garden for the cars and lines it out with concrete. 'It's a pit,' he says. You'd think he were seven.

'Whatever you want a pit for?'

'To get at 'em,' he says. Then they drives one car or another over the pit and they crawls down underneath and they fiddles about, breaking things off and welding things on and hammering and grunting. Every night after work and half of Sundays. Transistors blaring. Saturdays is the Scramble with the bikes. Always bikes and cars and lads. Girls never.

Might be war-games to look at them on a night. In the pit. He used to play war-games when he were seven. *And* ten. *And* fourteen if you want to know. His poor father he used to go mad – machine guns racketing, bombs squealing down. 'Git out o' them bushes. If yer don't shut up I'll brae yer.' Poor Syd. He were too heavy. He should never of let hisself get upset, a heavy man like him. He just dropped down. Outside the bathroom door. Yelling at our Tony he was then, too. 'In the bloody bathroom half the morning,' he yells, and then thump and a crash and I flew. I said, 'You've done it now. You've done it this time all right,' and Tone unlocks the door and stands there all foam on his face and his shaving brush in his hand and he looks and he says, 'We'd best not shift him. Get a doctor.'

That's all he said and he'd killed his father.

Oh, I've been daft. I've been daft to put up with him. Not that he's not helped. He's earned good money, not like Mrs Morgan's lot. Still students at thirty hers are, writing books and that and their mother on tranquillisers.

No, our Tone pays the gas and electricity, his father not having thought ahead. No reason why he shouldn't, mind, the amount of electricity he gets through. He's got yards of these cables with electric light bulbs stuck on the ends of them, all trailed out over the garden to light up his pit. Sets them up like a blessed telly studio. Then he gets revving up the engines till all hours.

I can't face the neighbours. I mean it. I can't face them. They're foreigners both sides and they don't seem to care and they make enough of a racket theirselves but still I'm ashamed. I says to one side one day – Mrs Palmer, she's Jamaican: Mrs Morgan on the other side, on the tranquillisers, she's Welsh – 'Mrs Palmer,' I says, 'I'm that sorry about the noise.'

'I don't hear no noise,' she says.

'I mean the engines. It's my Tone.'

'Oh, we like a bit of noise,' she says. 'You ought to come and make a bit of noise yourselves when we all have a Get-Together.' Then she starts asking me to these sing-songs they have Saturday nights. She belongs to some funny Church where they all believe in love and that. So I had to draw back.

She says – Mrs Palmer – when there's more bits of cars and bikes than usual over the lawn and me just standing helpless thinking of Syd and his lobelias and the hours he used to spend on his edgings and how he wouldn't even let Tone have a rabbit-hutch out there because it left a yellow mark – 'Mrs James dear,' she says (dear!), 'that beautiful young boy of yours, he ought to have a girlfriend.'

Well, I just went into the house. I wasn't having that.

'Bringing home a bird Saturday,' he says.

'Saturday's tomorrow,' I says.

'That's right,' he says.

'And so it's me got to make the house right,' I says, 'and get food in and that?' My heart were thudding away still. I felt right queer. Excited like. Daft. I don't know why I do it somehow, the way I go on at Tone.

'You don't want your supper then?' (Saturday's his steak and kidney and a sponge.)

'No,' he says, 'I'll be getting it out. When I pick her up.'

'What, after the Scramble?'

'That's it.'

Didn't seem hardly worth bringing her home that time, I thought. And then a real terrible thing strikes me. He looks at me – great lump. He'll have to watch his weight or he'll go down like his father – *and* sooner –

'You don't need to get owt right,' he says. 'She's comin' in with me.'

Then he thunders off to bed singing like an opera (and he has got a lovely voice, I'll say that. He could of got to the D'Oyly Carte), bumping and crashing about. When he passes me on the landing he gives me a bold great look like to say 'and there's not a blind thing you can do about it, is there?'

And there's not. All next day in the shoe shop I'm all over the place. 'Whatever's the matter with you then, Mrs James?' (Mr Hinton, the manager.) 'You're looking tired.' He's a bit sweet on me, the manager, if you want to know. Says I make him laugh. He thinks I'm funny the way I'm always worried. And he was good to me over Syd. He seemed to understand I was upset about not being upset, if you see what I mean. 'Enjoy yourself then, Mrs James,' he says when it's a real bad day like Sales times. 'Relax and enjoy it, Confucius he say,' and all these little girls – that Sandra! – with their great bottoms and their tight skirts lounging about while I take the customers, they just snigger. He'll be talking about tranquillisers next and have me blinkin' my eyes and yawning like that Mrs Morgan. That Sandra blinks her eyes and yawns anyway. Put her on tranquillisers and she'd drop off in a coma. She fetches me a cup of tea though, and Saturday's busy. Don't know how she stays awake to watch the kettle.

Saturday's busy. Saturday's always busy. This Saturday's murder. Thirty-seven customers and all with feet like elephants or feet like them Australian things with beaks. I used to make Tone laugh about the customers long since. Tone can laugh. Syd could never laugh. I don't believe he ever laughed at anything except in a bitter sort of a way. 'Why do you do it then?' he used to say when I was going on about the shoe shop. 'I earn good money,' he said. It's funny how he always thought he earned good money. He did maybe. He made mirrors. Unusual job. But there was none at the last. Maybe I should of packed in the shoe shop and he'd of done better. Maybe I should of been home a bit more and kept Syd and Tone apart. They did fight.

But the money come in useful for Tone's training. He were a Late Developer but good with his hands and with his figures. I don't think he'd of ever bothered to get hisself on at all if I hadn't worked to pay for his training at the engineering. He's got a lot to thank me for. His father used to say that. 'You've got a lot to thank your mother for. It's more'n I'd of done for you,' he said. 'Not reading till you was nine.'

Funny thing is Tone never looked the happier for it when I give him his money on a Friday night. Maybe I should just of left him alone.

And now this.

And he's going to sleep with her.

Just some girl or other he's picked up.

In this house. In Eastern View. His father's house. I dare say it's more like his house now since he pays the rates and that and the bit of mortgage and all the instalments. But I can't take it. I can't take it. The place his father and I went mad for, coming from Bootle, and kept decent – beautiful – nineteen years. Stepping into bed with her, just like it was on a bus!

If he's turning to this style why can't he take her to some hotel? Or go round her place? Wherever that is. Port Sunlight likely. I don't like it. I'm not used. I hear enough of it at the shop.

I wonder if he's done it before? Outside? It's possible. Things being what they are. I think I'll die. And we had him at the United Reform Sunday Schools till he were past fourteen.

I ran round home dinnertime to see to his meal – best end, dumplings, potatoes, rice-pudding and treacle – and he were all togged up in his leather jacket with the studs, fixing on his round black helmet and trying to buckle on his belt. Far too fat he is.

'Did you get your dinner?'

'I did.'

'Was it all right for you then?'

'Grand.'

'So yer off? Scrambling?'

'I am.'

'And you'll be late back?'

'After me tea.'

I rinsed off his plates at the sink and made a cup of tea for meself and didn't look at him. He was racketing about for something.

'And you're bringing back this –?'

'I am. Where's me gauntlets?'

'How do I know where you put your gauntlets? Where she from?'

'Who?'

'This bird.'

'Oh – I dunno. Asia somewhere. She's Asian. Chinese.'

And he come over and bless me he gives me a kiss.

Well, this time I nearly did die. No wonder he gives me a kiss. Chinese! I nearly did die. I *looked* dead. I could tell by the way they all skimmered at me sideways round the shop. 'Talking to herself now,' I heard one of them say – that Sandra – in the boxes. 'Goin' on something terrible.' 'Just her age dear.' (Mr Hinton, the manager.) 'Heart of gold,' he says. That's all he knows.

Well, I gets home and it's nearly dark. They won't be that long. But there's Mrs Palmer still hanging out over my fence with the baby. One of the babies.

'Now, hello there, Mrs James,' she sings out as I puts my key in the door. 'You not happy today now, Mrs James? You ought to come to our Get-Together tonight.' She leans her whole side against the fence. Syd would of gone spare. I looks away – over at the curtains in Mrs Morgan's all drawn anyhow and not washed this side of Christmas. Thank God Syd's not here to see what's happened in this road. The baby starts laughing and clapping its hands. It's a bonny child, mind. It's a real beauty. You can't help wanting to pick it up and love it. You want to pat all that frizz. It's like the heather up above Bolton.

I says all of a sudden, 'Our Tone's bringing a girl back tonight.'

'Well now, that's nice now, Mrs James. Where she from?'

'Your parts somewhere. Asia somewhere.'

'What – is she Jamaican girl?'

'Some of them parts,' I says. 'Asia, China somewhere.'

She laughs like nobody's business. Don't know how it is, she never stops laughing. She's better off than Mrs Morgan anyway.

'Your Tone's a big boy now, Mrs James,' she says. 'Time he had a nice girl. Chinese girls make wonderful wives,' she says. 'Why not you all come round here to our sing-song?'

Well, I went in and I couldn't eat my tea. I cleaned out the kitchen. 'Let her see how to keep a place clean,' thinks I. 'Just let her see the polish on this kitchen floor. Chinese, he says. Always on about how clean they are, the Chinese. Well, let her see what clean is. You'll get nothing cleaner than Eastern View in any of your Asias.'

I'd put my top polish on my vinyl and rubbed down all my working surfaces. I went over all my blind slats – variegated pastels – and shone up my brass ornaments and washed over the leaves on the pot plant on the ledge and I looked round very satisfied. *Very* satisfied. She'll get a right shock when she sees this, thinks I. After seeing our Tone all over mud and grease she'll not think he comes from this style. She'll walk in here all little and grinny on them wobbly little feet they all have – it's their grand-mothers having them in bandages. Inherited bad ankles. I read it in the *Shoe News* – and she'll look round and she'll think, My word! Here's somebody knows what's what.

I moved the plant so's her eye'd catch it first go off. Very keen on flowers the Chinese. It's like their religion, the way they arrange them about. It was on the telly. Little white hands they've got, all dainty. Never think they did a thing. Mind, all that cook-ing – all them little different bits – that must take a time. If they do it all themselves that is and not just open tins like they do down the Chinese take-away. I got one of them once – a tin of that stuff they eat – queer white fruits. I took it in the supermarket by mis-take for mandarins. Never got round to changing it neither, come to think.

And before I knew it I went over to my store-cupboard and I got this tin out. Then I got the opener and I was opening it up. Nasty little round white things they were inside. 'Lychees' it said. Sort of slimy moth balls. Not my style. I poured them in my cut-glass fruit dish and set them down in the middle of the kitchen table.

Daft.

Then I went quick into the front room. I'm tired out from the cleaning and that and it's nearly dark now. No sign of Tone. I've got this bit of polyester and cotton I'm supposed to be making up for that Sandra in the shop, since she's got no idea. Girls can't do nothing these days. She wants a blouse and she's give me the pat-tern. Far too low-cut.

One thing about Chinese girls is they dress decent. They don't go in for low-cut like Mrs Palmer. And Mrs Morgan come to that. Nice straight backs, too. Little high collars and long sleeves. There was one in the shop today with five little ones with her all good as gold sitting on the row of chairs. Three on them still had their legs stuck out straight in front. I like to see children that size. Before their legs hang down. Up to nearly three they're like that. All colours the same.

Good as gold they were, all on them. Little pale faces and black eyes. Wonder why they're called yellow-skinned? There's nothing yellow about them. Black, black eyes, shape of petals. Ten petals. Twelve if you count hers. The mother's. Didn't look much older than them, the mother. They stay young the Chinese. Still like children when they're forty. Lovely little things really.

She bought a nice pair of shoes that woman. Careful about them. Knew what she were after. Tiny little feet. And all them little things in their helmets and mittens and good coats, quiet like dolls. They'll feel the cold likely, China being the tropics. They were that *good*.

I sat there with my scissors, daft as a brush, and down the garden path I could just see in the half-dark this little trail coming. Down through our garden. To Eastern View. The five on them and this little pretty woman coming behind with two big shopping bags dragging the grass. I sees myself running out. 'Here,' says I. 'Give us hold. Mind the pit. Come here then. You can't carry that lot – all that rice and the sweet-and-sour and these Chinese Leaves you see in the supermarkets and nobody buys but stands there saying they look just as good as lettuces. "Better," they say. I've said it myself, though I've never bought none. Maybe I ought. They're probably all right. Well, passable.'

I think of the fruit bowl full of them lychee things and they don't seem much to offer somehow. After a long day. I dare say that great lad's taken her out like he said he would but it'll only be fish and chips or the pub, knowing him.

Down go my scissors and I'm back in the kitchen and putting out tea and biscuits and plates and cups and the blue-handled knives that were wedding presents from Syd's sister – they were good ones. Binns's of Newcastle. The biscuit tin's got pagodas on it, black and gold. It's a thing I'd never do in the ordinary way but I leave them in the tin. On account of the pagodas. To look more friendly.

I've no china tea – she'll have to make do with the PG tips in the bags. Somewhere there was a willow-pattern sugar basin once but I think that cat he had broke it. He's that mad about animals I didn't dare say a word. Looking for it – the basin – I came upon these Chinese fig things in my Christmas drawer. They've been there a few years. They're a bit black. Like old bits of Syd's shag tobacco. Or used-up brillo pads. Still, maybe the children'll like them.

And I sits down very sudden and I thinks, well, there it is then! That's it. They're right. You have gone off it. *What* children? The ones in the shoe shop? It's just the *one* coming – one girl. A girlfriend. His girlfriend. I'm going round the twist. Maybe I ought to go and talk to Mr Hinton –

They'll come in soon. Just the pair on them. Tone and his girlfriend. I make myself see them, step by step so's I'll be ready. Tone, the great lump – and this little girl.

Suppose she's not little, though?

She may be one of them great big fat ones. The Chairman Mao style in the siren suits. You see them on the telly all marching about in thousands with all the same haircuts, shouting out slogans and firing off rifles. Nasty angry faces they've got, too; saying how well off they are with plenty to eat and never had it so good and that. Funny really, when everything's going so much better for them why they always look so furious. They say there's nobody poor in China now. Nobody hungry. No nappies to wash since there's machines and old folk to look after the children. The nappies'll be paper ones likely. There's a lot of paper in China – like rice paper. Even the houses are paper because of the earthquakes. Though that might be Japan. All the women except for the baby-minders are out growing rice or making munitions like we did in the War.

We were never furious in the War though – it wasn't slogans and firing rifles off. It was cups of tea and laughs and Workers Playtime: 'You are my Sunshine'. That style. Tell you the truth I liked the War. Syd looked grand in khaki. I met him at a Naafi dance and he looked that sensible – and crinkly hair and thin. Something after Leslie Howard if you remember. Fantastic to think he ever could of, really. He'd got all purple towards the end and he'd lost his neck. Well, it was maybe my fault. I think I irritated him.

If this girl's the Chairman Mao style we'll not get on. She'll start trying to run everything. They're the sort. You can tell. She'll be making me eat lunch and shouting slogans. Little Red Books and that. Making me get my veins done. Just to think of it makes me het up.

I pick up the lychees and I starts walking about with them thinking, 'She's not to have them. I'll put them in the fridge.'

But where's the use? Tone'll never eat them. He wouldn't touch them. Maybe Mrs Palmer might. She'd eat them. I wouldn't give them to Mrs Morgan, she gets enough out of tins already, being too tranquillised to cook for herself: but Mrs Palmer, she'd eat them. I can't bring myself just to put them down the sink somehow – first because it seems a shame when they've managed to grow them and send them all this way over the Atlantic and that, after being so poor; and second because I couldn't ever be able to press them down the sink grid. Like pressing eyeballs.

I'll give them to Mrs Palmer then. I won't go to the Get-Together but I'll just go round and knock on the door and hand them in. In a pudding basin. Not the glass dish. It was my auntie's from Southport and very good taste. It wouldn't last in Mrs Palmer's ten minutes even if they do all look like angels from heaven with heather on their heads. I'll just slip round later when Tone and this Chairman Mao begins to go –. When they starts to go up to –.

If Syd was here he'd die. He'd die.

'You're not bringin' this style here,' he'd shout. When she started with her slogans he'd shout worse ones back. The Enoch Powell variety. He'd of thrown Tone out years ago anyway. Maybe I've been daft not to. Never growing up. Great daft lump. I wonder if I ought to put out clean sheets?

And I'm fiery red. Sitting here all by myself I'm fiery red.

I can't stay here. Not tonight. Well, can I? Not with them in his bed. Just across the landing. It's a small house, Eastern View. It's a single bed. It's the bed he's had since he were nine, with the oak headboard and the raised lozenge.

Well, I starts running round the kitchen putting everything away – figs and dishes and knives and pagodas. I grabs at a pudding bowl and I pounces at the lychees and I tries to decant the one into the other in mid-air so to speak and the juice runs all down my wrists and up my arm and I slip and I'm flat on my vinyl. There's broken glass and broken basin and these filthy foreign things all over everywhere, scattering and rolling for miles (it's the nylon thread runner, it never was that safe when there's been a top polish), and I lets out a wail. Spread out there on the floor I lets out a very long, awful, queer sort of a wail. My face and my dress and my tights are all over lychees. There's juice right down to my shoes and right up to my Tuesday's shampoo and set.

And I hears the front door.

Dear God, the front door!

I'm up like an ice-skater falling down in a competition and pretending he'd meant it and I'm into my coat and rinsing my hands and – let the nasty things lie there. I don't care. I'm over to the door to the back garden and I'm off. Now. Into the dark. I don't know where. I'll maybe go round and lie in the pit till morning and they'll find me dead. Tone and that great fat creature. Or the little skinny one. Loose women the pair on them. When they see me lying down that pit they'll see what morals are. They'll see I don't like it. They'll of learned something. It's not everyone thinks it's all right, they'll of learned. NOT WHEN YOU'RE NOT MARRIED.

There now. I've said it. I'm not ashamed. It's nothing to do with the sexual liberations or the race defamatory act or the women's lib. It's just not my style. Mrs Palmer'd laugh at me and that Sandra at the shop, she's no better, and Mrs Morgan wouldn't understand at all, being Welsh. They're very immoral, the Welsh. That's why Alfred the Great had to move them out. I heard it on Magnus Magnusson. And look at *How Green was my Valley*!

James Bond is worse, I dare say, but for him it's different, in his surroundings and with his looks. All them empty beaches and the sound of the surf and afterwards all them waiters with trays of pink gins and bits of fruit floating in them.

But Eastern View's not like that. Tone's not James Bond. You can't see James Bond's bedroom all model aeroplanes and daft Snoopy mobiles and bits of transistors. And Syd and me never. And we had chance often enough, two years courting. Round his parents every Saturday afternoon while they were at the pictures. Many a time we could of. But we never.

Bringing her home and me in the house! 'Bringing this bird home Saturday,' he says. 'Saturday's tomorrow,' I says. 'That's it,' he says.

Well then, here's my gloves and hat because I'm not nobody and I'm off. There's no one outside to see the stick on my face.

And here they come. I see his shadow first coming down the passage through the glass door with the art bubbles. I've not reached the back door.

'Where'yer off? What's that on yer face? What's the mess? What's them awful things on the floor? Looks like you been layin' eggs.' I stands. 'Mum,' he says, 'where'yer off then?'

'Mrs Palmer's.' (Down the pit.)

'Mrs Palmer's!' He looks that disappointed. 'Aren't yer goin' to come in and see her then? She's in the front room.' His helmet's off and his curly hair's all over the place. He's got a nice face, I'll say that for him. Looks about ten when he's disappointed. Looks like he did when he brought them newts home and his father made him pour them out.

And all of a rush I sees these little black-eyed children again and they've all got curly hair. They're all round the kitchen table eating a good sponge and they're all singing – when they've put their spoons and forks together – like the D'Oyly Carte. And in nice little dresses that I've shown their mother how to run up of an evening for next to nothing. Good as gold they are, and she's out in the kitchen washing the Chinese Leaves.

I seem to have stood quiet a long time.

'I'd like to see her,' I says, a bit more dubious. 'But it's not right.'

'What's not right?'

'Me being here. I'm best away.'

'You're a good boy,' I says. 'It's you pays the instalments and it's you pays the bills. Don't think I'm not grateful. I'll just go and sleep next door with Mrs Palmer. Then I'll think what to do next.'

'Sleep with Mrs *Palmer*!' He turns purple. He has quite a look of Syd. 'Are you mad?'

'I'll go to the Get-Together.'

'You hate Get-Togethers.'

'Hold still,' he shouts, 'and I'll bring her through,' and he's off and back before I can get the door open into the garden. And he's carrying a cage.

A cage.

With a bird in it.

A bird.

'I's bringing a bird home –'

And it's the dingiest, ordinariest bird you ever saw. It's sullen-looking, bored-looking, insolent-looking, constipated-looking. It's down in the mouth. It's three parts asleep. It's probably on tranquillisers. It might be Mrs Morgan.

It's the colour of old dish-cloths – the kind you throw out. It's got a dirty blue smear down its chest like it's spilt something. It's got claws – nasty crude folded leathery claws. Vicious-looking. It looks at me and I look at it.

There's neither interest nor kindness nor slogans between us.

'She's Chinese,' he says. 'She's a Chinese Somethin'. In't she a beauty?'

'You'd of said no if I'd asked you,' he says in a bit, and I sits down heavy on my leatherette foam-top. I sits heavy.

He says, 'Look, Mum. I'll see to her. Have her down here with you if you like.'

'She'll be company,' he says. 'I'll see to her. She'll mek no extra.' I sits heavy. 'Mum,' he says, 'look, she's yours if you want her. I knows you gets lonely. Look, she don't *have* to be in with me.'

Well I cried.

THE MASK
OF THE BEAR

◆

Margaret Laurence

In winter my Grandfather Connor used to wear an enormous
coat made out of the pelt of a bear. So shaggy and coarse-furred
was this coat, so unevenly coloured in patches ranging from
amber to near-black, and so vile-smelling when it had become wet
with snow, that it seemed to have belonged when it was alive to
some lonely and giant kodiak crankily roaming a high frozen pla-
teau, or an ancient grizzly scarred with battles in the sinister forests of the north. In actuality, it had been an ordinary brown bear
and it had come, sad to say, from no more fabled a place than Gal-
loping Mountain, only a hundred miles from Manawaka. The skin
had once been given to my grandfather as payment, in the days
when he was a blacksmith, before he became a hardware merchant
and developed the policy of cash only. He had had it cobbled into
a coat by the local shoemaker, and Grandmother Connor had
managed to sew in the lining. How long ago that was, no one
could say for sure, but my mother, the eldest of his family, said she
could not remember a time when he had not worn it. To me, at
the age of ten and a half, this meant it must be about a century old.
The coat was so heavy that I could not even lift it by myself. I
never used to wonder how he could carry that phenomenal weight
on himself, or why he would choose to, because it was obvious
that although he was old he was still an extraordinarily strong
man, built to shoulder weights.

Whenever I went into Simlow's Ladies' Wear with my mother,

and made grotesque faces at myself in the long mirror while she tried on dresses, Millie Christopherson who worked there would croon a phrase which made me break into snickering until my mother, who was death on bad manners, tapped anxiously at my shoulders with her slender, nervous hands. 'It's you, Mrs MacLeod,' Millie would say feelingly, 'no kidding it's absolutely you.' I appropriated the phrase for my grandfather's winter coat. 'It's you,' I would simper nastily at him, although never, of course, aloud.

In my head I sometimes called him 'The Great Bear'. The name had many associations other than his coat and his surliness. It was the way he would stalk around the Brick House as though it were a cage, on Sundays, impatient for the new week's beginning that would release him into the only freedom he knew, the acts of work. It was the way he would take to the basement whenever a man came to call on Aunt Edna, which in those days was not often, because – as I had overheard my mother outlining in sighs to my father – most of the single men her age in Manawaka considered that the time she had spent working in Winnipeg had made more difference than it really had, and the situation wasn't helped by her flyaway manner (whatever that might mean). But if ever she was asked out to a movie, and the man was waiting and making stilted weather-chat with Grandmother Connor, Grandfather would prowl through the living-room as though seeking a place of rest and not finding it, would stare fixedly without speaking, and would then descend the basement steps to the rocking-chair which sat beside the furnace. Above ground, he would not have been found dead sitting in a rocking-chair, which he considered a piece of furniture suitable only for the elderly, of whom he was never in his own eyes one. From his cave, however, the angry crunching of the wooden rockers against the cement floor would reverberate throughout the house, a kind of sub-verbal Esperanto, a disapproval which even the most obtuse person could not fail to comprehend.

In some unformulated way, I also associated the secret name with Great Bear Lake, which I had seen only on maps and which I imagined to be a deep vastness of black water, lying somewhere very far beyond our known prairies of tamed fields and barbed-wire fences, somewhere in the regions of jagged rock and eternal ice, where human voices would be drawn into a cold and shadowed stillness without leaving even a trace of warmth.

One Saturday afternoon in January, I was at the rink when my grandfather appeared unexpectedly. He was wearing his formidable coat, and to say he looked out of place among the skaters thronging around the edges of the ice would be putting it mildly. Embarrassed, I whizzed over to him.

'There you are, Vanessa – about time,' he said, as though he had been searching for me for hours. 'Get your skates off now, and come along. You're to come home with me for supper. You'll be staying the night at our place. Your dad's gone away out to Freehold, and your mother's gone with him. Fine time to pick for it. It's blowing up for a blizzard, if you ask me. They'll not get back for a couple of days, more than likely. Don't see why he don't just tell people to make their own way in to the hospital. Ewen's too easy-going. He'll not get a penny nor a word of thanks for it, you can bet your life on that.'

My father and Dr Cates used to take the country calls in turn. Often when my father went out in the winter, my mother would go with him, in case the old Nash got stuck in the snow and also to talk and thus prevent my father from going to sleep at the wheel, for falling snow has a hypnotic effect.

'What about Roddie?' I asked, for my brother was only a few months old.

'The old lady's keeping care of him,' Grandfather Connor replied abruptly.

The old lady meant my Grandmother MacLeod, who was actually a few years younger than Grandfather Connor. He always referred to her in this way, however, as a calculated insult, and here my sympathies were with him for once. He maintained, quite correctly, that she gave herself airs because her husband had been a doctor and now her son was one, and that she looked down on the Connors because they had come from famine Irish (although at least, thank God, Protestant). The two of them seldom met, except at Christmas, and never exchanged more than a few words. If they had ever really clashed, it would have been like a brontosaurus running headlong into a tyrannosaurus.

'Hurry along now,' he said, when I had taken off my skates and put on my snow boots. 'You've got to learn not to dawdle. You're an awful dawdler, Vanessa.'

I did not reply. Instead, when we left the rink I began to take exaggeratedly long strides. But he paid no attention to my attempt to reproach him with my speed. He walked beside me steadily and silently, wrapped in his great fur coat and his authority.

The Brick House was at the other end of town, so while I shuffled through the snow and pulled my navy wool scarf up around my nose against the steel cutting edge of the wind, I thought about the story I was setting down in a five-cent scribbler at nights in my room. I was much occupied by the themes of love and death, although my experience of both had so far been gained principally from the Bible, which I read in the same way as I read Eaton's Catalogue or the collected works of Rudyard Kipling – because I had to read something, and the family's finances in the thirties did not permit the purchase of enough volumes of *Doctor Doolittle* or the *Oz* books to keep me going.

For the love scenes, I gained useful material from The Song of Solomon. 'Let him kiss me with the kisses of his mouth, for thy love is better than wine,' or 'By night on my bed I sought him whom my soul loveth; I sought him but I found him not.' My interpretation was somewhat vague, and I was not helped to any appreciable extent by the explanatory bits in small print at the beginning of each chapter: 'The church's love unto Christ.' 'The church's fight and victory in temptation,' et cetera. These explanations did not puzzle me, though, for I assumed even then that they had simply been put there for the benefit of gentle and unworldly people such as my Grandmother Connor, so that they could read the Holy Writ without becoming upset. To me, the woman in The Song was some barbaric queen, beautiful and terrible, and I could imagine her, wearing a long robe of leopard skin and one or two heavy gold bracelets, pacing an alabaster courtyard and keening her unrequited love.

The heroine in my story (which took place in ancient Egypt – my ignorance of this era did not trouble me) was very like the woman in The Song of Solomon, except that mine had long wavy auburn hair, and when her beloved left her, the only thing she could bring herself to eat was an avocado, which seemed to me considerably more stylish and exotic than apples in lieu of love. Her young man was a gifted carver, who had been sent out into the desert by the cruel pharaoh (pharaohs were always cruel – of this I was positive) in order to carve a giant sphinx for the royal tomb. Should I have her die while he was away? Or would it be better if he perished out in the desert? Which of them did I like the least? With the characters whom I liked best, things always turned out right in the end. Yet the death scenes had an undeniable appeal, a sombre splendour, with (as it said in Ecclesiastes) the mourners going about the streets and all the daughters of music brought low. Both death and love seemed regrettably far from Manawaka and the snow, and my grandfather stamping his feet on the front porch of the Brick House and telling me to do the same or I'd be tracking the wet in all over the hardwood floor.

The house was too warm, almost stifling. Grandfather burned mainly birch in the furnace, although it cost twice as much as poplar, and now that he had retired from the hardware store, the furnace gave him something to do and so he was forever stoking it. Grandmother Connor was in the dining-room, her stout body in its brown rayon dress bending over the canary's cage.

'Hello, pet,' she greeted me. 'You should have heard Birdie just a minute ago – one of those real long trills. He's been moulting lately, and this is the first time he's sung in weeks.'

'Gee,' I said enthusiastically, for although I was not fond of canaries, I was extremely fond of my grandmother. 'That's swell. Maybe he'll do it again.'

'Messy things, them birds,' my grandfather commented. 'I can never see what you see in a fool thing like that, Agnes.'

My grandmother did not attempt to reply to this.

'Would you like a cup of tea, Timothy?' she asked.

'Nearly suppertime, ain't it?'

'Well, not for a little while yet.'

'It's away past five,' my grandfather said. 'What's Edna been doing with herself?'

'She's got the pot-roast in,' my grandmother answered, 'but it's not done yet.'

'You'd think a person could get a meal on time,' he said, 'considering she's got precious little else to do.'

I felt, as so often in the Brick House, that my lungs were in danger of exploding, that the pressure of silence would become too great to be borne. I wanted to point out, as I knew Grandmother Connor would never do, that it wasn't Aunt Edna's fault there were no jobs anywhere these days, and that, as my mother often said of her, she worked her fingers to the bone here so she wouldn't feel beholden to him for her keep, and that they would have had to get a hired girl if she hadn't been here, because Grandmother Connor couldn't look after a place this size any more. Also, that the dining-room clock said precisely ten minutes past five, and the evening meal in the Connor house was always at six o'clock on the dot. And – and – a thousand other arguments rose up and nearly choked me. But I did not say anything. I was not that stupid. Instead, I went out to the kitchen.

Aunt Edna was wearing her coral sweater and grey pleated skirt, and I thought she looked lovely, even with her apron on. I always thought she looked lovely, though, whatever she was wearing, but if ever I told her so, she would only laugh and say it was lucky she had a cheering section of one.

'Hello, kiddo,' she said. 'Do you want to sleep in my room tonight, or shall I make up the bed in the spare room?'

'In your room,' I said quickly, for this meant she would let me try out her lipstick and use some of her Jergens hand lotion, and if I could stay awake until she came to bed, we would whisper after the light was out.

'How's *The Pillars of the Nation* coming along?' she asked.

That had been my epic on pioneer life. I had proceeded to the point in the story where the husband, coming back to the cabin one evening, discovered to his surprise that he was going to become a father. The way he ascertained this interesting fact was that he found his wife constructing a birch-bark cradle. Then came the discovery that Grandfather Connor had been a pioneer, and the story had lost its interest for me. If pioneers were like *that*, I had thought, my pen would be better employed elsewhere.

'I quit that one,' I replied laconically. 'I'm making up another – it's miles better. It's called *The Silver Sphinx*. I'll bet you can't guess what it's about.'

'The desert? Buried treasure? Murder mystery?'

I shook my head.

'Love,' I said.

'Good Glory,' Aunt Edna said, straight-faced. 'That sounds fascinating. Where do you get your ideas, Vanessa?'

I could not bring myself to say the Bible. I was afraid she might think this sounded funny.

'Oh, here and there,' I replied noncommittally. 'You know.'

She gave me an inquisitive glance, as though she meant to question me further, but just then the telephone rang, and I rushed to answer it, thinking it might be my mother or father phoning from Freehold. But it wasn't. It was a voice I didn't know, a man's.

'Is Edna Connor there?'

'Just a minute, please,' I cupped one hand over the mouthpiece fixed on the wall, and the other over the receiver.

'For you,' I hissed, grinning at her. 'A strange man!'

'Mercy,' Aunt Edna said ironically, 'these hordes of admirers will be the death of me yet. Probably Todd Jeffries from Burns' Electric about that busted lamp.'

Nevertheless, she hurried over. Then, as she listened, her face became startled, and something else which I could not fathom.

'Heavens, where are you?' she cried at last. 'At the station *here*? Oh Lord. Why didn't you write to say you were – well, sure I am, but – oh, never mind. No, you wait there. I'll come and meet you.

You'd never find the house –'

I had never heard her talk this way before, rattlingly. Finally she hung up. Her face looked like a stranger's, and for some reason this hurt me.

'It's Jimmy Lorimer,' she said. 'He's at the CPR station. He's coming here. Oh my God, I wish Beth were here.'

'Why?' I wished my mother were here, too, but I could not see what difference it made to Aunt Edna. I knew who Jimmy Lorimer was. He was a man Aunt Edna had gone around with when she was in Winnipeg. He had given her the Attar of Roses in an atomiser bottle with a green net-covered bulb – the scent she always sprayed around her room after she had had a cigarette there. Jimmy Lorimer had been invested with a remote glamour in my imagination, but all at once I felt I was going to hate him.

I realised that Aunt Edna was referring to what Grandfather Connor might do or say, and instantly I was ashamed for having felt churlishly disposed towards Jimmy Lorimer. Even if he was a cad, a heel, or a nitwit, I swore I would welcome him. I visualised him as having a flashy appearance, like a riverboat gambler in a movie I had seen once, a checkered suit, a slender oiled moustache, a diamond tie-pin, a dangerous leer. Never mind. Never mind if he was Lucifer himself.

'I'm glad he's coming,' I said staunchly.

Aunt Edna looked at me queerly, her mouth wavering as though she were about to smile. Then, quickly, she bent and hugged me, and I could feel her trembling. At this moment, Grandmother Connor came into the kitchen.

'You all right, pet?' she asked Aunt Edna. 'Nothing's the matter, is it?'

'Mother, that was an old friend of mine on the phone just now. Jimmy Lorimer. He's from Winnipeg. He's passing through Manawaka. Is it all right if he comes here for dinner?'

'Well, of course, dear,' Grandmother said. 'What a lucky thing we're having the pot-roast. There's plenty. Vanessa, pet, you run down to the fruit cellar and bring up a jar of strawberries, will you? Oh, and a small jar of chilli sauce. No, maybe the sweet mustard pickle would go better with the pot-roast. What do you think, Edna?'

She spoke as though this were the only important issue in the whole situation. But all the time her eyes were on Aunt Edna's face.

'Edna –' she said, with great effort, 'is he – is he a good man, Edna?'

Aunt Edna blinked and looked confused, a though she had been spoken to in some foreign language.

'Yes,' she replied.

'You're sure, pet?'

'Yes,' Aunt Edna repeated, a little more emphatically than before.

Grandmother Connor nodded, smiled reassuringly, and patted Aunt Edna lightly on the wrist.

'Well, that's fine, dear. I'll just tell Father. Everything will be all right, so don't you worry about a thing.'

When Grandmother had gone back to the living-room, Aunt Edna began pulling on her black fur-topped overshoes. When she spoke, I didn't know whether it was to me or not.

'I didn't tell her a damn thing,' she said in a surprised tone. 'I wonder how she knows, or if she really does? *Good*. What a word. I wish I didn't know what she means when she says that. Or else that she knew what I mean when I say it. Glory, I wish Beth were here.'

I understood then that she was not speaking to me, and that what she had to say could not be spoken to me. I felt chilled by my childhood, unable to touch her because of the freezing burden of my inexperience. I was about to say something, anything, however mistaken, when my aunt said 'Sh,' and we both listened to the talk from the living-room.

'A friend of Edna's is coming for dinner, Timothy,' Grandmother was saying quietly. 'A young man from Winnipeg.'

A silence. Then, 'Winnipeg!' my grandfather exclaimed, making it sound as though Jimmy Lorimer were coming here straight from his harem in Casablanca.

'What's he do?' Grandfather demanded next.

'Edna didn't say.'

'I'm not surprised,' Grandfather said darkly. 'Well, I won't have her running around with that sort of fellow. She's got no more sense than a sparrow.'

'She's twenty-eight,' Grandmother said, almost apologetically. 'Anyway, this is just a friend.'

'Friend!' my grandfather said, annihilating the word. Then, not loudly, but with an odd vehemence, 'You don't know a blame thing about men, Agnes. You never have.'

Even I could think of several well-placed replies that my grandmother might have made, but she did not do so. She did not say anything. I looked at Aunt Edna, and saw that she had closed her eyes the way people do when they have a headache. Then we heard Grandmother's voice, speaking at last, not in her usual placid and unruffled way, but hesitantly.

'Timothy – please. Be nice to him. For my sake.'

For my sake. This was so unlike my grandmother that I was stunned. She was not a person who begged you to be kind for her sake, or even for God's sake. If you were kind, in my grandmother's view, it was for its own sake, and the judgement of whether you had done well or not was up to the Almighty. 'Judge not, that ye be not judged' – this was her favourite admonition to me when I lost my temper with one of my friends. As a devout Baptist, she believed it was a sin to pray for anything for yourself. You ought to pray only for strength to bear whatever the Lord saw fit to send you, she thought. I was never able to follow this advice, for although I would often feel a sense of uneasiness over the tone of my prayers, I was the kind of person who prayed frantically – 'Please, God, please, please *please* let Ross MacVey like me better than Mavis.' Grandmother Connor was not self-effacing in her lack of demands either upon God or upon her family. She merely believed that what happened to a person in this life was in Other Hands. Acceptance was at the heart of her. I don't think in her own eyes she ever lived in a state of bondage. To the rest of the family, thrashing furiously and uselessly in various snarled dilemmas, she must often have appeared to live in a state of perpetual grace, but I am certain she didn't think of it that way, either.

Grandfather Connor did not seem to have heard her.

'We won't get our dinner until all hours, I dare say,' he said.

But we got our dinner as soon as Aunt Edna had arrived back with Jimmy Lorimer, for she flew immediately out to the kitchen and before we knew it we were all sitting at the big circular table in the dining-room.

Jimmy Lorimer was not at all what I had expected. Far from looking like a Mississippi gambler, he looked just like everybody else, any uncle or grown-up cousin, unexceptional in every way. He was neither overwhelmingly handsome nor interestingly ugly. He was okay to look at, but as I said to myself, feeling at the same time a twinge of betrayal towards Aunt Edna, he was nothing to write home about. He wore a brown suit and a green tie. The only thing about him which struck fire was that he had a joking manner similar to Aunt Edna's, but whereas I felt at ease with this quality in her, I could never feel comfortable with the laughter of strangers, being uncertain where an including laughter stopped and taunting began.

'You're from Winnipeg, eh?' Grandfather Connor began. 'Well, I guess you fellows don't put much store in a town like Manawaka.'

Without waiting for affirmation or denial of this sentiment, he continued in an unbroken line.

'I got no patience with these people who think a small town is just nothing. You take a city, now. You could live in one of them places for twenty years, and you'd not get to know your next-door neighbour. Trouble comes along – who's going to give you a hand? Not a blamed soul.'

Grandfather Connor had never in his life lived in a city, so his first-hand knowledge of their ways was, to say the least, limited. As for trouble – the thought of my grandfather asking any soul in Manawaka to give aid and support to him in any way whatsoever was inconceivable. He would have died of starvation, physical or spiritual, rather than put himself in any man's debt by so much as a dime or a word.

'Hey, hold on a minute,' Jimmy Lorimer protested. 'I never said that about small towns. As a matter of fact, I grew up in one myself. I came from McConnell's Landing. Ever heard of it?'

'I heard of it all right,' Grandfather said brusquely, and no one could have told from his tone whether McConnell's Landing was a place of ill-repute or whether he simply felt his knowledge of geography was being doubted. 'Why'd you leave, then?'

Jimmy shrugged. 'Not much opportunity there. Had to seek my fortune, you know. Can't say I've found it, but I'm still looking.'

'Oh, you'll be a tycoon yet, no doubt,' Aunt Edna put in.

'You bet your life, kiddo,' Jimmy replied. 'You wait. Times'll change.'

I didn't like to hear him say 'kiddo'. It was Aunt Edna's word, the one she called me by. It didn't belong to him.

'Mercy, they can't change fast enough for me,' Aunt Edna said. 'I guess I haven't got your optimism, though.'

'Well, I haven't got it, either,' he said, laughing, 'but keep it under your hat, eh?'

Grandfather Connor had listened to this exchange with some impatience. Now he turned to Jimmy once more.

'What's your line of work?'

'I'm with Reliable Loan Company right now, Mr Connor, but I don't aim to stay there permanently. I'd like to have my own business. Cars are what I'm really interested in. But it's not so easy to start up these days.'

Grandfather Connor's normal opinions on social issues possessed such a high degree of clarity and were so frequently stated that they were well known even to me – all labour unions were composed of thugs and crooks; if people were unemployed it was due to their own laziness; if people were broke it was because they were not thrifty. Now, however, a look of intense and brooding sorrow came into his face, as he became all at once the champion of the poor and oppressed.

'Loan company!' he said. 'Them bloodsuckers. They wouldn't pay no mind to how hard up a man might be. Take everything he has, without batting an eye. By the Lord Harry, I never thought the day would come when I'd sit down to a meal alongside one of them fellows.'

Aunt Edna's face was rigid.

'Jimmy,' she said. 'Ignore him.'

Grandfather turned on her, and they stared at one another with a kind of inexpressible rage but neither of them spoke. I could not help feeling sorry for Jimmy Lorimer, who mumbled something about his train leaving and began eating hurriedly. Grandfather rose to his feet.

'I've had enough,' he said.

'Don't you want your dessert, Timothy?' Grandmother asked, as though it never occurred to her that he could be referring to anything other than the meal. It was only then that I realised that this was the first time she had spoken since we sat down at the table. Grandfather did not reply. He went down to the basement. Predictably, in a moment we could hear the wooden rockers of his chair thudding like retreating thunder. After dinner, Grandmother sat in the living-room, but she did not get out the red cardigan she was knitting for me. She sat without doing anything, quite still, her hands folded in her lap.

'I'll let you off the dishes tonight, honey,' Aunt Edna said to me. 'Jimmy will help with them. You can try out my lipstick, if you like, only for Pete's sake wash it off before you come down again.'

I went upstairs, but I did not go to Aunt Edna's room. I went into the back bedroom to one of my listening posts. In the floor there was a round hole which had once been used for a stove-pipe leading up from the kitchen. Now it was covered with a piece of brown painted tin full of small perforations which had apparently been noticed only by me.

'Where does he get his lines, Edna?' Jimmy was saying. 'He's like old-time melodrama.'

'Yeh, I know.' Aunt Edna sounded annoyed. 'But let me say it, eh?'

'Sorry. Honest. Listen, can't you even –'

Scuffling sounds, then my aunt's nervous whisper.

'Not here, Jimmy. Please. You don't understand what they're –'

'I understand, all right. Why in God's name do you stay, Edna? Aren't you ever coming back? That's what I want to know.'

'With no job? Don't make me laugh.'

'I could help out, at first anyway –'

'Jimmy, don't talk like a lunatic. Do you really think I could?'

'Oh hell, I suppose not. Well, look at it this way. What if I wasn't cut out for the unattached life after all? What if the old leopard actually changed his spots, kiddo? What would you say to that?'

A pause, as though Aunt Edna were mulling over his words.

'That'll be the day,' she replied. 'I'll believe it when I see it.'

'Well, Jesus, lady,' he said, 'I'm not getting down on my knees. Tell me one thing, though – don't you miss me at all? Don't you miss – everything? C'mon now – don't you? Not even a little bit?'

Another pause. She could not seem to make up her mind how to respond to the teasing quality of his voice.

'Yeh, I lie awake nights,' she said at last, sarcastically.

He laughed. 'Same old Edna. Want me to tell you something, kiddo? I think you're scared.'

'Scared?' she said scornfully. 'Me? That'll be the fair and frosty Friday.'

Although I spent so much of my life listening to conversations which I was not meant to overhear, all at once I felt, for the first time, sickened by what I was doing. I left my listening post and tiptoed into Aunt Edna's room. I wondered if someday I would be the one who was doing the talking, while another child would be doing the listening. This gave me an unpleasantly eerie feeling. I tried on Aunt Edna's lipstick and rouge, but my heart was not in it.

When I went downstairs again, Jimmy Lorimer was just leaving. Aunt Edna went to her room and closed the door. After a while she came out and asked me if I would mind sleeping in the spare bedroom that night after all, so that was what I did.

I woke in the middle of the night. When I sat up, feeling strange because I was not in my own bed at home, I saw through the window a glancing light on the snow. I got up and peered out, and there were the northern lights whirling across the top of the sky like lightning that never descended to earth. The yard of the Brick House looked huge, a white desert, and the pale gashing streaks of light pointed up the caverns and the hollowed places where the wind had sculptured the snow.

I could not stand being alone another second, so I walked in my bare feet along the hall. From Grandfather's room came the sound of grumbling snores, and from Grandmother's room no sound at all. I stopped beside the door of Aunt Edna's room. It seemed to me that she would not mind if I entered quietly, so as not to disturb her, and crawled in beside her. Maybe she would even waken and say, 'It's okay, kiddo – your dad phoned after you'd gone to sleep – they got back from Freehold all right.'

Then I heard her voice, and the held-in way she was crying, and the name she spoke, as though it hurt her to speak it even in a whisper.

Like some terrified poltergeist, I flitted back to the spare room and whipped into bed. I wanted only to forget that I had heard anything, but I knew I would not forget. There arose in my mind, mysteriously, the picture of a barbaric queen, someone who had lived a long time ago. I could not reconcile this image with the known face, nor could I disconnect it. I thought of my aunt, her sturdy laughter, the way she tore into the housework, her hands and feet which she always disparagingly joked about, believing them to be clumsy. I thought of the story in the scribbler at home. I wanted to get home quickly, so I could destroy it.

Whenever Grandmother Connor was ill, she would not see any doctor except my father. She did not believe in surgery, for she thought it was tampering with the Divine Intention, and she was always afraid that Dr Cates would operate on her without her consent. She trusted my father implicitly, and when he went into the room where she lay propped up on pillows, she would say, 'Here's Ewen – now everything will be fine,' which both touched and alarmed my father, who said he hoped she wasn't putting her faith in a broken reed.

Late that winter, she became ill again. She did not go into hospital, so my mother, who had been a nurse, moved down to the Brick House to look after her. My brother and I were left in the adamant care of Grandmother MacLeod. Without my mother, our house seemed like a museum, full of dead and meaningless objects, vases and gilt-framed pictures and looming furniture, all of which had to be dusted and catered to, for reasons which everyone had forgotten. I was not allowed to see Grandmother Connor, but every day after school I went to the Brick House to see my mother. I always asked impatiently, 'When is Grandmother going to be better?' and my mother would reply, 'I don't know, dear. Soon, I hope.' But she did not sound very certain, and I imagined the leaden weeks going by like this, with her away, and Grandmother MacLeod poking her head into my bedroom doorway each morning and telling me to be sure to make my bed because a slovenly room meant a slovenly heart.

But the weeks did not go by like this. One afternoon when I arrived at the Brick House, Grandfather Connor was standing out on the front porch. I was startled, because he was not wearing his great bear coat. He wore no coat at all, only his dingy serge suit, although the day was fifteen below zero. The blown snow had sifted onto the porch and lay in thin drifts. He stood there by himself, his yellowish-white hair plumed by a wind which he seemed not to notice, his bony and still-handsome face not averted at all from the winter. He looked at me as I plodded up the path and the front steps.

'Vanessa, your grandmother's dead,' he said.

Then, as I gazed at him, unable to take in the significance of what he had said, he did a horrifying thing. He gathered me into the relentless grip of his arms. He bent low over me, and sobbed against the cold skin of my face.

I wanted only to get away, to get as far away as possible and never come back. I wanted desperately to see my mother, yet I felt I could not enter the house, not ever again. Then my mother opened the front door and stood there in the doorway, her slight body shivering. Grandfather released me, straightened, became again the carved face I had seen when I approached the house.

'Father,' my mother said. 'Come into the house. Please.'

'In a while, Beth,' he replied tonelessly. 'Never you mind.'

My mother held out her hands to me, and I ran to her. She closed the door and led me into the living-room. We both cried, and yet I think I cried mainly because she did, and because I had been shocked by my grandfather. I still could not believe that anyone I cared about could really die.

Aunt Edna came into the living-room. She hesitated, looking at my mother and me. Then she turned and went back to the kitchen, stumblingly. My mother's hands made hovering movements and she half rose from the chesterfield, then she held me closely again.

'It's worse for Edna,' she said. 'I've got you and Roddie and your dad.'

I did not fully realise yet that Grandmother Connor would never move around this house again, preserving its uncertain peace somehow. Yet all at once I knew how it would be for Aunt Edna, without her, alone in the Brick House with Grandfather Connor. I had not known at all that a death would be like this, not only one's own pain, but the almost unbearable knowledge of that other pain which could not be reached nor lessened.

My mother and I went out to the kitchen, and the three of us sat round the oilcloth-covered table, scarcely talking but needing one another at least to be there. We heard the front door open, and Grandfather Connor came back into the house. He did not come out to the kitchen, though. He went, as though instinctively, to his old cavern. We heard him walking heavily down the basement steps.

'Edna – should we ask him if he wants to come and have some

tea?' my mother said. 'I hate to see him going like that – there –'

Aunt Edna's face hardened.

'I don't want to see him, Beth,' she replied, forcing the words out. 'I can't. Not yet. All I'd be able to think of is how he was – with her.'

'Oh honey, I know,' my mother said. 'But you mustn't let yourself dwell on that now.'

'The night Jimmy was here,' my aunt said distinctly, 'she asked Father to be nice, for her sake. For her sake, Beth. For the sake of all the years, if they'd meant anything at all. But he couldn't even do that. Not even that.'

Then she put her head down on the table and cried in a way I had never heard any person cry before, as though there were no end to it anywhere.

I was not allowed to attend Grandmother Connor's funeral, and for this I was profoundly grateful, for I had dreaded going. The day of the funeral, I stayed alone in the Brick House, waiting for the family to return. My Uncle Terence, who lived in Toronto, was the only one who had come from a distance. Uncle Will lived in Florida, and Aunt Florence was in England, both too far away. Aunt Edna and my mother were always criticising Uncle Terence and also making excuses for him. He drank more than was good for him – this was one of the numerous fractured bones in the family skeleton which I was not supposed to know about. I was fond of him for the same reason I was fond of Grandfather's horse-trader brother, my Great-Uncle Dan – because he had gaiety and was publicly reckoned to be no good.

I sat in the dining-room beside the gilt-boned cage that housed the canary. Yesterday, Aunt Edna, cleaning here, had said, 'What on earth are we going to do with the canary? Maybe we can find somebody who would like it.'

Grandfather Connor had immediately lit into her. 'Edna, your mother liked that bird, so it's staying, do you hear?'

When my mother and Aunt Edna went upstairs to have a ciga-rette, Aunt Edna had said, 'Well, it's dandy that he's so set on the bird now, isn't it? He might have considered that a few years earlier, if you ask me.'

'Try to be patient with him,' my mother had said. 'He's feeling it, too.'

'I guess so,' Aunt Edna had said in a discouraged voice. 'I haven't got Mother's patience, that's all. Not with him, nor with any man.'

And I had been reminded then of the item I had seen not long before in the Winnipeg *Free Press*, on the social page, telling of the marriage of James Reilly Lorimer to Somebody-or-other. I had rushed to my mother with the paper in my hand, and she had said, 'I know, Vanessa. She knows, too. So let's not bring it up, eh?'

The canary, as usual, was not in a vocal mood, and I sat beside the cage dully, not caring, not even trying to prod the creature into song. I wondered if Grandmother Connor was at this very moment in heaven, that dubious place.

'She believed, Edna,' my mother had said defensively. 'What right have we to say it isn't so?'

'Oh, I know,' Aunt Edna had replied. 'But can you take it in, really, Beth?'

'No, not really. But you feel, with someone like her – it would be so awful if it didn't happen, after she'd thought like that for so long.'

'She wouldn't know,' Aunt Edna had pointed out.

'I guess that's what I can't accept,' my mother had said slowly. 'I still feel she must be somewhere.'

I wanted now to hold my own funeral service for my grandmother, in the presence only of the canary. I went to the bookcase where she kept her Bible, and looked up Ecclesiastes. I intended to read the part about the mourners going about the streets, and the silver cord loosed and the golden bowl broken, and the dust returning to the earth as it was and the spirit unto God who gave it. But I got stuck on the first few lines, because it seemed to me, frighteningly, that they were being spoken in my grandmother's mild voice – 'Remember now thy Creator in the days of thy youth, while the evil days come not –'

Then, with a burst of opening doors, the family had returned from the funeral. While they were taking off their coats, I slammed the Bible shut and sneaked it back into the bookcase without anyone's having noticed.

Grandfather Connor walked over to me and placed his hands on my shoulders, and I could do nothing except endure his touch.

'Vanessa –' he said gruffly, and I had at the time no idea how much it cost him to speak at all, 'she was an angel. You remember that.'

Then he went down to the basement by himself. No one attempted to follow him, or to ask him to come and join the rest of us. Even I, in the confusion of my lack of years, realised that this would have been an impossibility. He was, in some way, untouchable. Whatever his grief was, he did not want us to look at it and we did not want to look at it, either.

Uncle Terence went straight into the kitchen, brought out his pocket flask, and poured a hefty slug of whisky for himself. He did the same for my mother and father and Aunt Edna.

'Oh Glory,' Aunt Edna said with a sigh, 'do I ever need this. All the same, I feel we shouldn't, right immediately afterwards. You know – considering how she always felt about it. Supposing Father comes up –'

'It's about time you quit thinking that way, Edna,' Uncle Terence said.

Aunt Edna felt in her purse for a cigarette. Uncle Terence reached over and lit it for her. Her hands were unsteady.

'You're telling me,' she said.

Uncle Terence gave me a quizzical and yet resigned look, and I knew then that my presence was placing a constraint upon them. When my father said he had to go back to the hospital, I used his departure to slip upstairs to my old post, the deserted stove-pipe hole. I could no longer eavesdrop with a clear conscience, but I justified it now by the fact that I had voluntarily removed myself from the kitchen, knowing they would not have told me to run along, not today.

'An angel,' Aunt Edna said bitterly. 'Did you hear what he said to Vanessa? It's a pity he never said as much to Mother once or twice, isn't it?'

'She knew how much he thought of her,' my mother said.

'Did she?' Aunt Edna said. 'I don't believe she ever knew he cared about her at all. I don't think I knew it myself, until I saw how her death hit him.'

'That's an awful thing to say!' my mother cried. 'Of course she knew, Edna.'

'How would she know,' Aunt Edna persisted, 'if he never let on?'

'How do you know he didn't?' my mother countered. 'When they were by themselves.'

'I don't know, of course,' Aunt Edna said. 'But I have my damn shrewd suspicions.'

'Did you ever know, Beth,' Uncle Terence enquired, pouring himself another drink, 'that she almost left him once? That was before you were born, Edna.'

'No,' my mother said incredulously. 'Surely not.'

'Yeh. Aunt Mattie told me. Apparently Father carried on for a while with some girl in Winnipeg, and Mother found out about it. She never told him she'd considered leaving him. She only told God and Aunt Mattie. The three of them thrashed it out together, I suppose. Too bad she never told him. It would've been a relief to him, no doubt, to see she wasn't all calm forgiveness.'

'How could he?' my mother said in a low voice. 'Oh, Terence. How could he have done that? To Mother, of all people.'

'You know something, Beth?' Uncle Terence said. 'I think he honestly believed that about her being some kind of angel. She'd never have thought of herself like that, so I don't suppose it ever would have occurred to her that he did. But I have a notion that he felt all along she was far and away too good for him. Can you feature going to bed with an angel, honey? It doesn't bear thinking about.'

'Terence, you're drunk,' my mother said sharply. 'As usual.'

'Maybe so,' he admitted. Then he burst out, 'I only felt, Beth, that somebody might have said to Vanessa just now, *Look, baby, she was terrific and we thought the world of her, but let's not say angel, eh?* All this angel business gets us into really deep water, you know that?'

'I don't see how you can talk like that, Terence,' my mother said, trying not to cry. 'Now all of a sudden everything was her fault. I just don't see how you can.'

'I'm not saying it was her fault,' Uncle Terence said wearily. 'That's not what I meant. Give me credit for one or two brains, Beth. I'm only saying it might have been rough for him, as well, that's all. How do any of us know what he's had to carry on his shoulders? Another person's virtues could be an awful weight to tote around. We all loved her. Whoever loved him? Who in hell could? Don't you think he knew that? Maybe he even thought sometimes it was no more than was coming to him.'

'Oh –' my mother said bleakly. 'That can't be so. That would be – oh, Terence, do you really think he might have thought that way?'

'I don't know any more than you do, Beth. I think he knew quite well that she had something he didn't, but I'd be willing to bet he always imagined it must be righteousness. It wasn't. It was – well, I guess it was tenderness, really. Unfair as you always are about him, Edna, I think you hit the nail on the head about one thing. I don't believe Mother ever realised he might have wanted her tenderness. Why should she? He could never show any of his own. All he could ever come out with was anger. Well, everybody to his own shield in this family. I guess I carry mine in my hip pocket. I don't know what yours is, Beth, but Edna's is more like his than you might think.'

'Oh yeh?' Aunt Edna said, her voice suddenly rough. 'What is it, then, if I may be so bold as to enquire?'

'Wisecracks, honey,' Uncle Terence replied, very gently. 'Just wisecracks.'

They stopped talking, and all I could hear was my aunt's uneven breathing, with no one saying a word. Then I could hear her blowing her nose.

'Mercy, I must look like the wreck of the Hesperus,' she said briskly. 'I'll bet I haven't got a speck of powder left on. Never mind. I'll repair the ravages later. What about putting the kettle on, Beth? Maybe I should go down and see if he'll have a cup of tea now.'

'Yes,' my mother said. 'That's a good idea. You do that, Edna.'

I heard my aunt's footsteps on the basement stairs as she went down into Grandfather Connor's solitary place.

Many years later, when Manawaka was far away from me, in miles and in time, I saw one day in a museum the Bear Mask of the Haida Indians. It was a weird mask. The features were ugly and yet powerful. The mouth was turned down in an expression of sullen rage. The eyes were empty caverns, revealing nothing. Yet, as I looked, they seemed to draw my own eyes towards them, until I imagined I could see somewhere within that darkness a look which I knew, a lurking bewilderment. I remembered then that in the days before it became a museum piece, the mask had concealed a man.

INFIDELITY AND
SECOND
MARRIAGES

MY MISTRESS

—— ◆ ——

Laurie Colwin

My wife is precise, elegant, and well-dressed, but the sloppiness of my mistress knows few bounds. Apparently I am not the sort of man who acquires a stylish mistress – the mistresses in French movies who rendezvous at the cafés in expensive hotels and take their cigarette cases out of alligator handbags, or meet their lovers on bridges wearing dashing capes. My mistress greets me in a pair of worn corduroy trousers, once green and now no colour at all, a grey sweater, an old shirt of her younger brother's which has a frayed collar, and a pair of very old, broken shoes with tassels, the backs of which are held together with electrical tape. The first time I saw these shoes I found them remarkable.

'What are those?' I said. 'Why do you wear them?'

My mistress is a serious, often glum person, who likes to put as little inflection into a sentence as she can.

'They used to be quite nice,' she said. 'I wore them out. Now I use them for slippers. They are my house shoes.'

This person's name is Josephine Delielle, nicknamed Billy. I am Francis Clemens, and no one but my mistress calls me Frank. The first time we went to bed, my mistress fixed me with an indifferent stare and said: 'Isn't this nice. In bed with Frank and Billy.'

My constant image of Billy is of her pushing her hair off her forehead with an expression of exasperation on her face. She frowns easily, often looks puzzled, and is frequently irritated. In movies men have mistresses who soothe and pet them, who are consoling, passionate, and ornamental. But I have a mistress who is mostly grumpy. Traditional things mean nothing to her. She does not flirt, cajole, or wear fancy underwear. She has taken to referring to me as her 'little bit of fluff', or she calls me *her* mistress, as in the sentence: 'Before you became my mistress I led a blameless life.'

But in spite of this I am secure in her affections. I know she loves me – not that she would ever come right out and tell me. She prefers the oblique line of approach. She may say something like: 'Being in love with you is making me a nervous wreck.'

Here is a typical encounter. It is between two and three o'clock in the afternoon. I arrive and ring the doorbell. The Delielles, who seem to have a lot of money, live in a duplex apartment in an old town house. Billy opens the door. There I am, an older man in my tweed coat. My hands are cold. I'd like to get them underneath her ratty sweater. She looks me up and down. She gives me her edition of a smile – a repressed smile that is half smirk, half grin.

Sometimes she gets her coat and we go for a bracing walk. Sometimes we go upstairs to her study. Billy is an economic historian who teaches two classes at the business school. She writes for a couple of highbrow journals. Her husband, Grey, is the resident economics genius at a think tank. They are one of those dashing couples, or at least they sound like one. I am no slouch either. For years I was an investment banker, and now I consult from my own home. I too write for a couple of highbrow journals. We have much in common, my mistress and I, or so it looks.

Billy's study is untidy. She likes to spread her papers out. Since her surroundings mean nothing to her, her workplace is bare of ornament, a cheerless, dreary little space.

'What have you been doing all day?' she says.

I tell her. Breakfast with my wife, Vera; newspaper reading after Vera has gone to work; an hour or so on the telephone with clients; a walk to my local bookstore; more telephoning; a quick sandwich; her.

'You and I ought to go out to lunch some day,' she says. 'One should always take one's mistress out for lunch. We could go dutch, thereby taking both mistresses at once.'

'I try to take you for lunch,' I say. 'But you don't like to be taken out for lunch.'

'Huh,' utters Billy. She stares at her bookcase as if looking for a misplaced volume and then she may give me a look that might translate into something tender such as: 'If I gave you a couple of dollars, would you take your clothes off?'

Instead, I take her into my arms. Her words are my signal that Grey is out of town. Often he is not, and then I merely get to kiss my mistress which makes us both dizzy. To kiss her and know that we can go forward to what Billy tonelessly refers to as 'the rapturous consummation' reminds me that in relief is joy.

After kissing for a few minutes, Billy closes the study door and we practically throw ourselves at one another. After the rapturous consummation has been achieved, during which I can look upon a mistress recognisable as such to me, my mistress will turn to me and in a voice full of the attempt to stifle emotion say something like: 'Sometimes I don't understand how I got so fond of a beat-up old person such as you.'

These are the joys adulterous love brings to me.

Billy is indifferent to a great many things: clothes, food, home decor. She wears neither perfume nor cologne. She uses what is used on infants: baby powder and Ivory soap. She hates to cook and will never present me with an interesting post-coital snack. Her snacking habits are those, I have often remarked, of a dyspeptic nineteenth-century English clubman. Billy will get up and present me with a mug of cold tea, a plate of hard wheat biscuits, or a squirt of tepid soda from the siphon on her desk. As she sits under her quilt nibbling those resistant biscuits, she reminds me of a creature from another universe – the solar system that contains the alien features of her real life: her past, her marriage, why I am in her life, what she thinks of me.

I drink my soda, put on my clothes, and, unless Vera is out of town, I go home to dinner. If Vera and Grey are out of town at the same time, which happens every now and again, Billy and I go out to dinner, during the course of which she either falls sleep or looks as if she is about to. Then I take her home, go home myself, and have a large steadying drink.

I was not entirely a stranger to adulterous love when I met Billy. I have explained this to her. In all long marriages, I expound, there are certain lapses. The look on Billy's face as I lecture is one of either amusement or contempt or both. The dinner party you are invited to as an extra man when your wife is away, I tell her. You are asked to take the extra woman, whose husband is also away, home in a taxi. The divorced family friend who invites you in for a drink one night, and so on. These fallings into bed are the friendliest thing in the world, I add. I look at my mistress.

'I see,' she says. 'Just like patting a dog.'

My affair with Billy, as she well knows, is nothing of the sort. I call her every morning. I see her almost every weekday afternoon. On the days she teaches, she calls me. We are as faithful as the Canada goose, more or less. She is an absolute fact of my life. When not at work, and when not with her, my thoughts rest upon the subject of her as easily as you might lay a hand on a child's head. I conduct a mental life with her when we are apart. Thinking about her is like entering a secret room to which only I have access.

I, too, am part of a dashing couple. My wife is an interior designer who has dozens of commissions and consults to practically everyone. Our two sons are grown up. One is a securities analyst and one is a journalist. What a lively table we must be, all of us together. So I tell my mistress. She gives me a baleful look.

'We can get plenty of swell types in for meals,' she says.

I know this is true and I know that Billy, unlike my gregarious and party-giving wife, thinks that there is no hell more hellish than the hell of a social life. She has made up a tuneless little chant, like a football cheer, to describe it. It goes:

They invited us
We invited them
They invited us
We invited them
They invited us
We invited them

Billy and I met at a reception to celebrate the twenty-fifth anniversary of one of the journals to which we are both contributors. We fell into a spirited conversation during which Billy asked me if this reception wasn't the most boring thing I had ever been to. I said it wasn't, by a long shot. Billy said: 'I can't stand these things where you have to stand up and be civilised. People either yawn, itch, or drool when they get bored. Which do you do?'

I said I yawned.

'Huh,' said Billy. 'You don't look much like a drooler. Let's get out of here.'

This particular interchange is always brought up when intentionality is discussed: Did she mean to pick me up? Did I look available? And so on. Out on the street we revealed that we were married and that both our spouses were out of town. Having made this clear, we went out to dinner and talked shop.

After dinner Billy said why didn't I come have a drink or a cup of tea. I did not know what to make of this invitation. I remembered that the young are more casual about these things, and that a cup of tea probably meant a cup of tea. My reactions to this offer are also discussed when cause is under discussion: Did I want her to seduce me? Did I mean to seduce her? Did we know what would happen right from the start?

Of her house Billy said: 'We don't have good taste or bad taste. We have no taste.' Her living-room had no style whatsoever, but it was comfortable enough. There was a portrait of what looked like an ancestor over the fireplace. Otherwise it was not a room that revealed a thing about its occupants except solidity, and a lack of decorative inspiration. Billy made us each a cup of tea. We continued our conversation, and when Billy began to look sleepy, I left.

After that, we made a pass at social life. We invited them for dinner, along with some financial types, a painter, and our sons and their lady friends. At this gathering Billy was mute, and Grey, a very clever fellow, chatted interestingly. Billy did not seem at all comfortable, but the rest of us had a fairly good time. Then they invited us, along with some financial types they knew and a music critic and his book designer wife. At this dinner, Billy looked tired. It was clear that cooking bothered her. She told me later that she was the sort who, when forced to entertain, did every little thing, like making and straining the veal stock. From the moment she entered the kitchen she looked longingly forward to the time when all the dishes would be clean and put away and the guests would all have gone home.

Then we invited them, but Grey had a bad cold and they had to cancel. After that, Billy and I ran into one another one day when we were both dropping off articles at the same journal and we had lunch. She said she was looking for an article of mine – we had been sending each other articles right from the start. Two days later, after rummaging around in my files, I found it. Since I was going to be in her neighbourhood, I dropped it off. She wrote me a note about this article and I called her to discuss it further. This necessitated a lunch meeting. Then she said she was sending me a book I had said I wanted to read, and then I sent her a book, and so it went.

One evening I stopped by to have a chat with Billy and Grey. I had just taken Vera, who was off to California, to the airport. I decided to ring their bell unannounced, but when I got there it turned out that Grey was out of town, too. Had I secretly been hoping that this would be the case? Billy had been working in her study, and without thinking about it, she led me up the stairs. I followed her and at the door of her study, I kissed her. She kissed me right back and looked awful about it.

'Nothing but a kiss!' I said, rather frantically. My mistress was silent. 'A friendly kiss,' I said.

My mistress gave me the sort of look that is supposed to make your blood freeze, and said: 'Is this the way you habitually kiss your friends?'

'It won't happen again,' I said. 'It was all a mistake.'

Billy gave me a stare so bleak and hard that I had no choice but to kiss her again and again.

After all this time it is still impossible for me to figure out what was and is going on in Billy's life that has let me in it. She once remarked that in her opinion there is frequently too little kissing in marriage, through which frail pinprick a microscopic dot of light was thrown on the subject of her marriage – or was it? She is like a Red Indian and says nothing at all, nor does she ever slip.

I, however, do slip, and I am made aware of this by the grim, sidelong glance I am given. I once told Billy that, until I met her, I had never given kissing much thought – she is an insatiable kisser for an unsentimental person – and I was rewarded for this utterance by a well-raised eyebrow and a rather frightening look of registration.

From time to time I feel it is wise to tell Billy how well Vera and I get along.

'Swell,' says Billy. 'I'm thrilled for you.'

'Well, it's true,' I say.

'I'm sure it's true,' says Billy. 'I'm sure there's no reason in the world why you come and see me all the time. It's probably just an involuntary action, like sneezing.'

'But you don't understand,' I say. 'Vera has men friends. I have women friends. The first principle of a good marriage is freedom.'

'Oh, I see,' says Billy. 'You sleep with your other women friends in the morning and come over here in the afternoon. What a lot of stamina you have, for an older person.'

One day this conversation had unexpected results. I said how well Vera and I got along, and Billy looked unadornedly hurt.

'God hates a mingy lover,' she said. 'Why don't you just say that you're in love with me and that it frightens you and have done with it?'

A lump rose in my throat.

'Of course, maybe you're not in love with me,' said Billy in her flattest voice.

I said: 'I *am* in love with you.'

'Well, there you are,' said Billy.

My curiosity about Grey is a huge, violent dog on a very tight leash. He is three years older than Billy, a somewhat sweet-looking boy with rumpled hair who looks as if he is working out problems in higher maths as you talk to him. He wears wire-rimmed glasses and his shirt tail hangs out. He has the body of a young boy and the air of a genius or someone constantly preoccupied by the intense pressure of a rarefied mental life. Together he and Billy look not so much like husband and wife as co-conspirators.

What are her feelings about him? I begin preliminary queries by hemming and hawing. 'Umm,' I say, 'it's, um, it's a little hard for me to picture your life with Grey. I mean, it's hard to picture your everyday life.'

'What you want to know is how often we sleep together and how much do I like it,' says Billy.

Well, she has me there, because that is exactly what I want to know.

'Tell you what,' says my mistress. 'Since you're so forthcoming about *your* marriage, we'll write down all about our home lives on little slips of paper and then we'll exchange them. How's that?'

Well, she has me there, too. What we are doing in each other's lives is a well-tended mystery.

I know how she contrasts to my wife: my wife is affable, full of conversation, loves a dinner party, and is interested in clothes, food, home decor, and the issues of the day. She loves to entertain, is sought out in times of crisis by her numerous friends, and has a kind or original word for everyone. She is methodical, hardworking, and does not fall asleep in restaurants. How I contrast to Grey is another matter, a matter about which I know nothing. I am considerably older and perhaps I appeal to some father-longing in my mistress. Billy says Grey is a genius – a thrilling quality but not one that has any real relevance to life with another person. He wishes, according to his wife, that he were the conductor of a symphony orchestra and for this reason he is given musical scores, tickets, and batons for his birthday. He has studied Russian and can sing Russian songs. He is passionately interested in the natural sciences and also wishes he were a forest ranger.

'He sounds so charming,' I say, 'that I can't imagine why you would want to know someone like me.' Billy's response to this is pure silence.

I hunt for signs of him on Billy – jewellery, marks, phrases. I know that he reads astronomy books for pleasure, enjoys cross-country skiing, and likes to travel. Billy says she loves him, but she also says she loves to read the works of Cardinal Aidan Gasquet, the historian of monastic life.

'If you love him so much,' I say, taking a page from her book, 'why are you hanging around with me?'

'Hanging around,' repeats Billy in a bored monotone.

'Well?'

'I am large and contain multitudes,' she says, quoting a line from Walt Whitman.

This particular conversation took place en route to a cottage in Vermont which I had rented for five days when both Grey and Vera happened to be out of town at the same time on business.

I remember clearly with what happy anticipation I presented the idea of this cottage to her.

'Guess what?' I said.

'You're pregnant,' said Billy.

'I have rented a little cottage for us, in Vermont. For a week when Grey and Vera are away on their long trips. We can go there and watch the leaves turn.'

'The leaves have already turned and fallen off,' said Billy faintly. She looked away and didn't speak for some time.

'We don't have to go, Billy,' I said. 'I only sent the cheque yesterday. I can cancel it.'

There appeared to be tears in my mistress's eyes.

'No,' she said. 'Don't do that. I'll split it with you.'

'You don't seem pleased,' I said.

'Being pleased doesn't strike me as the appropriate response to the idea of sneaking off to a love nest with your lover,' said Billy.

'What *is* the appropriate response?' I said.

'Oh,' Billy said, her voice now blithe, 'sorrow, guilt, horror, anticipation.'

Well, she can run but she can't hide. My mistress is given away from time to time by her own expressions. No matter how hard she tries to suppress the visible evidence of what she feels, she is not always successful. Her eyes turn colour, becoming dark and rather smoky. This is as good as a plain declaration of love. Billy's mental life, her grumpiness, her irritability, her crotchets are like static that, from time to time, give way to a clear signal, just as you often hit a pure band of music on a car radio after turning the dial through a lot of chaotic squawk.

In French movies of a certain period, the lovers are seen leaving the woman's apartment or house. His car is parked on an attractive side street. She is carrying a leather valise and is wearing a silk scarf around her neck. He is carrying the wicker basket she has packed with their picnic lunch. They will have the sort of food lovers have for lunch in these movies: a roasted chicken, a bottle of champagne, and a goat cheese wrapped up in leaves. Needless to say, when Billy and I finally left to go to our love nest, no such sight presented itself to me. First of all, she met me around the corner from my garage after a number of squabbles about whose car to take. She was standing between a rent-a-car and an animal hospital, wearing an old skirt, her old jacket, and carrying a ratty canvas overnight bag. No lacy underwear would be drawn from it, I knew. My mistress buys her white cotton undergarments at the five-and-ten-cent store. She wears an old T-shirt of Grey's to sleep in, she tells me.

For lunch we had hamburgers – no romantic rural inn or picnic spot for us – at Hud's Burger Hut off the throughway.

As we drew closer to our destination, Billy began to fidget, reminding me that having her along was sometimes not unlike travelling with a small child.

In the town nearest our love nest we stopped and bought coffee, milk, sugar, and cornflakes. Because I am a domestic animal and not a mere savage, I remembered to buy bread, butter, cheese, salami, eggs, and a number of cans of tomato soup.

Billy surveyed these items with a raised eyebrow.

'This is the sort of stuff you buy when you intend to stay indoors and kick up a storm of passion,' she said.

It was an off-year Election Day – congressional and Senate races were being run. We had both voted, in fact, before taking off. Our love nest had a radio which I instantly switched on to hear if there were any early returns while we gave the place a cursory glance and put the groceries away. Then we flung ourselves onto the unmade bed, for which I had thoughtfully remembered to pack sheets.

When our storm of passion had subsided, my mistress stared impassively at the ceiling.

'In bed with Frank and Billy,' she intoned. 'It was Election Day, and Frank and Billy were once again in bed. Election returns meant nothing to them. The future of their great nation was inconsequential, so busy were they flinging themselves at one another they could barely be expected to think for one second of any larger issues. The subjects to which these trained economists could have spoken, such as inflationary spirals or deficit budgeting, were as mere dust.'

'Shut up, Billy,' I said.

She did shut up. She put on my shirt and went off to the kitchen. When she returned she had two cups of coffee and a plate of toasted cheese on a tray. With the exception of her dinner party, this was the first meal I had ever had at her hands.

'I'm starving,' she said, getting under the covers. We polished off our snack, propped up with pillows. I asked Billy if she might like a second cup of coffee and she gave me a look of remorse and desire that made my head spin.

'Maybe you wanted to go out to dinner,' she said. 'You like a proper dinner.' Then she burst into tears. 'I'm sorry,' she said. These were words I had never heard her speak before.

'Sorry?' I said. 'Sorry for what?'

'I didn't ask you what you wanted to do,' my mistress said. 'You might have wanted to take a walk, or go for a drive or look around the house or make the bed.'

I stared at her.

'I don't want a second cup of coffee,' Billy said. 'Do you?'

I got her drift and did not get out of bed. The forthrightness of her desire for me melted my heart.

During this excursion, none of my expectations came to pass. We did not, for example, have long talks about our respective marriages or our future together or apart. We did not discover what our domestic life might be like. We lived like graduate students or mice and not like normal people at all. We kept odd hours and lived off sandwiches. We stayed in bed and were both glad when it rained. When the sun came out, we went for a walk and observed the bare and almost bare trees. From time to time I would switch on the radio to hear the latest election results and commentary.

'Because of this historic time,' Billy said, 'you will never be able to forget me. It is a rule of life that care must be taken in choosing whom one will be in bed with during Great Moments in History. You are now stuck, with me and this week of important congressional elections twined in your mind forever.'

It was in the car on the way home that the subject of what we were doing together came up. It was twilight and we had both been silent.

'This is the end of the line,' said Billy.

'What do you mean?' I said. 'Do you mean you want to break this up?'

'No,' said Billy. 'It would be nice, though, wouldn't it?'

'No, it would not be nice,' I said.

'I think it would,' said Billy. 'Then I wouldn't spend all my time wondering what we are doing together when I could be thinking about other things, like my dissertation.'

'What do you think we are doing together?' I said.

'It's simple,' said Billy. 'Some people have dogs or kitty cats. You're my pet.'

'Come on.'

'Okay, you're right. Those are only child substitutes. You're my child substitute until I can make up my mind about having a child.'

At this, my blood freezes. Whose child does she want to have?

Every now and then when overcome with tenderness – on those occasions naked, carried away, and looking at one another with sweetness in our eyes – my mistress and I smile dreamily and realise that if we dwelt together for more than a few days, in the real world and not in some love nest, we would soon learn to hate each other. It would never work. We both know it. She is too relentlessly dour, and too fond of silence. I prefer false cheer to no cheer at all and I like conversation over dinner no matter what. Furthermore we would never have proper meals and, although I cannot cook, I like to dine. I would soon resent her lack of interest in domestic arrangements and she would resent me for resenting her. Furthermore, Billy is a slob. She does not leave towels lying on the bathroom floor, but she throws them over the shower curtain rod any old way instead of folding them or hanging them properly so they can dry. It is things like this that squash out romance over a period of time.

As for Billy, she often sneers at me. She finds many of my opinions quaint. She thinks I am an old-time domestic fascist. She refers to me as 'an old-style heterosexual throwback' or 'old hetero' because I like to pay for dinner, open car doors, and often call her at night when Grey is out of town to make sure she is safe. The day the plumber came to fix a leak in her sink, I called several times.

'He's gone,' Billy said. 'And he left big, greasy paw prints all over me.' She found this funny, I did not.

After a while, were we to cohabit, I believe I would be driven nuts and she would come to loathe me. My household is well run and well regulated. I like routine and I like things to go along smoothly. We employ a flawless person by the name of Mrs Ivy Castle who has been flawlessly running our house for years. She is an excellent housekeeper and a marvellous cook. Our relations with her are formal.

The Delielles employ a feckless person called Mimi-Ann Browning who comes in once a week to push the dust around. Mimi-Ann hates routines and schedules, and is constantly changing the days of the people she works for. It is quite something to hear Billy on the telephone with her.

'Oh, Mimi-Ann,' she will say. 'Please don't switch me. I beg you. Grey's awful cousin is coming and the house is really disgusting. Please, Mimi, I'll do anything. I'll do your mother-in-law's tax return. I'll be your eternal slave. *Please*. Oh, thank you, Mimi-Ann. Thank you a million times.'

Now why, I ask myself, does my mistress never speak to me like that?

In the sad twilight on the way home from our week together, I asked myself, as I am always asking myself: could I exist in some ugly flat with my cheerless mistress? I could not, as my mistress is always the first to point out.

She said that the small doses we got of one another made it possible for us to have a love affair but that a taste of ordinary life would do us in. She correctly pointed out that our only common interest was each other, since we had such vast differences of opinion on the subject of economics. Furthermore, we were not simply lovers, nor were we mere friends, and since we were not going to end up together, there was nothing for it.

I was silent.

'Face it,' said my tireless mistress. 'We have no *raison d'être*.'

There was no disputing this.

I said: 'If we have no *raison d'être*, Billy, then what are we to do?'

These conversations flare up like tropical storms. The climate is always right for them. It is simply a question of when they will occur.

'Well?' I said.

'I don't know,' said my mistress, who generally has a snappy answer for everything. A wave of fatherly affection and worry came over me. I said, in a voice so drenched with concern it caused my mistress to scowl like a child about to receive an injection: 'Perhaps you should think about this more seriously, Billy. You and Grey are really just starting out. Vera and I have been married a long, long time. I think I am more a disruption in your life than you are in mine.'

'Oh, really,' said Billy.

'Perhaps we should see each other less,' I said. 'Perhaps we should part.'

'Okay, let's part,' said Billy. 'You go first.' Her face was set and I entertained myself with the notion that she was trying not to burst into tears. Then she said: 'What are you going to do all day after we part?'

This was not a subject to which I wanted to give much thought.

'Isn't our *raison d'être* that we're fond of one another?' I said. 'I'm awfully fond of you.'

'Gee, that's interesting,' Billy said. 'Just last week you broke down and used the word "love". How quickly things change.'

'You know what I mean.'

'Whatever our status quos are,' Billy said, 'they are being maintained like mad.'

This silenced me. Billy and I have the world right in place. Nothing flutters, changes, or moves. Whatever is being preserved in our lives is safely preserved. It is quite true, as Billy, who believes in function, points out, that we are in each other's life for a reason, but neither of us will state the reason. Nevertheless, although there are some cases in which love is not a good or sufficient reason for anything, the fact is, love is undeniable.

Yes, love is undeniable and that is the tricky point. It is one of the sobering realisations of adult life that love is often not a propellant. Thus, in those romantic movies, the tender mistress stays married to her stuffy husband – the one with the moustache and the stiff tweeds – while the lover is seen walking through the countryside with his long-suffering wife and faithful dog. It often seems that the function of romance is to give people something romantic to think about.

The question is: if it is true, as my mistress says, that she is going to stay with Grey and I am going to stay with Vera, why is it that we are together every chance we get?

There was, of course, an explanation for this, and my indefatigable mistress came up with it, God bless her.

'It's an artistic impulse,' she said. 'It takes us out of reality and gives us an invented context all our own.'

'Oh, I see,' I said. 'It's only art.'

'Don't get in a huff,' Billy said. 'We're in a very unusual situation. It has to do with limited doting, restricted thrall, and situational adoration.'

'Oh, how interesting,' I said. 'Are doting, thrall, and adoration things you actually feel for me?'

Naturally Billy would never deign to answer a leading question.

Every adult knows that facts must be faced. In adult life, it often seems that's all there is. Prior to our weekend together, the unguarded moments between us had been kept to a minimum. Now they came more frequently. That week together haunted us. It dogged our heels. It made us long for and dread – what an unfortunate combination! – each other.

One evening I revealed to her how I sometimes feel as I watch her walk up the stairs to the door of her house. I feel she is walking into her real and still fairly young life. She will leave me in the dust, I think. I think of all the things that have not yet happened to her, that have not yet gone wrong, and I think of her life with Grey, which is still fairly unlived.

One afternoon she told me how it makes her feel when she thinks of my family table – with Vera and our sons and their friends and girlfriends, of our years of shared meals, of all that lived life. Billy described this feeling as a band around her head and a hot pressure in the area of her heart. I, of course, merely get a lump in my throat. Why do these admittings take place at twilight or at dusk, in the gloomiest light when everything looks dirty, eerie, faded, or inevitable?

Our conversation comes to a dead halt, like a horse baulking before a hurdle, on the issue of what we want. I have tried my best to formulate what it is I want from Billy, but I haven't got very far. Painful consideration has brought forth this revelation: I want her not ever to stop being. This is as close as grammar or reflection will allow.

One day the horse will jump over the hurdle and the end will come. The door will close. Billy will doubtless do the closing. She will decide she wants a baby, or Grey will be offered an academic post in London, or Billy will finish her dissertation and get a job in Boston, and the Delielles will move. Or perhaps Vera will come home one evening and say that she longs to live in Paris or San Francisco, and we will move. What will happen then?

Perhaps my mistress is right. A love affair is like a work of art. The large store of reference and jokes, the history of our friendship, our trip to Vermont, our numberless phone calls, this edifice, this monument, this civilisation known only to and constructed by the two of us will be – what will it be? Billy once read me an article from one of Grey's nature magazines about the last Coast Salish Indian to speak Wintu. All the others of his tribe were dead. That is how I would feel, deprived of Billy.

The awful day will doubtless come. It is like thinking about the inevitability of nuclear war. But for now, I continue to ring her doorbell. Her greeting is delivered in a bored monotone. 'Oh, it's you,' she will say.

I will follow her upstairs to her study and there we will hurl ourselves at one another. I will reflect, as I always do, how very bare the setting for these encounters is. Not a picture on the wall, not an ornament. Even the quilt that keeps the chill off us on the couch is faded.

In one of her snootier moments, my mistress said to me: 'My furnishings are interior. I care about what I think about.'

As I gather her into my arms, I cannot help imagining all that interior furniture, those hard-edged things she thinks about, whatever is behind her silence, whatever, in fact, her real story is.

I imagine that some day she will turn to me and with some tone in her voice I have never heard before say: 'We can't see each other any more.' We will both know the end has come. But meanwhile she is right close by. After a fashion, she is mine. I watch her closely to catch the look of true love that every once in a while overtakes her. She knows I am watching, and she knows the effect her look has. 'A baby could take candy from you,' she says.

Our feelings have edges and spines and prickles like a cactus, or porcupine. Our parting when it comes will not be simple, either. Depicted it would look like one of those medieval beasts that have fins, fur, scales, feathers, claws, wings, and horns. In a world apart from anyone else, we are Frank and Billy, with no significance to anyone but the other. Oh, the terrible privacy and loneliness of love affairs!

Under the quilt with our arms interlocked, I look into my mistress's eyes. They are dark, and full of concealed feeling. If we hold each other close enough, that darkness is held at bay. The mission of the lover is, after all, to love. I can look at Billy and see clear back to the first time we met, to our hundreds of days together, to her throwing the towels over the shower curtain rod, to each of her gestures and intonations. She is the road I have travelled to her, and I am hers.

Oh, Billy! Oh, art! Oh, memory!

COMING SOUTH

———— ◆ ————

Celia Dale

Fancy me just happening to see it in the newspaper! Right down at the bottom of an inside page it was, only a few lines, I could easy have missed it. DEATH IN PRISON, it said, and underneath: 'Frank Wisbey, sentenced to life imprisonment in 1961 for the murder of his wife Edna, has died in Hackenfield Prison. He was fifty-eight.'

It gave me a turn, I can tell you. After all these years. Death comes to us all, of course; and of course, if it hadn't been for them changing the law Frank Wisbey would have been hung. Still, no matter what they found him guilty of, one wouldn't want that, would one, it's not nice to think about.

Well, when I read that piece in the evening newspaper I had to sit down. My legs just gave way. After a bit I got up and made myself a cup of tea, and as I sat and drank it of course I knew what I had to do. I'd always known, of course. But somehow it made me feel ever so funny. Ever such a funny mixture, I felt.

So the next morning I said to Mr Harding I had to have a few days off on account of urgent business. He didn't like it much and grumbled a bit but in the end he had to agree. I'm the best typing pool supervisor he's ever had and he knows it. I can keep those silly young girls in order like nobody's business, some of them have been there nearly six months and their work's as good as you'll find anywhere. I have my standards and I see they keep to them. They're only bits of girls, they respect authority if it's done with a smile. And I always smile. Whatever I feel inside, seething I may be, but I keep a smile.

So in my lunch hour I went to the travel agent and got my ticket to London for the next day. Tell you the truth, I quite looked forward to it. I hadn't been south for – oh, donkey's years and one can always do with a bit of a break, specially when you're as conscientious a worker as I am, and frankly, there's lots of places I'd rather live than what they call the industrial north. But I will say this for them, there's plenty of Go in them up there and they mind their own business. On the whole I've not regretted it. I've a good position and a nice little flat a bit outside the city, right on the bus route. I keep it like a new pin, I can tell you, and I've lived very comfortable there these last few years, with no one to mess the place up and upset me or interfere. That's why I came in the first place.

Well, I packed a case and gave the flat a good clean (not that it needed it, but I like to have everything nice) and next morning I got on the train for London. I was nervous, I don't mind admitting it. But I've never let nerves stand in the way of what I've determined to do.

It's not that I'm nervous of travelling, I've got more sense than that. Though I've not been abroad like everyone else these days, I've been to Scotland on a coach trip and I even flew to Ireland on holiday one year – before the Troubles, of course – and I wasn't a bit nervous in the plane. You see those silly bits of stewardesses that do it all the time, with their fancy hair-dos and false eyelashes and nail varnish, and if they're not nervous it's not likely I'll be! No, I was nervous of going back. Yes I was, I was nervous.

Well, I needn't have been, of course. Not many people travelling, business gentlemen mostly, it being mid-week, and quite a nice clean train. I treated myself to a meal in the dining-car and it wasn't near so bad as what people make out. Quite nice really, and wonderful how those waiters don't spill anything. I closed my eyes for forty winks afterwards and it was dark by the time we got to London – and on time too. The railways aren't half so black as they're painted, if you ask me.

Anyway, I got a bus from the terminus (my word, how it's changed since I was there last!) and I found myself a room in a nice clean little hotel not far away and I took off my hat and coat and shoes and lay down on the bed, and here I am, going over it all in my mind. Until now, you see, I've just sort of acted automatic. After seeing that piece in the newspaper and getting over the shock, I'd known what I had to do, I made my plans and carried them through, just like I always do. But now, with nothing more to be done till tomorrow, I find it's all going round and round in my mind, over and over, just like I was reading it all in the newspaper again like it all came out at the trial, eleven years ago.

Frank Wisbey worked in the accounts department of one of them big factories out to the south of London, the real country not all that far away by car for a nice run at the weekend, and one of them big sewage farms, they call them, quite nearby, which wasn't all that nice really, I suppose, but you wouldn't notice it. He and his wife had a nice little house of their own, built in the 1920s, semi-detached, a nice bit of garden front and back. But what made it really nice was the back garden ran down to a foot-path along all the backs of the gardens and came out on a recreation ground, so it could never be built on. Cricket and football, a playground for the kiddies, a pond and a dirty old stream that fed it, more like a ditch really. But it was a really nice place to live and you'd never believe you was only a stone's throw away from the motorway – you know the kind of place.

They didn't have any children. She kept the house nice and he did the garden and they was as decent, respectable a couple as you could wish to meet. He was a bit younger than she was.

Well, she disappeared. Neighbours noticed they'd not seen her about, and when he was asked he gave out she'd gone to visit her auntie. Well, they thought it was funny, for no one had ever heard mention about no auntie. And then it began to come out he'd been seen around. With a girl. One of them young bits of things from his office, all long hair and – well, mini-skirts hadn't hardly come in then, but whatever it was, she wore it. Half his age, keen on music and all that stuff like he was.

People began to come out with they'd been seen about quite a bit long before the wife disappeared – after dark, of course, in the recreation ground down by the pond, or sitting in his car in a side road once or twice. Now they noticed she was going into the house and staying a bit too long. They noticed the car being driven in and out in the night the first weeks, and then, after a month of two, she moved in. Well, that started the tongues wagging even more, and to cut a long story short, the police stepped in.

He didn't deny it. He couldn't, could he, for the girl was living there as bold as brass and too many people had seen them together long before, people at his firm as well as the neighbours. But he said he didn't know nothing about his wife. No, she'd not written. No, she'd not taken her clothes or her Post Office book or the few bits of jewellery her mum had left her, as far as he could tell; only the things she stood up in.

Funny, they said. Had there been any disagreement?

Well, yes he said, there had been a few words. He had to admit it, you see, because the police already knew all about the girl. Had his wife found out about that, they said. No, he said, he'd told her. He wanted to make the break, he said, go away with the girl and marry her, if you please – half his age! Great love, real passion, touching romance, all that sort of nonsense. Disgusting, really. His lawyer made a great thing of it all at the trial but it didn't do any of them much good.

So how had his wife taken it, said the police. Quietly, he said. She'd said she must think it all over and did he know what he was doing? He'd said he did, and she'd said well, one thing was certain and that was she'd never give him his freedom. And he'd said then he'd go off with the girl anyway. And she'd said they must all think it over. There wasn't no row, he said. Next day when he come home from business she'd asked him had he changed his mind and he said he hadn't. She didn't say nothing more, he said, but when he come back from business the next evening she was gone – no note, nothing, just gone.

Well, naturally the police was suspicious. I mean, missing wife, young girl, it's too neat, isn't it? They searched the place, house, garden, recreation ground. And in the pond they found her dentures.

It's not very nice to talk about, but it all come out at the trial and the papers had a field day. Not the full set, just the bottoms, and the dentist checked they were hers. They found a shoe as well and a bangle she used to wear. And buried under the compost heap in the garden they found some underwear.

Well, you can imagine they just tore the place apart after – went through it all with a fine tooth comb, dug up the garden, had dogs and I don't know what – all up and down the path and the grounds, even went out to the sewage farm. But they never found nothing more.

Well, of course they arrested him. They had to. Even without the body it was obvious, wasn't it? They don't like being without the body, of course, but there's several cases they've had to do without, you remember them, I expect. They must have been pretty sure of themselves or they wouldn't have risked proceedings. Of course, it was all circumstantial, but it stood out a mile really. They fair took that sewage farm to pieces, but – well, it's not a very nice subject, is it? No wonder they couldn't find nothing more there, in the circumstances.

It was a big case. His lawyer made a good try for him, I will say that. Made out what a good chap he was, popular, kindly, wouldn't hurt a fly. Tried to make out his wife was a bit of a so-and-so, nagged him about the house and not smoking and wiping his feet, wouldn't have children. Made a great thing about the girl, like I said – great romance, all that stuff, how she'd sold her story to one of the newspapers just so she could pay for his trial, how she'd stand by him for ever, knew he was innocent. The other side soon put paid to that. He hadn't a chance, not with the way the case built up against him – although I will say the jury took their time about reaching the verdict, and one of them said afterwards in a newspaper interview that he was glad they didn't still have them hung.

Well, there it was. He got life. And she got nothing. She never even got him, not even after all her years of waiting, standing by him and all that lark. She'd be down her thirties now – a bit late to start again, especially without him. He'd have been out in a year or so, too, the way they do it now. Life sentence doesn't mean what it used to, more's the pity.

But I think she got the house. It was his, you see, and of course I never claimed it. Well, I couldn't, could I? She's welcome to it, I'm quite content where I am, thank you, with my own little place with no one messing it up and going behind my back and making a fool of me to all the neighbours. Throwing back in my face all the years I gave him, keeping the place nice, keeping respectable – carrying on with a silly bit of a girl young enough to be his daughter, sighing and sobbing, making big speeches, having sex . . . Disgusting.

I had a spare set, you see. It was easy. They was old, didn't fit as well as the ones I dumped in the pond with the other things after dark, but I found a good dentist up north after a year or two when the case was all forgotten, and he soon fixed me up. I took just the housekeeping and a coat I never wore much and pawned my engagement ring and got on the train with no one any the wiser. I touched up my hair a bit next day and wore my glasses and no one ever gave me a second look. They mind their own business up north. It was days before anyone knew I was gone except Frank, and he was keeping quiet about it naturally.

I never meant to come back really. Let them fry, I thought. But I'll go down to the house tomorrow, see if she's still there. Loss of memory, I'll say. No one can prove different.

I can't wait to see her face.

AN ACT OF REPARATION

Sylvia Townsend Warner

—— ◆ ——

> Lapsang sooshang – must smell like tar.
> Liver salts in *blue* bottle.
> Strumpshaw's bill – why *6d*.?
> Crumpets.
> Waistcoat buttons.
> Something for weekend – not a chicken.

So much of the list had been scratched off that this remainder would have made cheerful reading if it had not been for the last item.

Valerie Hardcastle knew where she was with a chicken. You thawed it, put a lump of marge inside, and roasted it. While it was in the oven you could give your mind to mashed potatoes (Fenton couldn't endure packet crisps), bread sauce and the vegetable of the season – which latterly had been sprouts. A chicken was calm and straightforward: you ate it hot, then you ate it cold; and it was a further advantage that one chicken is pretty much like another. Chicken is reliable – there is no apple-pie-bed side to its character. With so much in married life proving apple-pie-beddish, the weekend chicken had been as soothing as going to church might be if you were that sort of person. But now Fenton had turned – like any worm, she thought, though conscious that the comparison was inadequate – declaring that he was surfeited with roast chicken, that never again was she to put one of those wretched

193

commercialised birds before him.

'Think of their hideous lives, child! Penned up, regimented, stultified. They never see a blade of grass, they never feel the fresh air, all they know is chicken, chicken, chicken – just like us at weekends. Where is that appalling draught coming from? You must have left a window open somewhere.'

'What do you think I ought to get instead? I could do liver and bacon. But that doesn't go on to the next day.'

'Can't you get a joint?'

A joint. What joint? She had never cooked a joint. At home, Mum made stews. At the Secretarial College there was mince and shepherd's pie. No doubt a joint loomed in the background of these – but distantly, like mountains in Wales. When she and Olive Petty broke away from the college to share a bed-sitting room and work as dancing partners at the town's new skating rink their meals mainly consisted of chips and salami, varied by the largesse of admirers who took them to restaurants. Fenton, as an admirer, had expressed himself in *scampi* and *crêpes Suzette* – pronounced 'crapes', not 'creeps' – with never a mention of joints. Grey-haired, though with lots of it, he was the educated type, and theirs was an ideal relationship till Mrs Fenton, whom he had not mentioned either – not to speak of – burst out like a tiger, demanding divorce. The case was undefended. Six months later to the day, Fenton made an honest woman of her. Brought her down to earth, so to speak.

Marriage, said the registrar, was a matter of give and take. Marriage, thought Valerie, was one thing after another. Now it was joints. Sunk in marriage, she sat at a small polished table in the bank, waiting for Fenton's queries about his statement sheets to be thoroughly gone into, meanwhile enjoying the orderliness and impersonality of an establishment so unlike a kitchen or a bedroom.

And at an adjoining table sat the previous Mrs Hardcastle who for her part had come to withdraw a silver tea pot from the bank's strong room, examining with a curiosity she tried to keep purely abstract the young person who had supplanted her in Fenton's affections. Try as she might, abstraction was not possible. Conscience intervened, compunction and stirrings of guilt. It was all very well for Isaac; he had not drawn Abraham's attention to the ram in the thicket. It was all very well for Iphigenia, who had not suggested to the goddess that a hind could replace her at the sacrificial altar. Isaac and Iphigenia could walk off with minds untroubled by any shade of responsibility for the substituted victim. But she, Lois Hardcastle, writhing in the boredom of being married to Fenton, had snatched at Miss Valerie Fry, who had done her no harm whatever, and got away at her expense. And this, this careworn, deflated little chit staring blankly at a shopping list, was what Fenton had made of her in less than six months' matrimony.

'Oh dear!' said Lois, and sighed feelingly.

Hearing the exclamation and the sigh, Valerie glanced up to discover who was taking on so. She could see nothing to account for it. The woman was definitely middle-aged, long past having anything to sound tragic about. Indeed, she looked uncommonly healthy and prosperous, was expensively made up, wore a wedding ring, had no shopping bags – so why should she jar the polish and repose of a bank by sighing and exclaiming 'Oh dear'? Leg of lamb, leg of pork, leg of . . . did nothing else have legs? A bank clerk came up with a sealed parcel, saying 'Here it is, Mrs Hardcastle. If you'll just sign for it.'

'Here, you've made a mistake! Those aren't Mr Hardcastle's – ' As Valerie spoke, she saw the parcel set down in front of the other woman. Fenton's other one. For it was she, though so smartened up as to be almost unrecognisable. What an awkward situation! And what a pity she had drawn attention to herself by saying that about the parcel. Fortunately, Fenton's other one did not appear to have noticed anything. She read the form carefully through, took her time over signing it, exchanged a few words with the clerk about the time of year before he carried it away. Of course, at her age she was probably a bit deaf, so she would not have heard those give-away words. The give-away words sounded on in Valerie's head. She was still blushing vehemently when the other

Mrs Hardcastle looked her full in the face and said, cool as a cucumber, 'Mrs Lois Hardcastle, now. What an odd place we've chosen to meet in.'

Pulling herself together, Valerie replied, 'Quite a coincidence.'

'Such a small world. I've come to collect a tea pot. And you, I gather, are waiting for Fenton's statement sheets, just as I used to do. And it's taking a long time, just as it always did.'

'There were some things Mr Hardcastle wanted looked into.'

Not to be put down, Mr Hardcastle's earlier wife continued, 'Now that the bank has brought us together, I hope you'll come and have coffee with me. I'm going back to London tonight, so it's my only chance to hear how you both are.'

'I don't know that I can spare the time, thank you all the same, I'm behindhand as it is, and I've got to buy a joint for the week-end.'

'Harvey's or Ensten's?'

'Well, I don't really know. I'd rather thought of the Co-op.'

'Excellent for pork.'

'To tell the truth, I've not bought a joint before. We've always had a chicken. But now he's got tired of chicken.'

Five months of love and chicken . . .

'I'm afraid you've been spoiling him,' said Lois. 'Keep him on cold veal for a few weeks and he'll be thankful for chicken.'

'I hadn't thought of veal. Would veal be a good idea?'

'Here come your statement sheets. Now we can go and have some coffee and think about the veal.'

'Well, I must say, I'd be glad of it. Shopping gets me down.'

Tottering on stiletto heels and still a head shorter than Lois, the replacement preceded her from the bank, jostling the swinging doors with her two bulging, ill-assembled shopping bags. Lois took one from her. It was the bag whose handle Fenton, in a rush of husbandry, had mended with string. The string ground into her fingers – as fatal, as familiar, as ever.

The grey downs grew into lumps of sin to Guenevere in William Morris's poem, and as Fenton's wives sat drinking coffee the shopping bags humped on the third chair grew into lumps of sin to Lois. They were her bags, her burden; and she had cast them onto the shoulders of this hapless child and gone flourishing off, a free woman. It might be said, too, though she made less of it, that she had cast the child on Fenton's ageing shoulders and hung twenty-one consecutive frozen chickens round his neck . . . a clammy garland. Apparently it was impossible to commit the simplest act of selfishness, of self-defence even, without paining and inconveniencing others. Lost in these reflections, Lois forgot to keep the conversation going. It was Valerie who revived it. 'Where would one be without one's cup of coffee?'

For, considering how handicapped she was with middle age and morality, Fenton's other one had been putting up a creditable show of sophisticated broadmindedness, and deserved a helping hand – the more so since that sigh in the bank was now so clearly explainable as a sigh of regret for the days when she had a husband to cook for. Lois agreed that one would be quite lost without one's cup of coffee. 'And I always think it's such a mistake to put milk in it,' continued Valerie, who with presence of mind had refused milk, black coffee being more sophisticated. Two sophisticated women, keeping their poise on the rather skiddy surface of a serial husband, was how she saw the situation. For a while, she managed to keep conversation on a black-coffee level: foreign travel, television, the guitar. But you could see the poor thing's heart wasn't really in it; grieving for what could never again be hers, she just tagged along. Yes, she had been to Spain, but it was a long time ago. No, unfortunately, she had missed that programme. 'I never seem to have enough time. Do have another cake.' She seemed to have time enough now. The cake lay on her plate, the coffee cooled in her cup; still she sat brooding, and frowned as though she were calculating some odds, hatching some resolution. Could it be that she was going to turn nasty? All of a sudden, she looked up and exclaimed, 'I know. Oxtail.'

'I beg your pardon?'

'Oxtail. Instead of a joint. Come on.'

Well, if it made her happy . . .

It certainly did. A wife Fenton hadn't given her an idea of, a wife as animated and compelling as a scenic railway, swept Valerie to the butcher's, summoned old Mr Ensten himself, made him produce a series of outlandish objects totally unlike Valerie's conception of what could be called a joint, chose out the most intimidating of the lot, stiff as a poker and a great deal longer, watched with a critical eye as he smote it into coilability, swept on to a greengrocer to buy carrots, garlic, celery and button mushrooms, then to a grocer's shop, bafflingly small, dusky and undisplaying, where she bought peppercorns, bay leaves and a jar of anchovies, finally to a wine merchant where she bought half a bottle of claret. Whirled on in this career, consulted and assenting over God knew what next, abandoning all thought of the rest of her shopping list, Valerie fell from gasps to giggles. Why peppercorns, when pepper could be got ready ground? Why anchovies, when there was no thought of fish? And garlic? Now it was claret.

'And a taxi, please.'

As though it were perfectly normal for wine merchants to supply taxis, the taxi was fetched. Valerie was put into it; the parcels and shopping bags were put in after her.

'Seventeen Windermere Gardens,' said Lois.

Once, escaping from the Secretarial College, Valerie and Olive Petty bought half-crown tickets for a Mystery Drive. The bus, thundering through a maze of small streets, had taken them past the Corporation Gas Works into the unknown. It had dived into woods, skirted past villages with spires and villages with towers, shown them an obelisk on a hill-top, a reservoir, a bandstand, an Isolation Hospital, a glimpse of the sea, a waterfall, a ruined castle. Then, with a twirl through some unidentifiable suburbs, it set them down by the War Memorial, a stone's throw from the Secretarial College. Now it was to be the same thing. The Mystery Shopping Excursion would end at 17 Windermere Gardens. All that remained was to say something calm and suitable.

'Such an unexpected pleasure to meet you. You've quite changed the day for me.'

'But I'm coming, too. I'm coming to cook the oxtail. I hope you don't mind.'

'Mind? My God, I'd be thankful! And more.'

The ring of sincerity transformed the poor girl's voice. To say 'transfigured' would, however, be going too far. Transformed it. Unmuzzled it.

No act of reparation, thought Lois, sitting in the taxi, can be an exact fit. Circumstances are like seaweed: a moment's exposure to the air, an hour's relegation to the past tense, stiffens, warps, shrivels the one and the other. The impulse to ease even a fraction of the burden she had imposed on that very different Miss Valerie Fry of the divorce proceedings – an impulse first felt in the bank as an amused acknowledgement of a faint sense of guilt, which at the word 'joint' had fleshed itself in the possibility of a deed, and a compassion against which she had soon ceased to struggle – for only someone in a state of utter dejection could have eaten three of those appalling little cakes – would fit neither the offence nor the moment. Probably even the medium was ill-chosen. She happened to like oxtail herself, but very likely the girl would have preferred rolled ribs. Only one static element would resist the flux of time: Fenton's planet-like, unconjectural course. The Borough Offices where he worked as an architect closed at midday on Saturday. The planet-like course then took him to lunch at the Red Lion, and then to a healthful swim in the public baths, and then to his club; and he would be home at six.

'I'm afraid, as I wasn't expecting you, there won't be more than bread and cheese,' said the voice, now back in its muzzle.

'Nothing I should like better. It will give us more time to cook in. When does Fenton usually get home?'

'Four, or thereabouts.'

Even Fenton wasn't the same. She glanced with admiration at the young person whose society was two hours more alluring than hers had been; then at her wristwatch.

'Well, if I don't dawdle over my bread and cheese, that should be long enough. At any rate, it should be well on its way by then.'

'By then? All that time to cook a tail? You *must* be fond of cooking!'

The tone of spontaneous contempt, thought Lois, was just

what anyone trying to apply an act of reparation might expect, and therefore what she deserved.

The taxi turned down Windermere Terrace. Seeing the iteration of small houses, each carefully designed to be slightly at variance with the others, each with a small identical garage and small front gardens for demonstrations of individuality, Lois observed that in some of the gardens the ornamental shrubs had grown larger, in others had died. They entered the house.

'I should think it must feel a bit queer to you, coming back like this,' Valerie said.

'No. Rather homelike. What a pretty new wallpaper – new wallpapers, that is.' A pink wall with squiggles, a blue wall with stripes, a yellow wall with poodles, kiosks and the Eiffel Tower, a black wall with marbling. And did Fenton come home two hours earlier to gaze on these?

'I put them all on myself. And one with fishes in the bathroom. I expect you know your way to the bathroom?'

'I must not, will not, be censorious,' said Lois to herself. And Valerie, arranging ready-sliced bread and processed cheese for two, muttered to her four walls, when she was left alone with them, 'If she goes on being a condescending old ray of sunlight, I'll murder her.'

There was no time to expect that Lois knew her way to the kitchen. She was in it in a flash.

'I haven't really got around to decorating this yet. To tell the truth, I'm not all that struck on cooking.'

'Where do you keep the large stewpan?'

The large stewpan was traced to the cupboard under the stairs, where it held jam pots and spiders. But at some time it must have been used, for Lois had left it clean. The cooking knives were rusty, the wooden spoons had been used to stir paint. Moths and skewers were in every drawer she opened. Without a flutter of pity, of compunction, of remorse, of any of the feelings that should accompany an act of reparation as parsley and lemon accompany fried plaice or redcurrant jelly jugged hare, Lois searched, and cleaned, and sharpened, and by quarter to three the oxtail was in the large stewpan, together with the garlic, carrots, bay leaves, peppercorns and celery.

'What about the mushrooms?' Valerie inquired. She had rubbed the mushrooms and did not intend to see them slighted.

'They go in later on.'

'Well, as you seem to be managing all right, perhaps I'll . . .'

'Yes, do.'

One of the things Fenton particularly liked about Valerie was her habit of awaiting him. A man likes to be awaited. At the end of a dull day's architecture, to find a wife quietly sitting, undistracted by any form of employment, not even reading a book, but just sitting and waiting and ready to look pleased is very agreeable. Today he happened to be forty minutes later than usual, a conversation with a man called Renshaw having delayed him. His expectations were forty minutes livelier, and as he closed the garage and walked towards his door he said to himself that there was really quite a dash of the Oriental in him. The discovery of this dash – he had not been aware of it till Valerie – had even reconciled him to the prospect of baked beans or scrambled eggs on cold toast, if such was the price of being awaited. Besides, he always had a good substantial lunch at the Red Lion. But today Valerie was awaiting him amid a most exhilarating smell of cooking. It would be gross to comment on it immediately: to mulct her of the caresses of reunion, to fob off her proper desire to hear what he had been doing all day. And though she did not comment on his unpunctuality, he was at pains to tell her of his unforeseen encounter with Renshaw – not the Renshaw who skated and had been instrumental in bringing them together but his cousin E. B. Renshaw; to recount what E. B. Renshaw had said and to give a brief account of his character, career and accomplishments as a slow bowler. Only then did he say, 'No need to ask what you've been doing. What a wonderful smell! What is it?'

'Oxtail.'

'Of course! Oxtail. I thought I knew it.'

'Do you like oxtail?'

'Immensely – when it's not out of the tin. I can smell that this isn't.'

'Oh, no!'

He sniffed again. Lois had added the mushrooms and the anchovies and was now administering claret.

'Delicious! What's in it?'

'All sots of things. Button mushrooms.'

Her smile struck him as secretive – no wonder, with this talent up her sleeve. And all performed so casually, too, so unob-trusively; for there she sat, reposeful, not a hair out of place, none of the usual cook's airs of flurry and inattention, not a single 'Just wait one moment' while he was relating his day and the meeting with E. B. Renshaw.

'When will it be ready?' he said with ardour.

'Not just yet. Do you like my nail varnish? It's new. I bought it today.'

'Very pretty. Do you think you ought to go and stir it?'

'Oh no! She'll do all that.'

'She?' Had Valerie gone and got a cook? A cook from whom such odours proceeded would demand enormous wages, yet might almost be worth it. 'She? What she?'

'Your other wife. She's in there. She's been doing it all the afternoon.'

'Do you mean Lois?'

'Of course I mean Lois. You haven't any other wives, have you?'

This pertness when referring to his previous marriage was cus-tomary, and did not altogether displease. Now he didn't even notice it. He had a situation to grapple with, and the better to do so removed part of it off his knee.

'How did this happen?'

'We met at the bank – she'd gone there for some tea pot or other. We couldn't sit there glaring at each other, so we began to talk.'

About him, of course. What confidences had been exchanged? What invidious –

'She told me you liked cold veal.'

A total misrepresentation. Lois had always been malicious, seizing on some casually expressed liking to throw in his teeth. 'What else did she say?'

'Nothing much. I had to do most of the talking. And before I knew where I was, she was wanting to come and cook you an oxtail. I couldn't very well stop her, could I? Of course I paid for it. The worst of it is, she was in such a rush to get here that I hadn't a chance to ask Strumpshaw about that sixpence, or to get the waistcoat buttons or the right liver salts or your China tea. She isn't what I'd call considerate.'

'I shall have to go and see her.'

He would have to open the kitchen door, take the full assault of that witching smell, see Lois cooking as of old – an unassimilable answer to prayer. For of course she mustn't come again, she mustn't go on doing this sort of thing; nor was he a man to be won back by fleshpots. Yet he knew himself moved. Poor Lois, making her way back almost like an animal, forgetting her jealousy, her prejudice, all the awful things she had said at the time of the divorce, trampling on convention and *amour-propre*, just to cook him a favourite dish. What had impelled her to do this? Remorse, loneliness, an instinctive longing to foster and nourish? For many years her feeling for him had been almost wholly maternal – which made her insistence on the divorce even more uncalled-for. What had set it off? Seeing the tea pot, perhaps. They had both been fond of the tea pot. It was Georgian.

Or was it all a deliberate scheme to lure him back?

He sprang to his feet, straightened his waistcoat, left the sitting-room, entered the kitchen. It was empty. She had gone. Tied to the handle of the stewpan was a visiting card, on the back of which she had written: 'This will be ready by seven. It should simmer till then. *Don't let it boil.*'

THE WICKED
STEPMOTHER'S LAMENT

◆

Sara Maitland

The wife of a rich man fell sick and, as she felt that her end was drawing near, she called her only daughter to her bedside and said, 'Dear child, be good and pious, and then the good God will always protect you, and I will look down from heaven and be near you.' Thereupon she closed her eyes and departed. Every day the maiden went out to her mother's grave and wept, and she remained pious and good. When winter came the snow spread a white sheet over the grave and by the time the spring sun had drawn it off again the man had taken another wife . . .

Now began a bad time for the poor step-child . . . They took her pretty clothes away, put an old grey bedgown on her and gave her wooden shoes . . . She had to do hard work from morning to night, get up before daybreak, carry water, light fires, cook and wash . . . In the evening when she had worked until she was weary she had no bed to go to but had to sleep by the hearth in the cinders. And as on that account she always looked dusty and dirty, they called her Cinderella.

You know the rest I expect. Almost everyone does.

I'm not exactly looking for self-justification. There's this thing going on at the moment where women tell all the old stories again and turn them inside-out and back-to-front – so the characters you always thought were the goodies turn out to be the baddies, and vice versa, and a whole lot of guilt is laid to rest: or that at least is the theory. I'm not sure myself that the guilt isn't just passed on to the next person, *in tacta*, so to speak. Certainly I want to carry and cope with my own guilt, because I want to carry and cope with my own virtue and I really don't see that you can have one without the other. Anyway, it would be hard to find a version of this story where I would come out a shiny new-style heroine: no true version, anyway. All I want to say is that it's more complicated, more compex, than it's told, and the reasons why it's told the way it is are complex too.

But I'm not willing to be a victim. I was not innocent, and I have grown out of innocence now and even out of wanting to be thought innocent. Living is a harsh business, as no one warned us when we were young and carefree under the apple bough, and I feel the weight of that ancient harshness and I want to embrace it, and not opt for some washed-out aseptic, hand-wringing, Disneyland garbage. (Though come to think of it he went none-too-easy on stepmothers, did he? Snow White's scared the socks off me the first time I saw the film – and partly of course because I recognised myself. But I digress.)

Look. It was like this. Or rather it was more like this, or parts of it were like this, or this is one part of it.

She was dead pretty in a Pears soap sort of way, and, honestly, terribly sweet and good. At first all I wanted her to do was concentrate. Concentration is the key to power. You have to concentrate on what is real. Concentration is not good or bad necessarily, but it is powerful. Enough power to change the world, that's all I wanted. (I was younger then, of course; but actually they're starving and killing whales and forests and each other out there; shutting your eyes and pretending they're not doesn't change anything. It does matter.) And what she was not was powerful. She wouldn't look out for herself. She was so sweet and so hopeful; so full of faith and forgiveness and love. You have to touch anger somewhere, rage even; you have to spit and roar and bite and scream and know it before you can be safe. And she never bloody would.

When I first married her father I thought she was so lovely, so good and so sad. And so like her mother. I knew her mother very well, you see; we grew up together. I loved her mother. Really. With so much hope and fondness and awareness of her worth. But – and I don't know how to explain this without sounding like an embittered old bitch which I probably am – she was too good. Too giving. She gave herself away, indiscriminately. She didn't even give herself as a precious gift. She gave herself away as though she wasn't worth hanging on to. Generous to a fault, they said, when she was young, but no one acted as though it were a fault, so she never learned. 'Free with Kellogg's cornflakes' was her motto. She equated loving with suffering, I thought at one time, but that wasn't right, it was worse, she equated loving with being; as though she did not exist unless she was denying her existence. I mean, he was not a bad bloke, her husband, indeed I'm married to him myself, and I like him and we have good times together, but he wasn't worth it – no one is – not what she gave him, which was her whole self with no price tag on.

And it was just the same with that child. Yes, yes, one can understand: she had difficulty getting pregnant actually, she had difficulties carrying those babies to term too. Even I can guess how that might hurt. But her little girl was her great reward for suffering, and at the same time was also her handle on a whole new world of self-giving. And yes, of course she looked so lovely, who could have resisted her, propped up in her bed with that tiny lovely child sucking, sucking, sucking? The mother who denied her little one nothing, the good mother, the one we all longed for, pouring herself out into the child. Well, I'll tell you, I've done it too, it is hell caring for a tiny daughter, I know. Everything, everything drags you into hell: the fact that you love and desire her, the fact that she's so needy and vulnerable, the fact that she never leaves you alone until your dreams are smashed in little piles and shabby with neglect, the fact that pleasure and guilt come so precisely together, as so seldom happens, working towards the same end and sucking your very selfhood out of you. It is a peril-ous time for a woman, that nursing of a daughter, and you can only survive it if you cling to yourself with a fierce and passionate love, *and* you back that up with a trained and militant lust for justice *and* you scream at the people around you to meet your needs and desires *and* you do not let them off, *and* when all is said and done you sit back and laugh at yourself with a well-timed and not unmalicious irony. Well, she could not, of course she could not, so she did not survive. She was never angry, she never asked, she took resignation – that tragic so-called virtue – as a ninth-rate alternative to reality and never even realised she had been shortchanged.

So when I first married my husband I only meant to tease her a little, to rile her, to make her fight back. I couldn't bear it, that she was so like her mother and would go the same way. My girls were more like me, less agreeable to have about the house, but tough as old boots and capable of getting what they needed and not worrying too much about what they wanted or oughted, so to speak. I didn't have to worry about them. I just could not believe the sweetness of that little girl and her wide-eyed belief that I would be happy and love her if she would just deny herself and follow me. So of course I exploited her a bit, pushed and tested it, if you understand, because I couldn't believe it. Then I just wanted her to *see*, to see that life is not all sweetness and light, that people are not automatically to be trusted, that fairy godmothers are unreliable and damned thin on the ground, and that even the most silvery of princes soon goes out hunting and fighting and drinking and whoring, and doesn't give one tuppenny-ha'penny curse more for you than you give for yourself. Well, she could have looked at her father and known. He hardly proved himself to be the great romantic lover of all time, even at an age when that would have been appropriate, never mind later. He had after all replaced darling Mummy with me, and pretty damned quick too, and so long as he was getting his end off and his supper on the table he wasn't going to exert himself on her behalf, as I pointed out to her, by no means kindly.

(And, I should like to add, I still don't understand about that. I couldn't believe how little the bastard finally cared when it came to the point. Perhaps he was bored to tears by goodness, perhaps he was too lazy. He was a sentimental old fart about her, of course, his eyes could fill with nostalgic tears every time he looked at her and thought of her dead mother; but he never *did* anything; or even asked me to stop doing anything. She never asked, and he never had eyes to see, or energy or . . . God knows what went on in his head about her and as far as I'm concerned God's welcome. She loved him and trusted him and served him and he never even bloody noticed. Which sort of makes my point actually because he would never treat me like that, and yet he and I get on very well now; like each other and have good times in bed and out of it. Of course I'd never have let him tell me how to behave, but he might have tried, at least just once.)

Anyway, no, she would not see. She would not blame her father. She would not blame her mother, not even for dying, which is the ultimate outrage from someone you love. And she would not blame me. She just smiled and accepted, smiled and invented castles in the air to which someone, though never herself, would come and take her one day, smiled and loved me. No matter what I did to her, she just smiled.

So, yes, in the end I was cruel. I don't know how to explain it and I do not attempt to justify it. Her *wetness* infuriated me. I could not shake her goodwill, her hopefulness, her capacity to love and love and love such a pointless and even dangerous object. I could not make her hate me. Not even for a moment. I could not make her hate me. And I cannot explain what that frustration did to me. I hated her insane dog-like devotion where it was so undeserved. She treated me as her mother had treated him. I think I hated her stupidity most of all. I can hear myself almost blaming her for my belly-deep madness; I don't want to do that; I don't want to get into blaming the victim and she was my victim. I was older than her, and stronger than her, and had more power than her; and there was no excuse. No excuse, I thought the first time I ever hit her, but there was an excuse and it was my wild need, and it escalated.

So in the end – and yes I have examined all the motives and

reasons why one woman should be cruel to another and I do not find them explanatory – so in the end I was cruel to her. I goaded and humiliated and pushed and bullied her. I used all my powers, my superior strength, my superior age, my superior intelligence, against her. I beat her, in the end, systematically and severely; but more than that I used her and worked her and denied her pleasures and gave her pain. I violated her space, her dignity, her integrity, her privacy, even her humanity and perhaps her physical safety. There was an insane urge in me, not simply to hurt her, but to have her admit that I had hurt her. I would lie awake at night appalled, and scald myself with contempt, with anger and with self-disgust, but I had only to see her in the morning for my temper to rise and I would start again, start again at her with an unreasonable savagery that seemed to upset me more than it upset her. Picking, picking and pecking, endlessly. She tried my patience as no one else had ever done and finally I gave up the struggle and threw it away and entered into the horrible game with all my considerable capacity for concentration.

And nothing worked. I could not make her angry. I could not make her hate me. I could not stop her loving me with a depth and a generosity and a forgivingness that were the final blow. Nothing moved her to more than a simper. Nothing penetrated the fantasies and daydreams with which her head was stuffed so full I'm surprised she didn't slur her consonants. She was locked into perpetual passivity and gratitude and love. Even when she was beaten she covered her bruises to protect me; even when she was hungry she would not take food from my cupboards to feed herself; even when I mocked her she smiled at me tenderly.

All I wanted was for her to grow up, to grow up and realise that life was not a bed of roses and that she had to take some responsibility for her own life, to take some action on her own behalf, instead of waiting and waiting and waiting for something or someone to come shining out of the dark and force safety on her as I forced pain. What Someone? Another like her father who had done nothing, nothing whatever, to help her and never would? Another like him whom she could love generously and hopelessly and serve touchingly and givingly until weariness and pain killed her too. I couldn't understand it. Even when I beat her, even as I beat her, she loved me, she just loved and smiled and hoped and waited, daydreamed and night-dreamed, and waited and waited and waited. She was untouchable and infantile. I couldn't save her and I couldn't damage her. God knows, I tried.

And now of course it's just an ancient habit. It has lost its sharp edges, lost the passion in both of us to see it out in conflict, between dream and reality, between hope and cynicism. There is a great weariness in me, and I cannot summon up the fire of conviction. I do not concentrate any more, I do not have enough concentration, enough energy, enough power. Perhaps she has won, because she drained that out of me years and years ago. Sometimes I despair, which wastes still more concentration. We plod on together, because we always have. Sweetly she keeps at it, smile, smile, dream, hope, wait, love, forgive, smile, smile, bloody smile. Tiredly, I keep at it too: 'Sweep that grate.' 'Tidy your room.' 'Do your homework.' 'What can you see in that nerd?' 'Take out those damn earphones and pay attention.' 'Life doesn't come free, you have to work on it.' 'Wake up, hurry up, stop daydreaming, no you can't, yes you must, get a move on, don't be so stupid.' and 'You're not going to the ball, or party, or disco, or over your Nan's, dressed like *that*.'

She calls it nagging.

She calls me Mummy.

ALTERNATIVE
LOVE

ALMOST HUMAN

——— ◆ ———

Ruth Rendell

The Chief was stretched out on the settee, half-asleep. Monty sat opposite him, bolt upright in his chair. Neither of them moved as Dick helped himself to gin and water. They didn't care for strong drink, the Chief not even for the smell of it, though it wasn't his way to show his feelings. Monty would sometimes drink beer in the George Tavern with Dick. It was cigarette smoke that upset him, and now as he caught a whiff from Dick's Capstan, he sneezed.

'Bless you,' said Dick.

Better smoke the rest of it in the kitchen while he was getting their supper. It wasn't fair on Monty to start him coughing at his age, bring on his bronchitis maybe. There was nothing Dick wouldn't have done for Monty's comfort, but when he had taken the steak out of the fridge and gone once more into the sitting-room for his drink, it was the Chief he addressed. Monty was his friend and the best company in the world. You couldn't look on the Chief in that light, but more as a boss to be respected and deferred to.

'Hungry, Chief?' he said.

The Chief got off the settee and walked into the kitchen. Dick went after him. It was almost dark outside now but enough light remained to show Dick Monty's coat, the old check one, still hanging on the clothesline. Better take it in in case it rained in the night. Dick went out into the yard, hoping against hope old Tom, his next-door neighbour, wouldn't see the kitchen light and come out. Such hope was always vain. He'd got the first of the pegs out when he heard the door open and the cracked whining voice.

'Going to be a cold night.'

'Mmm,' said Dick.

'Shouldn't be surprised if there was to be a frost.'

Who cared? Dick saw the great angular shadow of the Chief appear in the rectangle of light. Good, that would fix him. Standing erect, as he now was against the fence, the Chief was a good head taller than old Tom, who backed away, grinning nervously.

'Come on, Chief,' said Dick. 'Suppertime.'

'Just like children, aren't they?' old Tom whined. 'Almost human. It's uncanny. Look at him. He understands every word you say.'

Dick didn't answer. He followed the Chief into the kitchen and slammed the door. Nothing angered him more than the way people thought they were paying compliments to animals by comparing them with people. As if the Chief and Monty weren't in every way, mentally, physically, morally, a hundred times better than any human being he'd ever known. Just like children – what a load of crap. Children wanting their supper would be crying, making a nuisance of themselves, getting under his feet. His dogs, patient, stoical, single-minded, sat still and silent, watching while he filled the earthenware bowls with steak and meal and vitamin supplement. And when the bowls were placed side by side on the floor, they moved towards them with placid dignity.

Dick watched them feed. Monty's appetite, at fourteen, was as good as ever, though he took longer about it than the Chief. His teeth weren't what they had been. When the old dog had cleared his plate he did what he'd always done ever since he was a pup, came over to Dick and laid his grey muzzle in the palm of the outstretched hand. Dick fondled his ears.

'Good old dog,' Dick said. He scorned the popular way of calling dogs boy. They weren't boys. Boys were dirty and smelly and noisy and uncontrolled. 'You're a cracker, you are. You're a fine old dog.'

The Chief behaved in a grander manner. Such signs of affection and gratitude would have been inconsistent with his pedigree and his dignified presence. Dick and Monty knew their place and they both stepped aside to allow the Chief to pass majestically through the doorway and resume his position on the settee. Dick pushed Monty's chair nearer to the radiator. Half-past six. He finished his gin.

'I have to go out now,' he said, 'but I'll be back by ten at the latest, so you get a bit of shut-eye and when I come back we'll all have a good walk. OK?'

Monty came to the front door with him. He always had and always would, though his hind legs were stiff with rheumatism. We all have to get old, Dick thought, I'll have to face up to it, I'm going to lose him this year or next . . . he knelt down by the door and did what he'd never done to a man, woman or child, performed that disgusting act which sickened him when he saw it done by human beings to human beings. Holding Monty's head in his hands, he pressed his lips to the wrinkled forehead. Monty wagged his tail and emitted little grunts of happiness. Dick closed the door and got his car out of the garage.

He drove it two or three hundred yards down the street to the phone box. For business he never used his own phone, but one or other of the call boxes between his house and the George Tavern. Five minutes to go and the bell inside it would begin to ring. Unless something went wrong again, of course. Unless, once more, things weren't working out the way she'd planned them. The stupid – what? Dick hated the habit of using the names of female animals – bitch, cow, mare – as insulting epithets for women. When he wanted to express his loathing for the sex he chose one of the succinct four-letter words or the five-letter one that was the worst he could think of – woman. He used it now, rolling it on his tongue. Stupid, bloody, greedy, God-damned *woman*!

When his watch showed nearly a quarter to seven, he went into the box. He only had to wait sixty seconds. The bell began to ring on the dot of a quarter to. Dick lifted the receiver and spoke the password that would tell her it was he and not some interfering busybody answering phones for the hell of it.

He'd never heard her voice before. It was nervous, upper-class, a thousand miles from any world in which he'd ever move. 'It's going to be all right tonight,' she said.

'About time.' All their previous transactions had been arranged through his contact and every plan had come to grief through a hold-up at her end. It was six weeks since he'd had the tip-off and the first instalment. 'Let's have it then.'

She cleared her throat. 'Listen. I don't want you to know anything about us – who we are, I mean. Agreed?'

As if he cared who they were or what dirty passions had brought her to this telephone, this conspiracy. But he said contemptuously:

'It'll be in the papers, won't it?'

Fear thinned her voice. 'You could blackmail me!'

'And you could blackmail me, come to that. It's a risk we have to take. Now get on with it, will you?'

'All right. He's not been well but he's better now and started taking his usual walk again. He'll leave this house at half-past eight and walk through the West Heath path towards the Finchley Road. You don't have to know why or where he's going. That's not your business.'

'I couldn't care less,' said Dick.

'It'll be best for you to wait in one of the lonelier bits of the path, as far from the houses as you can.'

'You can leave all that to me. I know the area. How'll I know it's him?'

'He's fifty, well-built, middle height, silver hair, small moustache. He won't be wearing a hat. He'll have on a black overcoat with a black fur collar over a grey tweed suit. He ought to get to the middle of the West Heath path by ten to nine.' The voice wavered slightly. 'It won't be too messy, will it? How will you do it?'

'D'you expect me to tell you that on the phone?'

'No, perhaps not. You've had the first thousand?'

'For six weeks,' said Dick.

'I couldn't help the delay. It wasn't my fault. You'll get the rest within a week, in the way you got the first . . .'

'Through the usual channel. Is that all? Is that all I have to know?'

'I think so,' she said. 'There's one other thing – no it doesn't matter.' She hesitated. 'You won't fail me, will you? Tonight's the last chance. If it doesn't happen tonight there's no point in its happening at all. The whole situation changes tomorrow and I shan't . . .'

'Goodbye,' said Dick, slamming down the receiver to cut short the voice that was growing hysterical. He didn't want to know any of the circumstances or be involved in her sick emotions. Bloody – *woman*. Not that he had any qualms. He'd have killed a hundred men for what she was paying him to kill one, and he was interested only in the money. What did it matter to him who he was or she was or why she wanted him out of the way? She might be his wife or his mistress. So what? Such relationships were alien to Dick and the thought of what they implied nauseated him, kissing, embracing, the filthy act they did like – no, not like animals. Animals were decent, decorous – like people. He spat into the corner of the kiosk and came out into the cold evening air.

As he drove up towards Hampstead, he thought of the money. It would be just enough to bring his accumulated savings to his target. For years, ever since he'd got Monty from the pet shop, he'd been working to this end. Confidence tricks, a couple of revenge killings, the odd beating up, casing places for robbery, they'd all been lucrative, and by living modestly – the dog's food was his biggest expense – he'd got nearly enough to buy the house he'd got his eye on. It was to be in Scotland, on the north-west coast and miles from a village, a granite croft with enough grounds round it for Monty and the Chief to run free all day. He liked to think of the way they'd look when they saw their own bit of moorland, their own rabbits to chase. He'd have sufficient left over to live on without working for the rest of his life, and maybe he'd get more animals, a horse perhaps, a couple of goats. But no more dogs while Monty was alive. That wouldn't be fair, and it seemed wrong, the height of treachery, to make plans for after Monty was dead . . . .

What there wouldn't be anywhere in the vicinity of his home were people. With luck he wouldn't hear a human voice from one month's end to another. The human race, its ugly face, would be excluded for ever. In those hills with Monty and the Chief he'd forget how for forty years they'd pressed around him with their cruelty and their baseness, his drunken savage father, his mother who'd cared only for men and having a good time. Then, later, the foster home, the reform school, the factory girls sniggering at his shyness and his pimply face, the employers who wouldn't take him because he had a record instead of an education. At last he'd have peace.

So he had to kill a man to get it? It wouldn't be the first time. He would kill him without passion or interest, as easily as the slaughterer kills the lamb and with as little mercy. A light blow to the head first, just enough to stun him – Dick wasn't worried about giving pain but about getting blood on his clothes – and then that decisive pressure just here, on the hyoid . . .

Fingering his own neck to site the spot, Dick parked the car and went into a pub for another small gin and water and a sandwich. The licensee's cat came and sat on his knee. Animals were drawn to him as by a magnet. They knew who their friends were. Pity really that the Chief had such a hatred of cats, otherwise he might have thought of adding a couple to his Scottish menagerie. Half-past seven. Dick always allowed himself plenty of time to do a job, take it slowly, that was the way. He put the cat gently on the floor.

By eight he'd driven up through Hampstead village, along Branch Hill by the Whitestone Pond, and parked the car in West Heath Road. A fine starry night, frosty too, like that old fool had said it would be. For a few minutes he sat in the car, turning over in his mind whether there was anything at all to connect him with the woman he'd spoken to. No, there was nothing. His contact was as reliable and trustworthy as any human being could be and the method of handing over the money was foolproof. As for associating him with the man he was going to kill – Dick knew well that the only safe murder is the murder of a complete stranger. Fortunately for him and his clients, he was a stranger to the whole world of men.

Better go up and look at the path now. He put the car in Templewood Avenue as near as he could to the point where the path left it to wind across West Heath. This was to be on the safe side. There weren't any real risks, but it was always as well to ensure a quick getaway. He strolled into the path. It led between the fences of gardens, a steep lane about five feet wide, with steps here and there where the incline grew too sharp. At the summit was a street lamp and another about fifty yards further on where the path became walled. Between the lights was a broader sandy space, dotted about with trees and shrubs. He'd do it here, Dick decided. He'd stand among the trees until the man appeared from the walled end, wait until he left the first pool of light but hadn't yet reached the second, and catch him in the darkest part. No roofs were visible, only the backs of vast gardens, jungly and black, and though the stars were bright, the moon was a thin white curve that gave little light.

Luckily, the bitter cold was keeping most people indoors. As soon as this thought had passed through his mind, he heard footsteps in the distance and his hand tightened on the padded metal bar in his pocket. But not yet, surely? Not at twenty-five past eight? Or had that fool woman made another of her mistakes? No, this was a girl. The click of her heels told him that, and then he saw her emerge into the lamplight. With a kind of sick curiosity he watched her approach, a tall slim girl yet with those nauseating repulsive bulges under her coat. She walked swiftly and nervously in this lonely place, looking with swift birdlike glances to the right and the left, her whole body deformed by the tight stupid clothes she wore and the stiff stance her heels gave her. No animal grace, no assurance. Dick would dearly have loved to give her a scare, jump on her and shake her till her teeth chattered, or chase her down those steps. But the idea of unnecessary contact with human flesh repelled him. Besides, she'd see his face and know him again when they found the body and raised the hue and cry. What would happen to Monty and the Chief if they caught him and put him inside? The thought made him shudder.

He let the girl pass by and settled down to wait again. A thin wrack of cloud passed across the stars. All to the good if it got a bit darker . . . Twenty to nine. He'd have left by now and be coming up to the Whitestone Pond.

Dick would have liked a cigarette but decided it wasn't worth the risk. The smell might linger and alert the man. Again he fingered the metal bar and the thin coil of picture cord. In a quarter of an hour, with luck, it would all be over. Then back home to the Chief and Monty for their evening walk, and tomorrow he'd get on to that house agent he'd seen advertising in the Sunday paper. Completely isolated, he'd say. It must be completely isolated and with plenty of land, maybe near the sea. The Chief would enjoy a swim, though he'd probably never had one in his life, spent as it had been in the dirty back street of a city. But all dogs could swim by the light of nature. Different from human beings who had to be taught like they had to be taught every damn-fool stupid thing they undertook . . .

Footsteps. Yes, it was time. Ten to nine, and evidently he was of a punctual habit. So much the worse for him. Dick kept perfectly still, staring at the dark hole between the walls, until the vague shape of his quarry appeared at the end of the tunnel. As the man came towards the light, he tensed, closing his hand over the bar. Her description had been precise. It was a stoutish figure that the lamp-light showed him, its gleam falling on thick silver hair and the glossy black fur of a coat collar. If Dick had ever felt the slightest doubt as to the ethics of what he was about to do, that sight would have dispelled it. Did scum like that ever pause to think of the sufferings of trapped animals, left to die in agony just to have their pelts stuck on some rich bastard's coat? Dick gathered saliva in his mouth and spat silently but viciously into the undergrowth.

The man advanced casually and confidently and the dark space received him. Dick stepped out from among the trees, raised his arm and struck. The man gave a grunt, not much louder than a hiccup, and fell heavily. There was no blood, not a spot. Bracing himself to withstand the disgust contact with a warm heavily fleshed body would bring, Dick thrust his arms under the sagging shoulders and dragged him under the lamp. He was unconscious and would be for five minutes – except that in five minutes or less he'd be dead.

Dick didn't waste time examining the face. He had no interest in it. He put his cosh back in his pocket and brought out the cord. A slip knot here, slide it round here, then a quick tightening of pressure on the hyoid . . .

A soft sound stayed him, the cord still slack in his hands. It wasn't a footstep he'd heard but a light padding. He turned sharply. Out of the tunnel, tail erect, nose to ground, came a hound dog, a black and tan and white basset. It was one of the handsomest dogs Dick had ever seen, but he didn't want to see it now. Christ, he thought, it'd be bound to come up to him. They always did.

And sure enough the hound hesitated as it left the darkness and entered the patch of light where Dick was. It lifted its head and advanced on him, waving its tail. Dick cursed fate, not the dog, and held out his hand.

'Good dog,' he whispered. 'You're a cracker. You're a fine dog, you are. But get out of it now, go off home.'

The hound resisted his hand with an aloof politeness and, bypassing him, thrust its nose against the unconscious man's face. Dick didn't like that much. The guy might wake up.

'Come on now,' he said, laying his hands firmly on the glossy tricolour coat. 'This is no place for you. You get on with your hunting or whatever.'

But the basset wouldn't go. Its tail trembled and it whined. It looked at Dick and back at the man and began to make those soft hound cries that are halfway between a whimper and a whistle. And then Dick loosened his hold on the thick warm pelt. A terrible feeling had come over him, dread coupled with nausea. He felt in the pocket of the black fur-collared coat and brought out what he was afraid to find there – a plaited leather dog leash.

That God-damned woman! Was that what she'd meant about one other thing but it didn't matter? That this guy would be coming along here because he was taking his dog for a walk? Didn't matter – Christ! It didn't matter the poor little devil seeing its owner murdered and then having to make its own way home across one of the busiest main roads out of London. Or maybe she'd thought he'd kill the dog too. The sheer inhumanity of it made his blood boil. He wanted to kick the man's face as he lay there, but didn't like to, couldn't somehow, with the dog looking on.

He wouldn't be done, though. His house in Scotland was waiting for him. He owed it to the Chief and Monty to get that house. All that money wasn't going to be given up just because she'd gone and got things wrong again. There were ways. Like putting the dog on the leash and taking him back across the road by the Whitestone Pond. He'd be safe then. And so by that time, thought Dick, would his owner who was already stirring and moaning. Or he could put him in the car. God knew, he was gentle enough, utterly trusting, not suspecting what Dick had done, was going to do . . . And then? Kill the man and take the dead man's dog home? Be seen with the dog in his car? That was a laugh. Tie him up to a lamp-post? He'd never in his life tied up a dog and he wasn't going to start now.

A cold despair took hold of him. He bore the dog no malice, felt for him no anger, nothing more than the helpless resignation of a father whose child has come into a room and interrupted his love-making. The child comes first – inevitably.

Slowly he put away the cord. He lifted the silver head roughly and the man groaned. There had been a hard metal object in the pocket where the leash was, a brandy flask. Dick uncapped it and poured some of the liquid down the man's throat. The hound watched, thumping its tail.

'Where – where am I? Wha – what happened?'

Dick didn't bother to answer him.

'I had a – a bang on the head. God, my head's sore. I was

mugged, was I?' He felt in his pocket and scrabbled with a wallet. 'Not touched, thank God. I'll – I'll try to sit up. God, that's better. Where's Bruce? Oh, there he is. Good boy, Bruce. I'm glad he's all right.'

'He's a fine dog,' Dick said remotely, and then, 'Come on, you'd better hang on to me. I've got a car.'

'You're most kind, most kind. What a blessing for me you came along when you did.'

Dick said nothing. He almost heaved when the man clung to his arm and leant on him. Bruce anchored to his leash, they set off down the steps to the car. It was a relief to be free of that touch, that solid weight that smelt of the sweat of terror. Dick got Bruce on to the back seat and stroked him, murmuring reassuring words.

The house he was directed to was a big one, almost a mansion on the East Heath. Lights blazed in its windows. Dick hauled the man out and propelled him up to the front door, leaving Bruce to follow. He rang the bell and a uniformed maid answered it. Behind her, in the hall, stood a tall young woman in evening dress.

She spoke the one word 'Father!' and her voice was sick with dismay. But it was the same voice. He recognised it just as she recognised his when, turning away from the glimpse of wealth in that hall, he said, 'I'll be off now.'

Their eyes met. Her face was chalk-white, made distorted and ugly by the destruction of her hopes. She let her father take her arm and then she snapped, 'What happened?'

'I was mugged, dear, but I'm all right now. This gentleman happened to come along at the opportune moment. I haven't thanked him properly yet.' He put out his hand to Dick. 'You must come in. You must let us have your name. No, I insist. You probably saved my life. I could have died of exposure out there.'

'Not you,' said Dick. 'Not with that dog of yours.'

'A lot of use he was! Not much of a bodyguard, are you, Bruce?'

Dick bent down and patted the dog. He shook off the detaining hand and said as he turned away, 'You'll never know how much use he was.'

He got into the car without looking back. In the mirror, as he drove away, he saw the woman retreat into the house while her father stood dizzily on the path, making absurd gestures of gratitude after his rescuer.

Dick got home by a quarter to ten. Monty was waiting for him in the hall, but the Chief was still in the sitting-room on the settee. Dick put on their leashes and his best coat on Monty and opened the front door.

'Time for a beer before the pub closes, Mont,' he said, 'and then we'll go on the common.' He and the dogs sniffed the diesel-laden air and Monty sneezed. 'Bless you,' said Dick. 'Lousy hole, this, isn't it? It's a bloody shame but you're going to have to wait a bit longer for our place in Scotland.'

Slowly, because Monty couldn't make it fast any more, the three of them walked up towards the George Tavern.

THE QUALITY
OF MERCY

———— ◆ ————

Patricia Ferguson

One day last August I was standing in a queue at the building society waiting to make a withdrawal when something very strange happened to me.

It was a sunny day. I'd got up very late and the sky had hurt my eyes when I'd first closed the front door behind me. I felt a bit frowsy in the building society, in that sweetish smell of new nylon carpeting. Everything looked very clean there and the people on either side of the counter were speaking across it in quiet subdued voices, as if they were in church.

I was tired because I'd slept so long. I took my building society book out and looked at the dots that made up the numbers and after a little while the strange thing happened.

For an instant it seemed that there was a great dim noise everywhere, and a sudden change in the light; that the ground had sighed and lolled over under my feet.

For an instant I heard the noise, saw the flickering, felt movement: perhaps through that same hopeful device that tries to protect you from your alarm clock by altering your dreams.

After the instant I understood that all the disturbance was a feeling, in me, because I had stopped believing in things. Everything around me, the building society office and its clean new smell, the other people in the queue, myself, my clothes, my handbag and Woolwich booklet, had all stopped being real, because something in me, some sentinel left in charge to concentrate on making things look real and whole had momentarily stopped thinking, passed out, or gone AWOL.

It was blankness and emptiness that I felt: the great abnormal dark that children fear.

None of this lasted very long. My trembling legs and bucketing heart were real enough, I noted them and felt real again. I looked round and saw that no one was staring at me: whatever had happened had passed unnoticed. Presently it was my turn at the counter and I stepped up and got the money out all right, and then I went outside.

The light was still dazzling. I walked up and down the street looking at the market stalls there, the little girls' frilly dresses and the bras pegged up on strings. I thought of the poor mad people I had looked after on the psychiatric ward, who had perhaps felt that stunning horror and its physical translation all the time, not just for a few seconds as I had but all the time, all the time. I saw how impossible everything would seem if it had to be played against such a backdrop: you wouldn't be able to do anything properly, sleep or work or wash your hair or go out for a drink, you just wouldn't be able to do anything.

I found a fruit stall and bought myself a bunch of rather expensive grapes. It occurred to me as I was handing over the money that I should get myself a steady job, no more short-term agency stuff or unemployment, but a proper responsible job where I'd get to know where everything was kept, and where I'd learn everyone's names and make sure they knew mine. I felt a lot better after deciding on this and caught a bus home considering where and what.

I had an interview at the end of the following week. It was at a hospital I'd done some agency at so I knew it fairly well. It was one of the old places, the sort with turrets, built as if to withstand a lengthy siege, and topped off here and there with bits of curly wrought iron, good tethering places, I'd more than once imagined, for transatlantic airships or hot-air balloons. There was a tiled corridor about a mile long too, on the ground floor: entering at one end you couldn't see the other, all the lines converged completely like an exercise in perspective.

I relaxed as soon as I saw the woman who was to interview me; I knew the job was mine. I'd met her once before when I was doing agency. She'd signed one of my timesheets and told me how nice it was, Staff, to see an agency nurse for once in a proper starched linen cap, and an apron. She'd batted her old eyelids and smiled at me as she spoke.

I'd felt rather a fraud; it was true I was immaculately turned out but I had my own obscure reasons for this. At home I was always washing and ironing things, I used to iron sheets and underwear and teatowels and starch my nursing aprons using old-fashioned hot-water starch. It all took ages but then I had little else to do. I used to put a record on and sing along as I ironed. I was partly aware that all this slavish domesticity wasn't quite natural to me but I didn't want to look into the whole thing too far. So I felt mildly guilty on being complimented about it.

She'd seemed a wistful old thing though, sitting there in her admin office behind a desk, but still wearing the ward nurse's jingling composite breastplate of pens and scissors and shiny hospital badges, so I didn't just smile back, I made a little speech about how much I regretted the passing of the old image, and that I thought nurses had somehow lost some public respect when they'd taken to zip fasteners and throwaway plastic aprons and paper caps.

I'd been sure this would be exactly what she wanted to hear and I'd been right, she'd just lapped it up, and finished by telling me that she hoped I'd work there again as she handed the timesheet back. I was pleased with her too: just because of her age she'd reminded me of some of the old-school ward sisters I'd known when I was doing my training, the sort who'd reduced me to public tears more than once. And yet here she was now just eating out of my hand. I thought, I wish I'd known then that all you have to do is sound confident and agree with them; still, it was pleasant enough to know it now, and we'd parted almost affectionately, having cheered one another up, if for all the wrong reasons.

Today for the interview she wore a name-badge: E. V. Holloway, I read, squinting at it over the desk. She remembered me; I knew she wanted to take me on, but I could see that all my qualifications made her a little uneasy, suspicious even.

'So you ah took a ah degree in English, Miss Markham?' She was holding the certificate in front of her as she asked.

'And *then* you went into nursing?' She looked down, it seemed doubtfully, at my other documents, GNC, hospital, midwifery certificate, the written references.

No, the whole lot's a forgery, I thought, but mildly. I could see one of the mad Rapunzel towers outside through her office window, and quickly sketched in the looming airship, the old R101, with a basketful of champagne-guzzling sophisticates waving from underneath. I smiled at Miss Holloway.

She was talking about the ward, Mercy ward, my ward: a male medico-geriatric ward, 'A little run down due to ah present ah circumstances – '

I knew exactly how run down the place could be, having worked briefly on its sister-ward, Patience, across the corridor. Besides hospitals usually promote their own, if their own stick around long enough: to advertise the post meant that staff turnover rates must be high. I smiled again and told Miss Holloway that I was especially looking for a challenging job with lots of responsibility, and how unsatisfying agency work had been in both these respects.

She liked this speech too and after a few more on similar lines she stood up and congratulated me and said that she wanted to welcome me aboard; and she called me Sister Mercy.

That was a real old-school touch; not many ward sisters are known by the ward's name these days. You can see why it's died out, when modern wards are called units, and numbered. You couldn't call someone Sister E5, or Sister unit 53. Besides the old way had meaning: it was for the old-school sisters, those starched pre-War dragons, professional maidens married to the job, whose wards were life itself.

Sister Mercy. It sounded rather a joke but still it seemed like safety for someone prone to mad horrors in building societies: better to live for a ward than get put away in one.

'Thank you so much, Miss Holloway,' I said, brightly, 'I shall do my very best.' I meant it, too, of course.

It didn't take me long to settle in. The work and the layout were all so familiar, I'd worked in a dozen similar places. Though none of them had been mine, as Mercy was. I was in charge of it all: the dingy ramshackle ward itself; the other nurses, short-term agency staff and slightly longer-term students; and the patients.

Mercy was a Nightingale ward, with one side-room partitioned in wood and glass like a greenhouse for isolation cases, a high ceiling, and smooth noisy wooden floors. At one end were my office, the treatment room, and the linen cupboard, this last a stifling walk-in affair, crammed from floor to ceiling with redundant foam pillows, knitted-square blankets all felted into some strange bendy substance like rubbery cardboard, never quite enough smooth white linen, and hardly ever enough pyjama bottoms. Tops we had: no bottoms. The bed-fast were often respectable only from the waist up, on Mercy.

At the far end of the ward stood the sluice-room and the bath-room. Two little hand basins had been plumbed into the walls in the early 1960s; they had sprinkler taps so feeble that no one ever tried to use them more than once. Only one sink, in the sluice, was large enough to take a bowl; the bedpan washer leaked, and broke down about once a month, giving warning before each bout of inertia by lavishly flooding the sluice-room floor; all three commodes had brakes so long defunct that the hinges were black with furry grime; and there was one bath. Twenty-seven patients: one bath.

The beds were all different makes and designs, almost a lesson in design evolution, from the heavy cage-like monster on fixed high legs, which could be tilted only by lifting it onto enormous splintery wooden blocks, to the state-of-the-art fixture with various foot pedals and levers to raise, lower, tilt, or sit up the patient, gently and effortlessly, as we pleased. We had two state-of-the-art-ers, and twenty-five assorted ancestors.

Many of the beds had little plaques set into the wall above the head, to commemorate an endowing charity or benefactor: THE

HORACE SPROAT BED or THIS BED DONATED BY THE AMERSHAM ROYAL EXCHANGE AMATEUR OPERATIC SOCIETY 1924 or IN MEMORY OF LADY CONSTANCE MILHAVEN 1919 and so on.

I felt a strong duty to read all these plaques whenever I got close enough, in the same way that you sometimes find yourself carefully reading gravestones in cemeteries; as if there's a sort of immortality attached to leaving names in print or stone, but only if the living take the trouble to read them. There was Lady Constance Milhaven relying on me to carry out my end of the bargain; she wore droopy muslins to curtsey in. And Horace Sproat, who had met his end at the Somme, stood coldly to attention, but with sad Wilfred Owen eyes, while the entire chorus of the Amersham Royal Exchange Amateur Operatic Society, a costumed bunch of flushed immortals, held hands to take their final final curtain, all courtesy of me: so I obliged. Presently I knew all the plaques off by heart. It was my ward.

The staff were harder to learn: they came and went so fast. Once early on I arrived unexpectedly to find my two current students clutching illicit mugs of tea in my office. They leapt to their feet, twin blushes; appalled guilt made them look almost identical, two schoolgirls caught smoking behind the bicycle sheds. I remember how I felt, seeing them, that delicious rush of power: I thought how pleasant it would be to be kind to them, how eagerly they would respond. Besides they worked so hard, twenty-seven patients, one bath.

Or rather, as I used to report clearly to Miss Holloway every month at the Sisters' Meeting, twenty-seven patients, one bath, and no hoist.

A hoist is a little crane, a nice easily manoeuvrable little crane with a seat, for lifting helpless people, swinging them up and over the rim of the bath, and gently lowering them into the water. It's for gerries or new amputees or old strokes, that sort. They usually enjoy it, too, there's a slight element of the funfair about it, swinging through the air on a neat little chair; and one slim nurse can bath a wardful of limp sixteen-stoners without even holding her breath.

Of course it was indefensible that Mercy ward should have twenty-seven patients, and one bath, and no hoist. No one was arguing about it, not even the Health Authority.

'But I'm afraid progress has to be piecemeal under the ah under the ah present circumstances,' Holloway would say every month.

Perhaps it was partly to annoy her that I went on trying. I was always in the minutes:

New Business

1. Sister Markham (Mercy) asked that urgent funding be sought for the purchase of a patient-lifting device for Mercy ward. Miss Holloway undertook to re-state the case for this requisition to the appropriate administrative officers.

But in the previous few weeks Miss Holloway had found me out; caught me swearing in my office and seen me lighting a cigarette in the canteen; she knew I'd thrown out that hallowed geriatric-ward institution, the bath book; she knew I sometimes let my old boys lie in bed past nine in the morning if they wanted to; she knew I was friendly with the equally raffish Sister Patience across the corridor. She also knew I had rather pretty legs, which I liked to cross, sighingly, in front of her while she was monthly Undertaking to Re-state: an underhand weapon, I knew, so small that she could hardly be aware of where the sting came from, but still it was the only sting I could needle her with. I knew she'd never give me that damn hoist. I'd found her out too.

My predecessor on Mercy ward hadn't prised a hoist out of her either.

'They didn't have hoists in her day,' said Phyllis Morgan on Patience ward one late shift after another Sisters' Meeting, 'so she doesn't see why you should need one now.'

'They didn't have antibiotics either,' I said.

'Or hot water.'

'Or bandages. They had to rip up their petticoats.'

'They had a vocation.'

'They had Miss Nightingale. How *was* Scutari?'

'Magnificent,' said Phyllis happily, 'but it wasn't war. Want a refill?' She was holding the tea pot.

'No thanks. I've got to get back.' I looked out of the window. The view from Phyllis's office was the rear view of mine: crossing the corridor was like walking through a mirror. It was a dark afternoon, I saw the Rapunzel turrets looming unlit from behind.

'And my sodding bedpan-washer's on the blink again,' I said, standing up and brushing the crumbs off my skirt.

'I don't know,' said Phyllis. 'Why do we stick it?'

'God knows.'

Of course I knew too. I hadn't forgotten what unreality had felt like, I knew why I needed the job. But I hadn't expected it to work quite so well; I had forgotten what nursing can be. It was true that Mercy ward had no hoist and one bath, but it also had the twenty-seven patients. Twenty-seven strangers, all old: the easiest people in the world to please.

I wanted to be needed, I wanted to be recognised. I tried to learn my patients, as far as I could. I tried to be whatever they wanted me to be.

Once in the October of that year, listening to the radio while I did some ironing (I was doing slightly less ironing by then, it had occurred to me that ironing underwear was rather a point-less thing to do), I heard a programme all about prostitution, vox pop stuff with lots of voices, women's voices. It had ended with someone singing, rather sadly, in time to her own street-walking stilettos:

> If you want to end your cares
> Come along and climb my stairs,
> Love for Sale.

I went on ironing my pillow-case, a tricky flounced thing, and thought that the song had got it wrong, that prostitutes offered sex for sale; it was nurses who sold love. It made me smile to myself, the thought of selling my love. I turned the pillow-case over. Why not sell love, if you couldn't find anyone to give it to; no one was willing to *take* it, anyway.

And it was easy to be tender with my old men. Age had made all of them weak and gentle. It took old Fred Sawby fifteen laborious and vituperative minutes to push his Zimmer frame out to the bathroom. Had he ever struck his wife or bullied his children? They were safe from him now. Had he really fed a machine-gun at the Somme? He couldn't hold a teacup now.

Because they were so old, my old men, they told me stories of their youth. I saw the young men they had been while I tended the great-grandfathers they had become, as if there had been no years in between, no gradual decline, but a sudden step from that world to this. They all remembered a war, old men always have a war to remember. It was the Great War for the oldest ones. They talked history, they remembered events so farcically distant, it seemed to me, that it might as well have been the Trojan wars they'd fought in, or Agincourt.

They remembered being visited in the trenches by Horatio Bottomley, they harboured hatred still for Churchill, for Gallipoli; had landed at Archangel, to destroy Lenin; had suffered frostbite, fighting with the Russian Imperial Army in 1915. And there they lay, each under his little plaque, survivors from another world, talking to me as if they knew me, turning on me eyes that had seen the ships go down off Scapa Flow.

You had to feel privileged, you had to feel reverence, talking to such old age. And I tried to be whatever they wanted in return: respectful and grave, or, if they were still sprung with some masculine cheek, the ghostly shade of their old male force, flirtatious and teasing, to help pretend that the shade still had substance. And yet they weren't relations, but clients: I didn't have to hear the stories over and over again, and I was free at the end of my eight-hour shift.

At night when the yellow lights were lit and shining back from each high window, and the night nurses were settled at the centre desk with their crocheting and *Nursing Mirrors*, I'd stand at the door with my apron folded over my arm and bid all my old men a goodnight.

'Goodnight, gentlemen!'

And those that could reply did so: 'Goodnight, Sister,' or

'Night-night, lovey,' or 'Goodbye, gorgeous!' as they pleased.

It was that differing chorus that made me feel I'd perfected an art.

So it was a rhetorical question Phyllis had been asking me that evening after the Sisters' Meeting: Phyllis loved her old ladies, who remembered the details of special dresses, antique childbirth, scrubbing floors by candlelight, or eating turbot at Simpson's in 1912.

'I don't know. Why do we stick it?'

'God knows.'

But Phyllis knew too, and so did I. Love for sale: price, a small wage, and sanity. Love for sale.

It was at the following Sisters' Meeting, in November, that Holloway told me Mercy ward was to be closed, initially for Christmas, and for an indefinite period afterwards.

'But not, we of course hope, for more than a few weeks,' she went on. Her powdery old face had gone quite scarlet as she spoke. I felt simply panicky, my eyes filled. I looked down and stared hard at her shapeless ankles.

'What about the patients?' asked Phyllis fiercely. 'What about them?'

They were to be split up, disbanded, discharged early, sent all over the hospital to wherever a bed could be found. Some of them were to go to Patience ward, when enough Patience ward old ladies had been shunted elsewhere.

'I'm sure the old folk will enjoy their ah get-together during the festive season,' said Holloway.

I looked up to meet Phyllis's eyes at this. She couldn't believe it either.

'I'm afraid I can't accept that, I can't accept that at all,' she said rapidly. Her voice was trembling with rage. I wished I could feel angry too, instead of just beaten.

'I'm afraid there's no question of acceptance; or, or, of not accepting,' said Holloway, losing control a bit but still enjoying herself. She batted her eyelids. 'It's hardly my decision, Sister

Patience, I need hardly tell you that – '

'The old bitch, the old bastard, I could strangle her,' said Phyllis. We were sitting in the pub over the road after the shift had ended. 'Enjoy their get-together, I mean, did you *hear* that – ' she gulped at her lager. 'I felt like saying to her, I really nearly said it, You're an old virgin, you're nearly as old as they are, how'd *you* like some strange man in the next bed seeing *you* in your nightie and hearing *you* asking for a bedpan, how'd *you* fucking well like it? The cow.'

I put a finger out and traced a clear path down the frosted side of my glass. I was to be relief sister while Mercy was closed. Relief sister, sent all over the place. No one would know who I was. No one would know my name.

'I'll go crazy,' I said to my glass. 'I'll go crazy, being relief sister.'

'No you won't,' said Phyllis crossly. 'Don't be so wet.'

I put my hand over my eyes. 'It'll kill George. It'll kill him, shunting him about.' George was my present favourite. He was eighty-five, a fragile trembly brigadier, a rare officer among my old men. He'd had his best suit on to come into hospital, red braces to keep his baggy trousers up and cufflinks in his best blue shirt; the cuffs all frayed, and scorch-marks at the shoulder where he'd ironed it himself. He was in the Horace Sproat bed. He might have met Horace. He'd have been the elder.

'Shunting George about.'

I rubbed at my eyes and my fingers came away all black, I'd forgotten I'd put mascara on. I'd only just started wearing it again, so I'd forgotten it.

'I'll look after George,' said Phyllis, 'he'll be all right. Honest.'

I looked at her. I thought for a moment of telling her what had happened to me at the building society, but decided against it.

Phyllis drank some more lager, set her glass down.

'Anyway. Listen, are you coming on Saturday then? You should.'

'Sorry?'

'Saturday. You know. Me and Ben are having that little do. Come on. You said you'd come.'

'Oh, I don't know, I – '

'Oh, come on! I mean it was, how long, eighteen bloody months ago, I bet *he's* not stopping in moping, I mean, eighteen months, you've got to get someone new.'

'I don't want someone new.'

Phyllis picked her drink up, scowling.

'Not unless they're old age pensioners, right?'

'Oh come on, you know it's not like that – '

Phyllis leant back suddenly in her chair, crossing her legs so abruptly that one knee knocked the table, and our drinks shivered. I saw that she felt herself to be surrounded by hopeless inadequacy, Holloway's public, mine private. Did she then regard me as another workplace-problem, something to be discussed with her husband or mentioned in passing to her mother?

'I'm sorry I'm such a trial,' I said.

'Oh give over,' snapped Phyllis.

So we didn't part friends.

Closing the ward took a long time. There was more to do than I'd realised. But it wasn't nearly as awful as I'd thought it would be, partly because I'd convinced myself that we'd be re-opening soon and partly because I'd been given a nice long-term agency nurse, a young man, and he cheered me up. It made a change having a young man about the place. Besides, male nurses nearly always lighten a ward's atmosphere, help to dispel that faint sour odour of feminine self-sacrifice that still pervades much of nursing, plastic aprons and zip-fasteners or no. They're such practised flirts, gay or straight. They get more female attention than anyone outside nursing could possibly imagine, except perhaps doctors, and doctors aren't equals; they give orders, they don't make beds with you.

Being surrounded, swamped, overwhelmingly outnumbered by young women makes male nurses rather pleased with themselves, makes the dullest feel, and so perhaps become, more attractive. No wonder they reach the top so fast; it's women who promote them.

Mike was attractive to start with, as prettily androgynous as a teenybopper idol. I saw straightaway from his badges that he'd trained in the same hospital as I had, which is a bit like two old soldiers discovering they've been in the same regiment. We exchanged the usual names and reminiscences, though we had few in common, since he was so much younger than me: he looked about twenty, though he must've been older than that.

Still, discovering that we'd twice worked on the same wards made us feel like old friends. I suppose I tended to treat him almost as if he were another woman but he didn't seem to mind. When he had blond streaks put in his hair I said to him, 'Mike, your hair! It looks great!' in just the same voice I'd have used to Phyllis, if it had been Phyllis's new look.

She'd called me early in December, after nearly a week's silence.

'Hello. Sister Markham.'

'Hello, ratbag. How's the quality of Mercy?'

'Strained,' I answered, as usual. I was surprised at how relieved I felt. 'Phyllis, I missed you.'

'I bet. Come over for tea. If you're feeling sociable.'

She rang off. I went through the mirror at 3.30. We ate cream buns supplied by some old lady's relative and groused about Miss Holloway, it was all very satisfying.

'Your young Michael's a bit of all right, isn't he,' said Phyllis.

'He's very sweet,' I said. I lit a cigarette. Phyllis pulled a face at me. 'And he works hard too,' I said. It was lovely doing lifts with Mike. He'd had a good training like mine, he knew how to do a proper Australian lift; that afternoon we'd lifted frail George right up his bed without hurting him at all, Ooh, that's *much* better, George had said, smiling: sometimes nurses don't know how to lift properly, you end up hauling people about by hooking the crook of your elbow under their armpits, and that hurts them.

'I suppose he's got to be gay,' said Phyllis, 'looking like that. Is he?'

I laughed. 'How on earth should I know?'

'Well he wears earrings doesn't he. Don't know how he gets away with it, we couldn't even wear sleepers, let alone a bloke doing it – I mean, what does Holloway say?'

'She's all over him,' I said, realising that his was so. 'She makes eyes at him.'

Phyllis wrinkled her nose and giggled. 'Yuck. Horrible old bag.'

I felt confused at this: that Phyllis thought it suitable for me to see Mike's charm, but unsuitable, disgusting even, for Holloway to see it too, as if there were some line she'd crossed, of age, or possibility. When would I cross it myself, and would I know it when I had?

'How's the closing going?'

'Oh, we're getting there. Half empty already.' We were empty-ing all the cupboards too. I'd discovered one I'd never seen before, inside the linen cupboard, behind a box of plastic-covered foam pillows. It had taken me twenty minutes to find a key that fitted. I had to stand on a chair to reach it and I nearly fell off it once I'd got the cupboard open, out of sheer surprise, because it had been crammed full with boxes of chocolates, stacks of them, all different, some in pretty wrapping paper. There were two bottles as well, one of wine, the other of sherry. An earlier Sister Mercy had clearly followed the old policy of locking away gifts from patients and relatives for special occasions, usually for a Christmas glut. Perhaps she'd forgotten this hoard. Everyone else had. The chocolates were inedible, every single boxful, the sweets all white and shrunken with age.

I'd handed them down, box after box, to Mike, who'd stuck his head out of the linen-room and shouted Treasure trove! at my one remaining student, but there was nothing to share out after all. I put the bottles in my office cupboard, and thought that I'd give all my last old boys a little drink on their final day on Mercy, if their doctors didn't object.

I told Phyllis about the chocolates and she told me how she'd recently come across a battered old cardboard box stuffed darkly away on Patience, and opened it to find three large pieces of heavily boned and studded elastic labelled 'One-size surgical corsetry' and how, in a quiet moment, she and two students had buckled and hooked one another into these objects, though nearly helpless with laughter, and how, encased and tearful, one-sized surgical corsets straining over their aprons, they had looked up to discover a particularly stuffy old consultant standing pop-eyed at the office door.

I was still grinning when I got back to Mercy ward. Mike was sitting at the centre table, writing the kardex. The student, Janet, was playing cards with George and Terry Sullivan, who was technically young for Mercy but had drunk himself as old as George.

I sat down beside Mike.

'We could do the curtains when you've finished?' I asked.

'Yeah . . . all right.'

I looked at him, at the curve of his cheek and his long eyelashes, at his hand as he wrote. Had George's hands once looked like that? It seemed impossible that Mike might ever grow as old as George. I thought that if he did there wouldn't be a war for him to talk about, because if there was a war now there'd be no survivors to remember it. Perhaps there would be no war; perhaps there would be a new thing in the world, a whole set of old men who'd never been soldiers.

'Oh, something I meant to tell you, something you'll just love to hear,' said Mike suddenly, sitting back.

'Oh?'

'You did agency here, didn't you, did you ever work on A3?'

This was in the new wing, far along the mile of tiled corridor.

'A3?' I thought. 'No.'

'Aha. Well I did. I did two shifts there last month. It's ENT, kids mostly, or young adults getting tonsils, right?'

'Yes?'

'Yeah, it's all spanking new, all the sink units match, you know, everything works, and, I just remembered it today, *and*,' he grinned at me, '*and* they've got a hoist.'

'What? You're kidding.'

'Nope. They've got a beautiful new bathroom and they've got a hoist. Never used of course – '

'Isn't it just typical – '

'Yes, kids and young adults. So they get a hoist. Well, because it's all new, I suppose they think, well, get it all right to start with – '

'Oh, I can't believe it, the times I've asked – '

'Mm. I suppose they'll get here eventually, you know, work their way along the corridor up this end, do up this end as well.'

'But under the ah the ah present circumstances,' I said, batting my eyelids, 'it'll be sometime in the next five hundred years,' Mike finished. We smiled at one another.

'Are you upset about it closing, I mean, are you out of a job?'

'No, not really. I was upset at first. I've got used to it. I'll miss my old men though.'

'Yeah,' Mike nodded.

'When I started my training, what, ten years ago,' I said, 'I did a geriatric ward then, and all the old boys were Victorian, they were all, you know, nineteenth century. It was *all* the First World War they'd been in. They're dying out now, old people are nearly all Edwardians now.' It felt a little risky saying this, but Mike said, 'I like it when they talk about the war, all those things you read about. I suppose there'll be more Edwardians, 'cos more of them missed the war, they didn't get killed off like the Victorians, like Horace Sproat, poor old Horace.'

I felt very pleased with him. 'You read the plaque,' I said.

'Yeah, Horace Sproat. What a name, eh, Horace Sproat.'

'Fred Sawby was at the Somme.'

'I know. So was my great-grandad actually. He got gassed.'

'I suppose it seems romantic because it was so long ago?'

'Fred Sawby's not romantic.'

I giggled. Then I said: 'No; he didn't get killed. If he'd been killed he'd have been one of those white crosses, those poppies in November. He'd've been in all that poetry – '

'Half the seed of Europe, one by one,' said Mike, and I was so pleased I touched his arm with delight.

'Oh, I thought of Wilfred Owen when I saw Horace's plaque, poor Horace – '

We talked about poetry we remembered while we unhooked

the heavy blue curtains round the empty beds and folded them up for cleaning. The ward looked even emptier without them.

Then it was suppertime. Messages about our depletion hadn't reached the kitchen yet, they were still sending us enough food for twenty-seven, tonight a huge Dickensian steak-and-kidney pie – you don't get individually wrapped plastic trays in hospitals with mad Rapunzel towers on. There are occasional advantages, you understand. The pie looked lovely, I cut everyone huge wedges and there was still enough for Janet and Mike and me. Janet went to the canteen anyway to meet a friend of hers who was undergoing an extremely complicated personal crisis, according to Janet's lurid and enjoyable reports, and Mike and I sat in the kitchen, talking and eating the leftover gooseberry tart while the patients drank their tea.

We'd barely finished when the night nursing officer came round, reconnoitring. He was a big blond man, he came into the kitchen and hung about chatting for a while. I don't think he even glanced at me, not once.

'Well, must be pressing on,' he said eventually. At the door he turned and wished me goodnight, but he was still looking at Mike.

As soon as his footsteps had died away we met one another's eyes and burst out laughing.

'Well, you have made a conquest,' I said.

'Happens all the time,' said Mike, mock-despairing, his hand to his forehead.

'He'll be asking you out tomorrow,' I said.

'I'll be busy,' said Mike, a little cool. I felt abashed.

'Shall we do some backrubs?'

'Okey-doke,' said Mike.

There was seldom a lot to do at that time of day but there was even less now we were half-empty. Everyone left seemed half-asleep as well, too much pie perhaps. No one wanted anything. After the late drug round we sat down at the centre table to wait for the night staff. I was wondering about Mike, whether he was unhappy about being gay, whether it had been a sort of sexual politeness in him to hint to me that he was straight, because to be outright gay is to tell a woman that you're never going to find her the least bit attractive. I looked covertly at his filmstar eyelashes and he turned and faced me and said in rather a low voice, so that Janet didn't hear, 'Coming for a drink after?'

'Oh, I can't tonight, I can't thanks,' I said, all flustered. Then I thought I'd make a joke of it. 'D'you always ask your ward sisters out?'

'No,' said Mike laughing, 'they usually ask me.'

Ten days later we closed the ward: the end of Mercy. Mike opened the wine for me and we gave all the remaining old men an inch each. Everyone's bed was loaded with belongings in bright yellow plastic bags. George lay in bed holding his slippers, waiting to be wheeled away. He was going to Patience.

'Goodbye, George. I'll come and visit you.'

'Goodbye, my dear,' said George. I tried to imagine him barking orders, inspiring terror in the ranks. I kissed his slack cheek. 'Take care of yourself.'

One by one we shunted them out, porter at one end, nurse at the other. They were all gone by lunchtime. We pushed the few remaining empty beds to one side, for the floor cleaners. No beds, no bed curtains.

'It looks like a deserted ballroom,' said Mike, looking round. Our footsteps sounded very loud on the wooden floors. Once, to save time the month before, I had bowled the ward keys along the boards to Janet, who'd wanted them at the far end of the ward, and she had stopped them neatly with her foot, winning an ironic patter of applause from the old boys nearby.

'Howzat!'

'We'll finish the cleaning after lunch,' I said. 'Come on.'

It was slow going. I was feeling so miserable that I infected the other two, and we cleaned the sluice-room almost in silence.

'You know what we should do,' said Mike suddenly, straightening up from the commode whose nasty jammed brakes he'd been listlessly poking at, 'we should go out in a blaze of glory, that's what we should do.'

I was re-lining the urine-testing cupboard. I'd found broken glass in it, from a smashed dropper, and three bottles of Labstix, all empty. Janet had disappeared altogether, in search, she'd said, of rubber gloves, because the Glitto was hurting her hands.

'That's what we should do.'

'How d'you mean?'

Mike looked round, and came closer. 'A blaze of glory. Yes? We steal the hoist.'

'What?' I turned round, laughing.

'Look. They don't need it. They don't use it. A3. We need it, they don't.'

'We're shut.'

'Not for long. Come on. We'll get it and then it'll be there for when you re-open.'

He pulled himself up to sit on the draining board. 'What d'you say?'

He sounded serious. So did I: 'It's the most idiotic thing I ever heard.'

'No, no, think about it. Really. It's not stealing really. It's borrowing. We go up there and we say, Look, we need this hoist and you don't, can we borrow it, you get it back if you need it. They won't mind.'

'Oh yes? What about Holloway?'

'What about her? She won't even notice, when did she last look in your bathroom? She never does, why should she?'

'She won't like it.'

'She won't know. Anyway who cares what she wants, she doesn't care about you lot does she, all your students hurting their backs, honest it's half-killed me working here and I'm a bloke!'

I bit my lip, staring into the urine-testing cupboard. Its wooden doors were all blotched with stains, I wondered what of.

'Come on,' said Mike, leaning towards me, his mouth close to my ear. 'Let's do it. Take it. Go on. Dare you.'

It was very difficult trundling the hoist along the mile of corridor. It wasn't built for long distances, it had awkward little wheels and kept trying to knock itself out against the tiled walls. We'd had a terrible struggle getting it in and out of the lift because the wheels stuck in the lift-door grooves and because we were laughing so much. It had a noble, pained look to it, that hoist, like a statue of some long-dead dignitary being knocked off its pedestal by a proletarian mob.

'Listen you bastard you're coming with us,' Mike had snarled, fighting it into the lift beside A3 while the A3 Sister looked on and giggled. Everyone had been full of the Christmas spirit on A3. The Sister had a piece of tinsel tied round her hospital badge in a bow. She'd been surprised at first, then amused, then eager to co-operate.

'Oh, Holloway, oh *her*. Take it, take it, why ever not?'

'See?' Mike had said, smiling sweetly at the A3 Sister, 'I told you they'd be nice.' He'd done nearly all the talking: he'd soon beat all the quick-promotion records, I'd thought rather sourly, my eyes on the A3 Sister's answering smile.

Now, stubborn unco-operative hostage, the hoist fought back as we panted up the last quarter-mile of corridor. There were crowds of people about because it was visiting-time but it's a common enough hospital sight, two people struggling fiercely with an awkward wheeled appliance, so no one stopped us, not even the big blond nursing officer who saw us from the door of admin; he merely smiled tenderly as Mike waved.

'Afternoon!' called Mike. We trundled past, red-faced.

'Ha!' said Mike as we reached Mercy's cramped little bathroom. 'Blazor glory!'

'Oh God, it won't fit,' I cried, anguished. Janet ran up to help us squeeze it past the doorjamb. It fitted, just. Janet instantly sat in the swing and we turned the wheel, lifted her, and, 'God bless all who sail in her,' said Mike, lowering Janet slowly into the empty bath. She sat there grinning till I put the plug in and turned the taps on, when she leapt out squawking.

'And we keep the door closed,' I said as I turned the taps off. 'Keep quiet about this, all right?'

'Right.'

'Come on, let's celebrate, there's some wine left,' said Mike, and we all went into the office and toasted the quality of Mercy, which was, I said, undeniably improved.

'And soon to re-open by popular demand,' said Mike. 'All those Edwardians.' Our eyes met, at that.

Then Janet's friend, the personal-crisis one, arrived and looked pleadingly into the office. It was quite late anyway and there were no late-shift nurses to give report to and no patients to report on, so I told Janet and Mike they could go home if they wanted to.

'I liked working here,' said Janet to me as she left. I thanked her and said I'd enjoyed having her, which she knew already from signing her ward report.

I turned back into the empty ward. It was getting dark already outside. I switched the main lights on. The little plaques looked down on nothing, no beds, no patients. There was no glad end-of-term feeling about it at all, despite the hoist and the blazor glory; it felt more like the end of the world.

'Deserted ballroom,' said Mike behind me. 'Care to dance?'

'I don't feel like dancing.'

'You're a barrel of laughs you are. Come on. Dance with me.'

'I can't dance.'

'You can waltz. Everyone can waltz.'

'I can't.'

'I'll teach you,' said Mike, 'look, it's easy, a waltz. Right, forward, side, together, right, one, two, three, forward side together – I mean, back, side together. Go on.'

'Back, side, together?'

'Right, see? Easy.' He took my hand, I put the other on his arm. We looked at our feet and moved off awkwardly.

'One two three.'

'Back, side, together.'

Mike began to hum the Blue Danube and we lurched about laughing, I kept tripping up unless I kept my eyes on my feet. Still, the ward was a big place to practise in and by the time we'd reached the bathroom and turned to come back down it felt more like dancing, more like that special metaphor. I remembered waltzing at school then, a hallful of girls all dancing with each other. Mike put his arm round my waist.

'Aren't you little,' he said. I looked up, he wasn't much taller than me. There was dark stubble on his chin; it contrasted rather nicely, I thought, with the dyed blond hair. He looked very raffish, the gold earrings glinting in the oblique light from the office.

'All those nurses asking you out,' I said.

'Such a burden,' he smiled.

'Women too?'

'Women mainly, dear,' said Mike, rather camp. 'Because I'm gentle, see,' he went on in his real voice, 'I'm never a threat. I look effeminate, and gentle.'

'Are you really so, then, or is it an act?'

'Oh well . . . No, I was gentle and effeminate to start with. But when I saw, you know, how it *worked* . . .'

'Slays 'em?'

'Every time. You know, when I first started nursing, well! I was in heaven: all those girls!' and he smiled down at me, not lasciviously, but happily, remembering delight. 'How old are you?'

'Twenty-three. How old are you?'

'Thirty-one.'

We smiled at one another, we stopped dancing.

'There. Now we've got that out of the way. Look. Can't I see you again?'

'What's the point?'

'Lots of point, I think. This ward. It'll be us one day, won't it? The Elizabethans.' We moved off again, no music. We danced past the plaques, Horace Sproat long gone, the Amersham chorus all silent now, Lady Constance gone to dust.

'Lots of point,' said Mike. His eyes were very gentle. As he knew. I thought of the past and going mad in building societies, and of how much simpler and safer it was to sell love rather than give it away. Then I smiled into his white coat, where he wore a hospital badge just like my own. I put my hand on his shoulder.

'Actually,' I said, 'I know how to polka. We learnt it at school. Shall I show you how?'

CASUALTIES
OF LOVE

GARTER

———— ◆ ————

Lisa St Aubin de Terán

For anyone passing along the uneven band of greyness that was the road between the South London Hospital for Women and the Clock Tower, the Common had a dour flat look with its alternate stretches of balding mud and windswept sweet papers. At best, it was a place to gather conkers, at worst, a short cut to run across, a place of menace whose edges held a frayed threat of their own.

Once a year a circus came, towing its marquees and trailers and camels and candy floss; and then the funfair with its young men in black leather who carried silvery chains and whose hair seemed to grow the wrong way in black spikes, and who tipped Fanta tins into the boating pond. We were never allowed to visit the circus, but we watched the preparations from the edge of the Common. We had also been warned never to so much as look at these young men in black leather, but we did.

After the funfairs and the circus had left, my sister and I used to cover the ground where they had been, discovering a hint of the thrill of the big top in the massive droppings and the fallen cartridge-cases. Once, we had even bought pass tickets into the circus ground, although we had no money for any of the side-shows, or for the big top itself. One of the side-shows had been a bearded lady, but we had already seen one of those on the 118 bus that stopped at the Old Town. Another of the side-shows was a fat lady, but she didn't seem at all unusual to us, it was the Siamese twins, 'born today', that we were most sorry to have missed.

It was after the departure of one of these funfairs that I first met Garter. I had noticed him once or twice on my way to school, sweeping by the plague pond in the middle of the lower hem of the Common. I had a fear of road-sweepers in general, a kind of social embarrassment and revulsion rolled into one. So, from the first time I had noticed him, I watched out from my coveted front seat on the upstairs of a number 118, with a sense of fascination. He was always there with his heavy-headed street-broom and his bottle-end glasses tied together with wire and string. He always wore the same threadbare grey suit. He didn't really move like other people, he was very slow.

I had pointed him out once to my mother, from the downstairs of the bus. She didn't like the smoke, and what she called the yobbos on the top, and I used to pretend that I didn't either when I was with her, but I did. She looked at my road-sweeper, almost through her nostrils, in a way she had, and she said that she wouldn't like to meet *him* on a dark night. This gave him a further air of mystery, and in the winter evenings, when his work had come full circle, and he was back by the plague pond, silhouetted against the willow on its island in the middle by the streetlights, I felt an urge to speak to my road-sweeper, and once, when I was on the inside of the aisle, and he couldn't see, I waved.

Later, I asked my mother to explain what she meant about him and the dark night, but I could get nothing from her, except that 'he was not the kind of man to be trusted with furry animals'. I had never known such a person, and when he spoke to me, from his avenue of sodden leaves beside the littered fair site, I was quick to reply. From then on, we spoke regularly, and I began to walk across the edge of the Common twice a day. He noticed all the days when I didn't come, and he took as keen an interest in the ups and downs of my tubercular glands as any of my doctors. He told me that his name was Garter, and whenever I asked him about his work or himself, he would always say, 'I'm doing all right,' then he would wait for what seemed like an uncomfortably long time, and finally add, 'but I would like you to do better.'

I was always very touched by this man's concern to keep me

from sweeping the gutter as he did. He worried about the illness in my glands, and I worried about his stammer and the way he dribbled when he spoke.

At Christmas I gave him a pound note, but he gave it back to me, saying, 'I d-don't want money, I want l-l-love.'

I was very hurt, and went home and gave the money to my sister. I didn't know how anyone could love Garter, with his grey suit thinned in the wind behind, and starched with years of OK sauce and egg down the front, and his lank greasy hair plastered down with the flakes of what I took to be a scalp infection.

On the days when my fever rose I didn't go out at all, and so I didn't get to see him, but I still thought about him, his refusal of my money, and, considering his appearance, what I thought to be his unreasonable demand for love. I tried to imagine him as the furry animal that my mother thought he could not be trusted with. As I lay in bed (and I was allowed to lie in my mother's double bed whenever I was ill, and use the wireless during the day, and borrow all my sister's pillows) I would close my eyes between the cramps in my side, and manage to imagine Garter as a kind of aging mole with a matted grey coat of fur, balding and caked in places like his suit, his tiny eyes strained away from both sunlight and lamps as though in pain, and his fingernails full of earth and compacted grime – it just seemed possible. I thought, someone could love him, but although he could move me, more perhaps than anyone else at the time, it couldn't be me. I wondered if he had a mother. Even Garter had to have a mother, and I set out to tell him this one morning, truanting from my sick-bed to do so.

He had worked his way along the slabs and gutters to the small lake, no bigger than a large concrete pond, where middle-aged men and children went at weekends to race their model boats. The walk had made me dizzy, and when I found him, Garter put his hand out to hold my arm. I shrank back from his touch, and then I was embarrassed. In those days, I shrank back from everybody's touch, I had a kind of neurasthenia of the skin, but he couldn't have known that.

'You must have a mother, Garter,' I told him.

'Course I have, Missus,' he said. He always called me Missus when I was alone with him.

'Well,' I said, 'she must love you.'

But Garter surprised me with his matter-of-fact reply.

'No, she never loved me, Missus, said I was soft.'

I was sorry to have introduced such an unsuccessful topic, and I tried to make amends.

'She probably did love you a little bit,' I said.

'No, Missus,' he said, and paused, the way he often did, with finality, but somehow always in mid-sentence. Then, after several minutes while we both shuffled uneasily on the pavement, Garter brightened, and said, 'But she did make me cakes.'

That was the one moment of perfect ease in our friendship. I didn't love this strange slow man either, but I, too, could make him cakes.

That night I made a batch of chocolate buns from Fanny Farmer's Boston Cookbook. It was the recipe that we always used, and the page itself was so caked with the ingredients that one could see at a glance all that was needed. Next morning I took the cakes to Garter. I had decided to miss school, and I took the long way across the Common.

This began on the corner of the 'SS murder', opposite the first entrance to the old war bunker that rose like a beached whale out of the grass, flanked by a pair of public lavatories that, like so many other things in that wasted area, we were not allowed to use. Then, still following the edge, up towards Wandsworth, where we never went, I walked along the avenue of peeling plane trees, past the scarred part where the circus came and squatted once a year. Then the walk turned in to the stunted may trees and the path to the swings and then, on the far side, the bandstand where boys on roller-skates tried to knock you down. As I neared the swings, I turned again, we were in trouble with the lady who doled out the drinking-water and broke up fights. Before I was even halfway across the indistinct football pitch, I could see Garter on the far side of the pond, sweeping in slow-motion as he always did.

In retrospect, I believe that our friendship changed from the day of the cakes. Garter began to confide in me, with what I now found an alarming insistence. The pauses between any word of his and the next could be so long that all meaning would be lost, but gradually I began to sense his drift. I was divided between my fear of his slowness, and my fear of hurting his feelings by letting our friendship drop.

Once, I remember, he asked me to put my hand in his pocket. He was smiling a strange leering smile such as I imagined him to have when he became the furry mole who had seen better times. I hesitated then, at least as long as he himself did. I considered everything. I considered running away, shouting for help, even drowning in the round pond that already held so many ancient corpses locked in its mud. Finally, I said, 'No.'

But Garter was ready for me, barring the pavement with his long broom-handle.

'Go on, Missus,' he said.

Again I waited, and then I put my gloved hand in his pocket with such loathing that I felt physically sick. I don't know what I expected to find, a dead newt, a slice of raw liver, a stag-beetle. But, from the seat of my dread, the last thing I expected to find was a bag of chocolate buttons.

'They're for you,' Garter stammered, 'I buyed them.'

Despite my relief, I didn't see Garter again for over a week. It was my longest absence yet. I had left the chocolate buttons and my gloves on the top of a bus, on purpose, but the gloves had been handed in at school, and my name-tabs brought them back to me. At least the sweets were gone. I threw the gloves at the railway-lines that run under the bridge from the gardens to the playing-fields, and it pleased me that they fell on to an oncoming train.

At last, I relented, and returned to our rendezvous, but Garter had gone. There was a new road-sweeper, and I was surprised to see that, by comparison, he seemed quite normal. After another week, I asked him where Garter was.

'They've moved him on again,' he said bluntly, and turned back to his work.

'Oh,' I said, turning to go as well, 'so he hasn't had an accident or anything?'

'Not yet,' his replacement told me, with a touch of unpleasantness in his voice. 'But you never know when a soft one like that will start molesting.'

'What do you mean?' I asked.

'Little girls,' he laughed, 'little girls like you.'

I couldn't resist asking him, 'What does he do to them?' But I could see that Garter's replacement was irked by my presence.

'How the hell should I know, but there's been a complaint. Now clear off, will you?'

Garter had told me earlier that he never spoke to anyone but me from one day to the next, and I was shocked to think that he had lost his place by the plague pond because of me. I began to read my mother's newspaper after her, scanning the columns for news of molesting, and asking questions, but I could find out nothing more specific about molesting, although I knew that it wasn't anything to do with moles, even if Garter sometimes did look a bit like one. It was always the same, I wanted to know what they did. I knew what a murderer was, we discussed the likes of them in the playground, but this new character, this so-called child-molester seemed to have no place in the spoken world around me. If it was a crime to touch me, then all the people who had held my face and kissed my head and rumpled my hair and who all without exception made me squirm, surely they should be 'moved on' first. However, there was something about Garter that made me feel ill. I decided that far from I being his victim, he was mine. During that time when I didn't see him, even the smell of a thousand spilt dinners that he carried around with him faded into the rich leafy smell of the Common.

It was just after my twelfth birthday that I found him again. I had become, once more, an out-patient at the South London Hospital which looked out over the bunker and the lavatories at the edge of the Common. I went in every day, before school, for an injec-

tion. One day, Garter was standing, leaning with his stubbly chin on his broom-handle outside the railings of the ambulance ramp. I couldn't decide what to do, whether to go back into the hospital and leave through another entrance, to ignore him or to say hello. But it was he who saw me first, miraculously through the dim lenses of his glasses. He was less than a mile away from where he had been before. He told me that he had nearly died, earlier, when they moved him down to Tooting, to the edge of the Common there. Garter seemed quite overcome, and I made him walk along the street in the hopes that no one would notice the rivulets of tears that were coming from under his glasses. After a while, I said, 'I have to go now, Garter, I'll see you again soon.'

He looked suddenly startled, as though remembering something that hurt.

'They moved me because of you, you know, Missus,' he said sadly, and then he paused. Two 118s came round the corner of Cavendish Road and up to the edge of the Common while I waited for Garter to speak again. He looked as though he might actually burst, such was his effort to overcome this phase of his silent stammer, suddenly he said, 'I need you, you're the only friend I've ever had. You never laugh at me, and you gave me some cakes and I buyed you some chocolate.'

This was the longest speech that he had ever made to me, and I squeezed his arm of my own accord, and wished that I had eaten those sweets, and ran away to catch my bus, laden with guilt.

After that, I spoke to him every day on my way to and from the hospital. I took upon myself the responsibility of keeping our meetings very brief, and of avoiding seeing him after dark. Every morning when I saw him, tears would gather and curl round the edges of his spectacles, and he would say, as regularly now as he had once said good morning, 'I thought you wasn't coming.'

I continued to see him daily for another six months. Sometimes, days in my mother's bed would keep me away. At other times, it would be hard to leave him crying in the street when I said I had to catch my bus again. But gradually he seemed to settle down into his new rhythm of sweeping leaves and salting sludge

and gathering up the endless sweet papers and the cigarette-ends. It seemed that Garter and I had found a way to live together.

I was questioned about Garter in May. I had feared that such a thing might happen the previous December, when we were reunited, and Garter used to walk beside me weeping, but by May he had stopped doing that. He was just a quiet elderly man with a worn grey suit and dirty hair. A harmless, motherless man who spent his days sweeping in slow-motion to suit his slow brain. But the officer who questioned me didn't think so. He asked me twice, 'Has he touched you?' And I lied for him, 'No.' Then he said, 'But he does talk to you. We've seen him.'

I nodded.

'What does he say?' he asked, kindlier now.

'Nothing,' I said, 'he doesn't say anything.'

'Well, he must say something,' he smiled.

'He just says he needs me,' I said, 'nothing else.'

'Well, that's all right then, isn't it,' the officer said, and I went home.

Next morning, Garter had gone. I looked for signs of him on the edge of the Common, both by the round pond and the bunker, and I even went down to Tooting on my bicycle and rode all day along the tree-lined streets. But I never found him again. All that year I walked on the Common, watching the horse chestnut leaves unfurling and falling, but the conkers and the funfair and the swings and even the bandstand lost their hold on me. Even the autumn leaves seemed dull, and it always seemed to be autumn. In November, the fevers returned, and I spent another year engrossed in my tubercular glands, and it was these that enabled me to stop searching for Garter with his grey suit and his stammer and his glasses tied together with wire and string, Garter who said that his proudest moment was when he 'buyed me the chocolate buttons'.